After Harry Met Sally

A Novel of Philosophical
Questioning

Stephen Paul Foster

After Harry Met Sally: A Novel of Philosophical Questioning is a work of fiction. All incidents and dialogue, and all characters with the exception of some well-known historical figures, are products of the author's imagination and are not to be construed as real. Where real-life historical figures appear, the situations, incidents, and dialogues concerning those persons are entirely fictional and are not intended to depict actual events or to change the entirely fictional nature of the work. In all other respects, any resemblance to actual persons, living or dead, events, or locales is entirely coincidental.

nephets.foster@gmail.com

www.fosterspeak.blogspot.com

First Edition

ISBN: 979-8530305245

For my Mother and her demons
– the good ones (*Eudaemons*)
and … the others.

"History is indeed little more than the register of the crimes, follies and misfortunes of mankind."

—**Edward Gibbon**, *Decline and Fall of the Roman Empire*

"[For] all mankind [there is] a perpetual and restless desire of power after power that ceases only in death. And the cause of this is not always that a man hopes for a more intensive delight than he has already attained, or that he cannot be content with a moderate power; but because he cannot assure the power and the means to live well which he has at present, without the acquisition of more."

—**Thomas Hobbes**, *Leviathan*

"Why tell how my heart burns hot with rage when I see the people hustled by a mob of retainers attending on one who has defrauded and debauched his ward, or on another who has been condemned by a futile verdict—for what matters infamy if the cash be kept?"

—**Juvenal**, *The Sixteen Satires*

"Man is conceived in sin and born in corruption and he passeth from the stink of the didie to the stench of the shroud. There is always something."

—**Willie Stark**, *All the King's Men*

"Go in fear of abstractions."

—**Ezra Pound**, "*A Few Don'ts by an Imagiste*"

1 The Ten Commandments Revisited

"Epigraph for a Condemned Book"

Quiet and bucolic reader,
Upright man, sober and naive,
Throw away this book, saturnine,
Orgiac and melancholy.

If you did not do your rhetoric
With Satan, that artful dean,
Throw it away, you'd grasp nothing,
Or else think me hysterical.

But if, without being entranced,
Your eye can plunge in the abyss,
Read me, to learn to love me;

Inquisitive soul that suffers
And keeps on seeking paradise,
Pity me!... or else, I curse you!

–Charles Baudelaire, *The Flowers of Evil*

Honor thy Father and thy Mother.

Who said that?

God.

Why would God say that?

It's one of His Ten Commandments. Those of you under the age of, say, fifty probably never heard of them. Why? Because as a patriarchal, judgmental old-guy, God's been on the outs for the last generation or two. So, who cares now about "commandments" from some non-existing, Fascist deity?

Nevertheless, He dispensed those commandments to another old-guy, Moses uh, Moses… Well, sorry. I don't remember his last name. Originally, they came chiseled on stone tablets. Eventually they made their way into the Book of Exodus in the Old Testament which precedes the New Testament, the Bible – not the *Bible of Golf* – the "Holy" one. You know. Maybe you don't. No matter. It was forced on me as a kid. It was the only book I ever read that "begat-ed" me into a deep sleep. The definition of "begat" in case you forgot means you produced offspring. Be patient. I throw this in because "having offspring" is what I'm going to have a lot to say about shortly. Getting one started is easy, too easy sometimes even when you didn't want to. Even with someone you didn't much care for. After that? Start practicing "*Que Sera, Sera*" with your fingers crossed.

Yes, these Ten Commandments came directly from God to a massively bearded bloke in flowing robes wandering around lost in a desert leading a horde of his feuding kinsmen. How lucky can a desperate guy get?

"Hey, Moses!"

"Say what? Who are you? Where are you?"

"It's God Q. Almighty. My friends call me Jehovah. To the Angels, I'm 'Mr. Big.' I'm high up above you. At the moment I'm invisible. But don't worry about it. Gird yourself and listen up. I don't chew my matzo balls twice. Ten rules, laws, commandments – whatever you want to call them, I don't care. Check that! I don't care, that is, so long as you and those bickering schlemiels you have in tow can pull your act together and do a number on those pesky Philistines – put the men to the sword and carry off their women-folk and, of course, the livestock. If you can't remember these, uh, commandments, grab the chisel over there. The stones are on your left. Stand by, Moses, my man. Pay close attention … chop-chop."

And so, they came to pass.

Fast forward a couple of millennia. The cigar-chomping, old cynic, H. L. Mencken, was to quip: "Say what you will about the Ten Commandments, you must always come back to the pleasant fact that there are only ten of them."

It's hard to argue with that. Still, the whole "commandment thing" for a millennium or two seemed like a half-decent way to keep mayhem, mischief and maleficence down to a dull roar at least some of the time. Thomas Hobbes, my favorite, tell-it-like-it-is, no-bullshit philosopher, put it this way: "[M]en have no pleasure (but on the contrary a great deal of grief) in keeping company where there is no power able to overawe them all." Which is why it's a good move to have commandments and a commander to, well, sort of "overawe them all." Anyone out there want to argue *against* less "grief"? Didn't think so. Not stealing, not coveting your neighbor's wife makes "keeping company" less complicated, more tolerable and safer for you, your neighbor and his missus. Maybe yours too. But for all those restless natives to shun such temptations they must be convinced that hijinks such as stealing and coveting are going to get them lined up for a hard, swift kick in the ass. Hence, the reminders in the form of commandments and the painful smack downs for those inclined to "forget."

Seems reasonable enough. It was for a long time. But alas. That simpler, direct approach to the management of malicious monkey business has been pushed aside. Now? We are "Waste Deep in the Big Muddy," the "Big Muddy" being this Oprah-era of manufactured self-esteem – "celebrating life," a euphemism for "kvelling for no obvious reason." Which means that we are caught up in these mysterious ceremonies that are supposed to affirm nothing more important or specific than … "you," whatever *you* happen to be at some arbitrary moment of exaltation and self-magnification. "The more you praise and celebrate your life," exhorts Oprah in one of her unique pronouncements of knowingness, "the more there is in life to celebrate." "Holy hole in a doughnut!" as Robin once hollered at Batman. She obviously doesn't know the meaning of the word "vacuous" and had never acquainted herself with Hobbes: "And therefore of absurd and false affirmations, in case they be universal, there can be no understanding; though many think they understand, then, when they do but repeat the words softly, or con them in their mind."

Don't hold back now – sensational, phenomenal "you" – even when it would be well counseled. Keep repeating to yourself: "I am wonderful." Praise and celebrate like there's no tomorrow until *you* are feeling, well, swell about *you*. Join the lemmings wallowing in the swamps of ritualized mumbo-jumbo. These alchemistic solemnities demand a minute-by-minute monitoring of your feelings and the secrets they reveal – and why they might be important to you or anyone else for more than, say, the next ten minutes. "Feel the power of focusing on what excites you," ("you" once again) from the *Conquistadora* of touchy-feely with that signature breathless delivery.

I wonder: how is that going to work long term for Hobbes's "keeping company" with less "grief"? I'm all for feeling powerful, very powerful – nothing quite like it. However, I'm guessing that lots of people focusing on what excites them rather than on the long-term benefits of self-restraint is a recipe for more, not less grief. That's particularly so when what excites them is more of them and less of you and me in the sharing of life's limited goodies. Hobbes called it the "state of nature," the "war of all against all."

It's all about "feelings" now. So, we're trapped in this helter-skelter pandemonium of non-stop scolding by *some* people who get worked up about people (like me) who hurt *other* people's feelings – sometimes even unintentionally. These nagging, two-legged, self-inflated rodents of coercive compassion don't overawe. They just whine, hector and tut-tut you to death for doing stuff you thought was mostly ok or at least not a big deal. It's stuff that they themselves do when they think nobody is paying attention. It's so confusing – and God-awful stupid. Scolding was once a semi-respectable calling reserved exclusively for preachers, priests, rabbis and weight loss gurus – fast-talkers who for the most part everyone ignored when they thought they weren't being watched.

This unpleasantly necessary, professional calling, however, has blown itself wide open with hucksters, hypocrites and phonies – aggrieved, small-minded authoritarians with personal agendas. They "work" full time to make you into their image of perfection – "a great deal of grief"… for you and me. These arriviste parsons pop up everywhere like in a game of Whack-a-Mole – universities, schools, corporations and government. Good luck trying to avoid these relentless martinets determined to make you into a pale imitation of them. You are always going to disappoint them and feel *their* pain when you do. It's inevitable. Here is a suggestion. The next time you hear someone prattling away about "*our* values," "how *I* feel," "having a conversation," "who we are," "changing the culture" and worst of all "making a difference" – reach for your Luger. Just kidding, *Waffenbruder*. But you should have one handy in case you need some fire power.

Maybe it slipped your mind. Feelings are not stable – never have been. They mutate like a flu virus. They move from person to person and within the same person with unpredictable, sometimes ugly manifestations. From one day to the next they change, sometimes by the hour.

> "Honey, I don't love you anymore. I want a divorce."
>
> "But you told me you loved me last Saturday, B.B."
>
> "Yeah, well, Baby… The thrill is gone."

Hmm… I think most of us have been there at some time on one side or the other. I wouldn't dare to argue with B.B. King or any tear-jerking blues singer about the coming and going of thrills. But here is how Hobbes put it, technically: "Because the constitution of a man's body is in continual mutation; it is impossible that all the same things should always cause in him the same appetites, and aversions: much less can all men consent in the desire of almost any one and the same object."

"Continual mutation." Got that? It leads to feelings-in-flux. The thrill – it came and it went – and "I *feel* so bad about it, but you'll have to deal with it!" It's all business as usual for *homo sapiens*. Which makes "not hurting anybody's *feelings*" as the solution for turning defective-me into someone else's version of "a perfect human being" ... a bit tricky. No, impossible. Most normal people, I suspect, have no desire to be perfect – too much pressure, too many unreasonable expectations, too much guilt. My second wife made a serious effort. She fell apart and kept threatening to jump off a bridge. Fortunately, there were no bridges nearby. But I'm already getting off track here.

Being a couple of candle-powers short of smarts than Hobbes, I must go with his commandments-commander view as the best way for folks to go about "keeping company" with each other – peaceful like. Most of those ten are easy enough (for me, anyway) to understand. Some, though, remain a bit of a challenge. "Thou shalt have no other gods before me." I'm hoping that not having *any* gods before anybody will get me over that hurdle. As for "no graven images"? Well, I looked up "graven images" in the dictionary. It's not a hot topic on social media these days. Here is why: "an object of worship carved usually from wood or stone." That was a relief. The only worship-object that ever came close to that for me was my black, fuel-injected, 450 horsepower Corvette. I washed it on a regular basis, which now that I mention it might be a weird kind of worshiping ritual. But it was "carved" out of fiberglass, and I totaled it long ago late one night, as far as I can recall, on a country road heading home from a wild party.

But it's the mother-father Commandment with honor attached that I keep trying to get my head around. What in the name of "Father Knows Best" was God thinking with this? It continues to intrigue me. Why? Maybe it's because my Mother was crazy. Maybe it's because I never discovered who my Father was until I was wandering around in my own private desert of confused, directionless adulthood having enthusiastically broken many of the Big Ten Cs. A bit of coveting now and again and some forgivable (I hope) carelessness with the "Lord's name." I never murdered anybody, however, at least that I can remember.

How then, is a mild-mannered palooka like me stuck with a mom and dad like these two, uh, slippery characters supposed to pull off this honor-gig?

For starters, what does it mean to "honor" someone? My resort? Again, the dictionary. "Honor" as a verb: "(1) to regard with great respect; (2) to fulfill (an obligation) or keep (an agreement)." Well, that put a serious dent in my plans. Both 1 and 2 didn't help me with sperm-donor-Dad, aka the amazing, disappearing deviant. My mother? "Crazy," I can assure you from direct experience, is not a straight road to a destination called "respect." And by "crazy" I don't mean crazy in a sweet, dizzy, flighty-flakey "I Love Lucy" sort of way. No, I mean nobody-can-stand-you-crazy, *DSM*-diagnosed-crazy as in a panoply of "disorders" and "disabilities" that only psychiatrists can decipher for a fee – those sourpuss, bill-by-the-hour quacks whose clutches you desperately try to avoid. It's the only professional class I know of that is more contemptible and less respectable than lawyers. Unlike lawyers, they invent clinically-sounding, unpronounceable labels that make your miseries sound worse than they are. They charge you to come and twiddle your thumbs in a waiting room for an hour. You study the cheap, knock-off paintings on the walls. You try to guess what sort of "crazy" possesses your rival occupants of this antechamber of angst who, like you, are not sure why they are here. Next, you enter and sit in their offices while they stare fish-faced at you and blink. Now that you are tense and nervous they invite you to talk about your dysphoria. Then they interrupt you with: "How does that make you feel?" You tell them: "I *feel* even worse." They answer: "That's good. You're making progress expressing your feelings." After which you say to yourself: "If this is what 'progress' feels like, I'm switching to the hard stuff." And, unlike with most products or services you're not happy with, there's no recourse for refunds. Think about the logic behind that for a moment. Before you went you felt bad: after you left you felt worse and were light a couple hundred bucks. Now, you understand: you are crazier and poorer than before your consultation. Life in a post-Hobbes world – more, not less "grief."

As I recollect, the only "obligation" I had to my mother was to try to pry her away from the low-life, grifter men she seemed life-long determined to flock to, like a moth to a lightbulb – not an obligation that I had much luck in fulfilling.

None of us had any say in the choice of those who "begat" us, to state the overly obvious. On the other side of the "begetting" coin, parents don't get to "choose" what *kind* of kid is going to result from their casual couplings of heavy breathing. A jaded buddy of mine with four kids once quipped after a few beers: "Following twenty minutes of pleasure comes twenty years of pain." Ouch! Let's face it. Spawning an offspring is a frightening, genetic crap-shoot. Is that kid going to be a Nobel Prize-winning chemist, a chess Grandmaster, a Cy-Young award-winning pitcher? Or, will he be that creepy flasher entertaining himself perched next to the trash barrel outside of a 7-Eleven? A higher probability, I would wager, that Junior is not going to be someone who will make you proud. Or worse. One of my close friends from early adulthood, G. Manny Williams, I later discovered, in fits of rage murdered two of his ex-girlfriends in Florida. One was with a hammer, the other with a kitchen knife. Who could have predicted it? Nobody. I swear to it. He was a perfect gentleman with a 138 IQ, fluent in four languages with a couple of impressive graduate degrees. He had many cool things to say about ethno-archaeology, Ludwig Wittgenstein and Arnold Schoenberg's method of atonality and 12-tone serialism. "Manny's relationship with his parents was invested with conflict and ambiguity." No kidding, Einstein. It took three psychiatrists and a court-appointed social worker in Ft. Lauderdale three months of expensive head scratching to figure out what was stunningly obvious to the average plumber or life-insurance salesman. And, completely irrelevant to the only important question relating to G. Manny's future: is there *any* good reason we shouldn't sit this lady-killer with the razzle-dazzle vocabulary down in Florida's trusty "Old Sparky" and run some high-voltage current through him until he turns crispy?

The parent-child relationship is always front-loaded with potential disaster. So many different ways things can go wrong on both ends. So, the next time you and the Mrs. are feeling romantic, take a cold shower instead and head off the potential of twenty years of grief.

In spite of my ruminations and determination, I was never able to get the mother-father command-ment off my to-do list. But that futile project did set me on a different path: not to honor my mother and father, since, well, you get the picture – but to under-stand them. As the French say: "*Tout comprendre c'est tout pardonner.*" Given my inclination toward unfor-giveness, and in view of the pathologies I was explor-ing, this would be a steep climb to the summit. At times I would come to a halt with the shortage of oxy-gen, return to base camp and consult with my per-sonal Sherpa, Hobbes. I would resume my ascent.

What follows is a deep-dive into the muck, the res-idue of the failed attempts of my mother and father to be decent human beings. My goal was to turn personal understanding into something more ambitious with a broader reach, if you catch my drift.

So, if contemplating disillusionment, dishonesty, alcoholism and sexual degeneracy put you out of sorts, stop reading. Maybe find some reruns of "Love Boat" on Hulu. Jump on your elliptical trainer. Read up on high-cholesterol or periodontal disease prevention.

Whatever. I understand completely. It's not your bag. But, before you retreat, let me ask: Do you worry about the future of Western civilization? Can you survive the trauma of learning that what you thought was normal turns out to be a sick joke? "Yes," you say? Then continue reading. Not fun, but it will be entertaining in a delicious, gruesome sort of way. It will be more enlightening than watching a slasher franchise series like "Halloween." You decide.

As I set out I slowly began to see how fortunate I was. Most peoples' Moms and Dads are good folks – good enough, anyway. Being good, obeying the rules and holding a steady job is the best way to get from point A, your joyous entry into the world, to point Z, your sad departure with the least amount of pain, or "grief," as Hobbes puts it. But a long life of quietly behaving yourself – with teacher praise, spouse approval, boss kudos, adding to your 401-K – is not all that attention grabbing. Cradle-to-grave happy-time, like it is for the *borgaren* of Sweden, may be desirable, but the contemplation of it could only be tedious and boring.

News headlines, movies and best-selling novels tend to be about misfits, scumbags and psychopaths. Add to that gangsters, con men, dope fiends, corrupt lawyers and politicians, serial adulterers. Don't forget mass-murders and war-mongering dictators. Ever wonder why that is? The answer to that question, I suspect, is connected to the curious practice of women who marry mass-murdering men who have been locked away in prisons, like the notorious Menendez brothers who slaughtered their parents and then went on to marry good looking women while serving life-sentences. Darkness rather than light draws them in. And, not just prison-groupie ladies.

Don't think so? Browse through the movie-series offerings on Netflix – homicide, adultery and various modes of betrayal seem to be the overriding preoccupation, particularly serial killers and the messy, multiple stuff they get into. Remember Shakespeare and the confession of Claudius in "Hamlet"?

> "O, my offence is rank it smells to heaven;
>
> It hath the primal eldest curse upon't,
>
> A brother's murder."

My good fortune was to have a mother and father whose lives *were* attention-grabbing – decadence and deviance that packed a wallop. Thanks to them, I had the material for the best kind of adventure chronicle – a combination of entertainment and enlightenment. Vice is the entertainment side. Connecting it to the raging pathologies of contemporary America is the enlightenment half of the equation. What was wrong with Mom and Dad was what was wrong with everything. Well, almost everything.

2 When Harry Met Sally

*"Ladies and gentlemen: the story you
are about to hear is true. Only the
names have been changed to protect the
~~innocent~~ guilty."*

—Introduction to TV series, *Dragnet*

To protect the guilty, my Mom I'll call "Sally," my Dad, "Harry."

Harry met Sally on a blind date in April of 1969 when they were both in college.

"April is the cruelest month, breeding

lilacs out of the dead land, mixing

memory and desire...."

—T.S. Eliot, *The Wasteland*

"Memory and desire" would be two of the most unreliable features of our lives, the "mixing" of which sometimes leads to "grief," sometimes to unforeseen disaster.

You must keep the following images in mind. The typical U.S. college experience in 1969 was a confection of bacchanalia and recreational vandalism known as "protesting." Which made "What part of 'no' don't you understand"? the most obvious question to pose for students on any campus other than Bob Jones University.

The blind date was fixed up by my future Dad's roommate, Larry Duggan, and his girlfriend, Elizabeth Bentley. Elizabeth's roommate was my future Mom. She had just broken up with Gus Hall, a degenerate, pot head drummer from a garage band called Orgasmic Explosion. It was rapidly imploding. Mom was acutely "bummed", as they put it back then, and up for an outing with a really "cute" guy. My Father, I am told, was a very "cute guy". Ok, so far so good. But ... this double date that started out with all due politeness and the usual blind-date reserve ended up at a drive-in movie theater. My future dad and mom, occupying the car's ample back seat, at some point put their bashfulness aside as they shared a pint of sloe gin – and became, uh, intimately acquainted.

In the back seat of Larry's 1962 Oldsmobile Starfire on Harry's and Sally's first and only date I was conceived. This maculate conception occurred during the unwatched double feature, "How the West was Won" and "Tom Jones." Most likely, if you think about it, it must have been during "Tom Jones." "Life imitates art" suggests that this had to be how it all "came off," so to speak.

I know what you're thinking about my mother, Sally. "Jeezus H. Christ! First date? A drive in? With a couple in the front seat?" But take a breath. Come on now Mr. and Mrs. Judgmental. Remember? This was freaking 1969. Give her a break! Liberation from rules then was the only rule. Those "feelings" as reliable guidelines I talked about – "in continual mutation" per Hobbes. Remember? They come and stay a while. Then, poof! Off they go like acid indigestion or an Excedrin migraine. "Feelings, nothing more than feelings. Trying to forget my feelings of love" – a couple of lines from one of the worst popular songs ever recorded, one that continues to spark "nothing more" than my own "feelings" of revulsion. Then there was the ruling maxim of the era that was in force that particular evening, "If it feels good do it" – whatever *feels* "natural." That would open up a whole lot of heretofore unchartered territory. With so much "natural," little remained of "unnatural" – mildly disturbing when you think about the implications. Unfortunately, this "feels good" guideline practiced with the wild abandon of those times put the kibosh on a wide spectrum of inhibitions. Some of them made good sense ever since the days saber tooth tigers were chasing cavemen around.

For helpful perspective on Sally's infelicitous flirtation that took place during the Age of Aquarius: this gin-lubricated, liberated act of "feel-good" occurred about the time the Yoko-smitten John Lennon unleashed his "living for today" deranged, sing-along yodel, or in mom's case that April, "living for tonight." "Imagine."

> "Imagine there's no heaven
> It's easy if you try
> No hell below us

Above us only sky

Imagine all the people living for today

Imagine there's no countries

It isn't hard to do

Nothing to kill or die for

And no religion too."

I've always thought that it was harder to imagine that there *was* a heaven, but maybe that's just me. Whatever you care to say about John Lennon, he sucked at being a theologian. East meets west as in the chronicle of John and Yoko was most unfortunate. Less Yoko, more Hobbes was in order, specifically on the bad stuff that happens when "there is no power to overawe" the young and the restless. Some pointers from Mr. Hobbes might have spiked that hirsute simpleton's spastic fit of fantasy and mercifully saved us from this crackpot anthem that aging, decrepit hippies still go weepy over. It continues to pollute the airwaves.

Living for today – what could be more fun? But for my Mom, "for today" and for tonight turned cruelly into – Yikes! – tomorrow. *Not* so hard to imagine, if you try. Then came next week, next month with no monthly – and for Sally's friends and family? Well, now … She had "some splainin' to do," per Ricky Ricardo when sternly holding poor wife Lucy to account for lesser kinds of, uh, screw ups. Sally must have been wishing that what had been so "easy if you try" hadn't been quite so easy in that back seat. She was thinking now that her future was going to be a lot less easy – how about "shitty" for starters? "No hell below us"? No, but the nausea and vomiting every morning post-blind date gave Mom a regular, little taste of hell right up here in Winter Wonderland Michigan in the privacy of her own bathroom. "Nothing to kill or die for"? Except a poor something or other in a lab that had to die – the cute little bunny rabbit that took one for the team, crumpled up into a stiff, furry ball after the syringe delivered a dose of Mom's pee-pee.

"You may say I'm a dreamer." No, John, I'd just say you had a brain-crippling bout of dementia.

"But I'm not the only one." Sigh. Yes, we know. It's unfortunate. It explains why so much has gone wrong.

But living on a particular day in the crazy, confused "I'm OK—You're OK" world of 1969, Sally found herself in Dr. Marcus Shelby's office digesting the inevitable and acutely embarrassing "bad news."

> "The hysterical bride in the penny arcade
>
> Screaming, she moans, 'I've just been made'
>
> Then sends out for the doctor, who pulls down the shade
>
> And says, 'My advice is to not let the boys in.'
>
> —**Bob Dylan**, *Tombstone Blues*

Bob Dylan does a "reality check" on John Lennon.

I try to "imagine" what getting that bad news must have been like for Sally. By the standards of the time she was not a wildly promiscuous young woman. Her misfortune that evening was to go up against Harry, a beguiling master of seduction the likes of whom she had never before encountered. With the gin as Harry's furtive accomplice, she had no chance to avoid surrender that fateful evening. Sally's feckless chaperone on that date was a guy named "Really Bad Luck".

> Doctor Shelby: "You are roughly two months pregnant, Miss."

He seemed to enjoy tacking on the "Miss" at the end of that sentence.

Sally turned pale and remained mute for several moments.

> Then: "That's impossible."

> Doctor Shelby blinked, smirked and remained silent. He was thinking: "Well, she did 'let the boys in.' Don't kids these days listen to Dylan?" In threateningly slow motion, he pushed the lab report with his notes across his desk toward Sally who recoiled from it like it was a giant spider charging toward her.

> Sally: Sob. "I'm not married. I don't even know the guy. What am I going to do?"

> Doctor Shelby smiled menacingly and showed his large white teeth: "Maintain a healthy diet and prepare for motherhood."

> Sally: "Oh God! What am I going to tell my parents? My Dad is a Baptist minister."

Too bad, Sally. The Doctor was a Unitarian. He worshipped a gentle and reasonable God – and only with a phlegmatic air that approached casual indifference. Which reflected the indifference of his non-judgmental God who was hoping to get around to "world peace" someday. His toothy smile beat a hasty retreat. An annoying sigh eased out of him as he defaulted to his rehearsed posture of fake sympathy and handed Sally a box of Kleenex.

> "You'll be fine." A canned, emotionless discharge so predictable and routine that even *he* must have found it unconvincing.

> Fine, yeah! "There, there, young lady. My advice is… Oh right, too late for that."

And just how far up from the bottom of your medical school class did you happen to graduate, Doctor Marcus, No-clue Douchebag?

Sorry, John Lennon, you blithering imbecile. With my parson grandad looming in the background, no way for *this* Mom-to-be to imagine "no religion too."

She was in what they used to call "the family way" way before a family was "Heather has Two Mommies." And where exactly was that one-night-stand Lothario, the slickster who had managed to get her in that old-fashioned, family way? "Imagine there's no countries"? How about no states, dipshit limey? How about no Ohio?

Ask Neil Young while you're at it.

> "Tin soldiers and Nixon coming,
>
> We're finally on our own.
>
> This summer I hear the drumming,
>
> Four dead in Ohio."

Harry's hearing "the drumming" too and figuring that he too is "on his own." And, with his college draft deferment about to expire, I suspect that his attempts to "imagine" away a country called the "Republic of South Vietnam" weren't getting much traction. Plus, there was at least one country he knew he didn't want to imagine away – Canada.

And, what *was* Sally going to tell her Dad?

3 When Harry Met Sally, Part II

"Well, a gal named Sally
Met a guy named Harry
And they got very merry
At the drive-in show

Harry talked so sweetly
Sally acted indiscreetly
On that big back seat
Of Larry's Oldsmobile

Sally wished she had been wiser
Wished someone had advised her
Not to get so lovey-dovey
In an Oldsmobile

Sally should have said "maybe"
'Why *did* I act so crazy?'
On that big back seat
Of Larry's Oldsmobile."

—**Backseat Baby**, *Love in an Oldsmobile*

Two and a half months pregnant, my Mom pulled herself together and teetered her way across the stage and through her university graduation ceremony. She had been cruising on overdrive until the middle of her last semester. This very smart lady was on her way to a happy summa cum laude finish line up until that April evening when Mr. Gallant knocked her up on the backseat of Larry's Oldsmobile.

Sally's mom and dad were in attendance. They were pleased to sit up straight, look attentive and endure the tedious formalities. Included were the usual banalities and bromides of false inspiration. They sat near the front row in the auditorium at Michigan State University in East Lansing – home of "the Spartans," although they called themselves the "Aggies" until 1925. Clifford M. Hardin, U.S. Secretary of Agriculture was the keynote speaker. Hardin, who displayed the stern countenance of suspicious benevolence, shared what passed for his "wisdom" with an unmoved congregation for a half an hour. Not a single memorable sentence was attempted, much less completed. No matter. Sally's parents were proud as punch of their academic achiever. Sally herself was looking a slight cast of green at the ceremony. This proud couple was still unaware, of course, that their daughter was six and a half months away from leaving them a special post-graduation "gift" – *moi*.

Since that unfortunate blind date Sally had caught a few, fleeting, on-campus sightings of Harry. You see, Harry was warming himself up to perfect what would be his life-long Great Disappearing Act. "When the going gets tough, I'm fucking outta here." I think that captures the essence of Harry Houdini's performance art. He was also riding out his final semester of a less than stellar academic performance. His challenging double major? Would you believe, draft dodging and draft beer? But, he was good at time management and managed to pick up a minor in womanizing along the way as well, a véritable *athlète de l'amour*. That made the rigors of his studies endurable. His four-year detour around adulthood and personal responsibility was rapidly drawing to an inconclusive conclusion. Now he was suddenly focused on trying to figure out what the rest of his life was supposed to look like. So far, the days of his youth had been the flat-out pursuit of self-indulgence, pursued, that is, by someone with the most unrefined sense of self. Most likely he had not given Sally, one of his many one-night inamoratas, and his back-seat romp with her much serious reflection. I'm guessing also the prospect of fatherhood in the near future for this young man from a family of "Primitive Methodists" was about as appealing as the thought of spending the rest of his life as a celibate Roman Catholic priest.

After Doc Shelby gave Sally the bad news a couple of weeks before graduation she set out in desperate search of the elusive escape artist. Finally, she tracked him down. He was ensconced in his late afternoon habitat, a rat shit bar called "Jimmy's." Jimmy's, five blocks from where Harry lived in Lansing, was an easy walk back to this apartment. Good thing for reasons that should be obvious.

Standing outside, if you were struggling to decide whether Jimmy's was worth a stop off, you'd be facing an old, two-story construction, finished in grimy red stucco with one big window. It was plastered with beer decals and probably was last washed when Harry Truman was President and American soldiers were getting killed in Korea for reasons that still remain obscure. Nothing on the outside would tempt you to enter. The block letters composing "Jimmy's" above the door had eroded somewhat with the top of the "J" partly missing and the "s" almost gone.

Inside, its walls were littered with the heads of deer, moose, black bear and assorted game fish, large-mouth bass mostly. Jimmy's was a sports bar before there were "sports bars" – a rustic *Field & Stream*, *Guns-n-Ammo* kind of hang out. No television screens. No perky, young waitresses in tight sweaters. No Expresso or Cranberry Martinis available from the bar. Ralphie, the bartender, was the fashion plate of the joint with a flat-top hair-cut and accoutered in a ratty sweatshirt. At 5'10" and around 280 pounds, this human battle tank had never in his forty or so years met a living soul he could not easily intimidate. With the disposition of an abused Rottweiler, Ralphie delivered service with a snarl. He also doubled as the bouncer, mostly a ceremonial function. To gain entry to the men's john in this den of dead critters you had to cross the path of a striped-helmeted sentry, a fierce, yellow-toothed badger mounted not far from the door. Courtesy of a (probably drunken) taxidermist was the moldy carcass of a northern Michigan Wild Cat perched high on a ledge behind the bar, jaws stretched menacingly wide-open, crouched and ready to spring. A 14-ounce jar of Carlings Black Label draft beer ran you 40 cents – from four to six p.m., two for half a buck. Achieving inebriation at Jimmy's (the only way to appreciate the nuances of its ambiance) was a risk-free venture – high return, so to speak, on low investment.

Harry had camped out in the back of the bar in a corner booth from where he could survey his humble kingdom. On this particular afternoon he was pondering his diminishing options. Taking meditative puffs on a Phillies cheroot, his right hand was fixed in its natural position, wrapped around a brown bottle beside an empty shot glass recently topped off with Jim Beam. Attached to the wall immediately above him were the massive head and antlers of a once proud, white-tailed buck whose glass eyes glowered suspiciously at the clientele as they wandered past. With Harry were two of his buddies, Dick Sorge and Mike Straight, both of whom resembled motley rejects from a police lineup. They were half-heartedly engaged in alcohol-tinged persiflage that was descending from almost-recognizable conversation into competing echoes of inebriated incoherence.

Sally was standing nervously outside Jimmy's listening to the din drifting out from the fusty inner sanctum. She couldn't help but wonder exactly what she would say to Harry if she found her one-night paramour in its cheesy bowels. How sober would he be? It was still early, so maybe. No matter. Here goes. She took a deep breath and pushed open the heavy wooden door to the tavern. Sally hesitated a moment and cautiously made her way into this funky smelling stowage of wild life cadavers and hebetudinous dipsomaniacs. Ralphie peered owlishly out from behind the bar and puzzled over what or who in this drab underworld under his jealous guardianship could possibly entice an unaccompanied, young woman with such admirable physical credentials to enter. Merle Haggard's "Okie from Muskogee" was wafting out of the jukebox. "We don't burn no draft cards down on Main Street. We like livin' right, and bein' free." Too late, Sally was thinking for "livin' right." "Bein' free"? Well, being a little *too* free was what got her into this sorry fix and standing in this dump. Sally then paused slightly and let her eyes adjust to the smoke and the gloomy darkness. She was momentarily at a loss for words that might capture the feel of Jimmy's and signal that it might be best to decamp. Somehow, "seedy", or "derelict" did not quite do it. No. Onward. In search of Harry, what did she expect? She moved cautiously toward the back of the bar then stopped. There was Harry slouched in that booth. Finally. Now what?

Harry looked up. She was standing a few feet away, silent, motionless, eyes fixed, staring at him. He reacted with a startle reflex, like that buck now on the wall above him when he snapped his head up just before the slug from the hunter's 308 Winchester rifle hit him behind the front shoulder, collapsing him onto the snow-covered ground. Recovering, then sheepishly to himself: "Damn! It's Sally. I should have called her. No way to avoid her now." He told his friends to take off which they did quickly. But before he could get up Sally quickly slid into the booth across from him. Coming to a stop, she bent and planked her elbows down on the table, face cupped in her hands, little girl-like. She was leaning over toward Harry with a big, fake smile not saying a word, waiting for the squirming, vanishing Romeo to figure out what to say – certainly an awkward moment for Mister Intrepid of one-night romances and rapid retreats. I'll relate the conversation that ensued as I've tried over the years to imagine how it unfolded. It must have been a doozy.

> Harry with insulting insincerity: "Hey, hey Sally. Uh, great to see you. I've been meaning to call you. How've you been?"

"Hell hath no fury like a woman scorned," as the Bard put it.

> Sally: "Hey, hey, ha, ha, glad you remembered my name, Terry. Oh wait, it's Larry, Jerry, whatever. How have *Iiiii* been? Guess what, Harrrry? Iiii'mm … whadda call it? Pa-reg-nant. Pregnant, asshole, knocked up, with child, bun in the oven – any and all of the above, just in case you've been wondering. So, how've *you* been? Where have you been? I thought maybe…"

Harry: "Whoa, whoa, whoa…"

This unfortunate word-choice of a horse-drawn carriage coachman drove Sally to translate her pent-up fury into an effusion of punishing sarcasm: "'Whoa,' 'whoa,' 'whoa'? No, Harry. Waaay too late. Maybe you don't remember: it was all go, go, go and no whoa-Nellie that night at the movies. So, where are we now? Well, *I'm* going to have *your* baby long about late December. Hey, a Christmas Baby-Jesus just for you, Joseph! Maybe we can find a stable near that hick town where you said you're from, and you can pitch in with the delivery. The angels singing from on high... 'My Baby does the Hanky-Panky.' Some of the sheep-buggering local shepherds you grew up with maybe will wander over from the near-by fields to get a peek at our little guy or gal in the manger. Any Wise Men you know from the east, Detroit, maybe, to make the trek and bring gifts?"

Harry was looking god-awful, desperate, like some low-life perp getting the third degree from Telly Savalas in an episode of "Kojak."

So, let's follow the exchange now as it moved rapidly downward, downward as in Elizabeth Kübler-Ross's "five stages of grief." Grief comes in many guises. Sally and Harry were feeling "a great deal of grief" as Hobbes might say, each in her and his own special way as well as with each other.

Jog my memory, could you, Reader? What's the first stage?

Ah, yes, "denial."

Harry: "You're sure you're pregnant? You're sure it's...?" Denial, of a very churlish sort.

Sally, as you can see, was already well past her brief stage of denial in Doc Shelby's office. She was deep into stage two, anger – anger of the simmering kind. She flinched and pulled back with a long, piercing stare. Then slowly she put up the *digitus infamis* of her right hand, pulling it slowly back toward her face. The stare turned into the nastiest sneer she could muster. Stage-two-anger expressed, you might say, with a hostile exclamation point.

Harry: "Ok, ok. Sorry. Wow. Jesus. Fuck..." Harry's denial was moving toward anger.

Mom: "Fuck? Oh perfect. That lousy, backseat fuckety-fuck you so quickly forgot about is why you and I are having this friendly conversation here in your charming taxidermist's happy hunting ground."

Harry took a long pull on his bottle of Drewrys Extra Dry. He was thinking, thinking, thinking. Well, something that weakly resembled thinking. Then, the next dumb ass question, just the one you'd predict.

Harry: "Is it too late to ... You know?" Stage three, bargaining, feckless bargaining.

Sally: "Tooo, you know, you know ... Too late to do what? Find some board-certified surgeon with a rusty coat hanger?" Stuck in anger.

Harry: "No, Jesus, an abortion, safely with a real doctor. It's gotta be legal somewhere." More feeble bargaining.

Sally: "Oh yeah, I'll just go ... somewhere! And with some money from ... somebody. And in quest of some 'real' doctor somebody or other. That's a plan that makes perfect sense, Harry. So simple, easy and affordable. Why didn't I think of that?" Can't move off anger cum sarcasm.

A long pause followed while they sat and stared hopelessly at each other. Stage four, depression, setting in for both.

Sally gave a deep sigh and teared up: "Look, ok, shit. I'm sorry, Harry. Not really. I'm losing it. I'm really pissed at you, but I was just as willing as you and even more stupid, if that's possible. I'm scared. You probably won't believe it, but 'that night' was not my usual dating etiquette. I don't know what I'm going to tell my folks. It would be one thing for me to tell them that my long-term boyfriend is the father. They wouldn't be happy, but they might forgive me for that. But, come on! Some guy I just happened to meet and just happened to hump on the first date? My parents are very, I mean, *very* Baptist. How do you think that is going to go over? 'Oh, that's wonderful, Honey. A little bundle of joy sent from heaven above – ok, from a drive-in movie down here below curtesy of Mr. Who-is-it now? Hey, but that's almost as good. Just what we were hoping for.'" Stage four, dripping with sarcasm.

Harry just sat in that booth across from my mom, his head down looking like one ashamed, pathetic, young man.

Finally.

"I'm really sorry, Sally. I don't know what to tell you. I'm broke. My student draft-deferment is over. Vietnam is calling. I'm working on a job possibility out of state in Kansas City, Missouri. It will pay well. But it's a long shot. If I can pull it off and dodge the draft, I can send you money."

Sally: "Sorry your ass. I'm a lot worse off than sorry. Ok, I really didn't expect you to do anything just now. I just needed you to know. You would want to know, right? Don't answer. I'm going ahead with the graduation ceremony in a couple of weeks for the sake of Mom and Dad. After that I'll have to tell them that I got knocked up on a blind date with a guy from... Where is it, again, you're from? Any suggestions on how to put a positive spin on it? Forget it.

It's really better for them and for me if you are out of the picture, at least for now. Here's my home address. Contact me when you get settled. I'll let you know – boy or girl. I *am* going to need money."

For Harry and Sally: stage five, "acceptance," of sorts.

"Having my baby....

The seed inside you…

Do you feel it growin'

Are you happy in knowin' that you're having my baby?"

—**Paul Anka**, *Having my Baby*

No.

4 Confession Time

"Confession has to be part of your new life."

—Ludwig Wittgenstein

The graduation ceremony left Sally brooding in a pit of melancholy and regret. Hours later, she gathered her belongings from her apartment and loaded them into her car. She bid a terse goodbye to her roommate Elizabeth and silently cursed her for helping to launch that disaster of a blind date. Sally needed to distribute the blame for her current fix in as wide a swath as possible. Harry was already gone – the inauguration of what would be his signature disappearing act. He'd skipped the graduation festivities. His past four years had been one long festivity. He'd left Sally in a less than festive frame of mind. She had talked to him once again just before he went to Kansas City. After that conversation, Sally briefly contemplated Voodoo and considered having a doll named Harry with some pins thrust through the torso and the legs.

Before that evening of infelicitous fornication with Harry, Sally had planned, post-graduation, to move to Chicago, get an apartment with one of her recently graduated friends and get a job. Instead, she was headed back to her home town to join mom and dad, Gladys and Richard. Oh, and to buck herself up for telling them about how Harry met Sally.

On that fateful movie night in April Sally had responded positively to what seemed to be the most casual of opportunities. But… "One only has to refuse a casual opportunity, and the curve of one's life commences a long, slow bending away from what it would have been." Yes, Mr. Kenner, looking back at all those "casual" opportunities in one's life – what a difference they make – the consents and the refusals. What different bends would that curve of Sally's life have taken had she refused that "opportunity" offered by a guy named Harry?

Sally's morning nausea had relented. Her appetite was revived. Three days at home had passed. The minister's daughter had put off what had to be done for as long as she could. It was "Come to Jesus" time. The summa cum laude graduate now sat at the family kitchen table suffused with an inner gloom that had been mounting as she prepared to divulge the circumstances and consequence of her recent impulsive transgression. Gladys was clearing the dishes from lunch while Sally watched her mother, working up the spunk to get this ugly business behind her. Her dad, Richard, was off somewhere. "Can't delay this any longer," she said to herself. This was as good a time as any to "drop the bomb." Mom first, then on to Dad – both of them together were simply beyond her limited confessional skill set at this time.

Gladys had missed her daughter and was brightened by having her at home again. Her mood was upbeat and cheerful. As she moved toward the sink, dishes in hand, she couldn't help but emit a burst of motherly bonhomie:

> "It's good to see you, Sally, eating more and putting on weight. A few more pounds won't hurt. You've always been so thin."

Finally. This was the opening Sally was waiting for.

> "I'm afraid it's temporary, Mom."

In mid-stride toward the sink Sally's mom stopped and stiffened. She slowly turned around and looked at Sally at first confused. That look quickly surrendered to the stern countenance of apprehension. An "edge" suddenly turned her voice from motherly-solicitous to motherly-suspicious.

> "What do you mean, 'temporary?'"

"Temporary." That word hung in the air giving off an ominous shadow that seemed to make the brightly lit kitchen suddenly darken.

Gladys's suspicioned-tinged rejoinder alchemized Sally into two Sallies: a scared, guilt-ridden Sally who was about to tell her mother about the "grief" of her impulsive act of fornication; a detached-Sally observing the anguish and confusion of two interlocutors.

Guilt-ridden Sally paused, took a deep breath as she prepared to discharge her dark secret. Well, the most elemental part of it. The painful extraction that would put *all* the seamy "details" completely out on the table would then follow.

> "I've been dreading this, Mom. Here goes.
> 'Temporary' as in I'm pregnant."

There, finally spoken out loud – that word, "pregnant," with its power to instantly change how people think about the future.

Gladys froze for a moment then moved in an austere silence back to the table. Slowly, almost cautiously, she descended into her chair as if it might not support the additional "weight" she suddenly felt bearing down on her. She carefully set the plates down in front of her, paused and pushed them to the side. With smoothly executed movements she retrieved her extended arms, gently clasped her hands together and took a deep breath – for several moments, immobilized. Fully erect in her chair, she then released her hands and folded her arms against her chest. Her eyes she fixed on Sally's now bloodless face. Gladys had assumed that easily recognizable, rigid posture of "self-defense" one takes against bad news that comes in suddenly and catches you off guard.

Her first, audible response came in a firm, soft voice:

> "How far along?"
>
> "Three months."

The shock had registered. Of course, Sally was pregnant. Gladys suddenly felt foolish. How could she have missed all the obvious signs? Immediately, she clasped on to a desperate hope for a denouement that would salvage the respectability of her daughter's imperiled future – marriage. But soon – matrimony with a known-commodity son-in-law to be. Yes. Then a few months after the baby's arrival she could relax. In a quiet evening over the dinner table she would gently sigh, then smile and say to Richard: "The marriage came late or the baby came early, but it doesn't matter now, does it, Dear?"

This desperate and, of course, futile fantasizing was creating a long, torturous pause for guilt-ridden Sally.

She was anxiously waiting. Detached-Sally was intrigued by the dramatic tension that was building and wondering how long before Gladys would ask "the question" – the question that would make her body double squirm.

Finally, from Gladys:

"The father?"

Silence.

Detached-Sally knew what the follow up from Gladys would be. Her mom had clutched at a dying-star in a human form, specifically in the form of ....

"Randy?"

Randy was Sally's steady boyfriend in high school as well as off and on during her university days. He too had gone to Michigan State University, and he always seemed to be somewhere in the picture – at least that's what Gladys thought. Sally's parents never knew about Gus from the garage band. Good thing. They liked Randy, though in a less than whole-hearted way. His parents were solid members of Richard's church. In an ideal world Randy would not be Gladys's first choice for a son-in-law, but...

"No, Mom. It's not Randy."

A body-blow. That hope was dashed by guilt-ridden Sally. Gladys was now looking even more stricken, and detached-Sally was bracing herself for the impact of the next seismic shockwave to hit Mom's parental universe.

"Not Randy?"

Guilt-ridden Sally shook her head in confirmation.

It took another few moments for this to sink in. No scenario was coming to Gladys's mind now but the worst case. She was beginning to grasp the unvarnished truth of Sally's "dilemma." Ok, the truth, the whole truth and nothing but the truth. Press on. "Just the facts, Ma'am," as Sergeant Joe Friday from "Dragnet" would demand from the ladies he questioned. Gladys's gaze had shifted away from Sally, now down toward the table. Then the dreaded question almost at a whisper:

"Well, who then?"

Sally in prolonged silence stared past her mother, futilely trying to obliterate the reality of the present moment and its feeling of intense discomfort. Finally, in a flat, emotionless ejaculation.

"Harry."

Gladys looked back up at Sally, again with a bewildered expression.

> "Harry?" She paused. She recoiled in her chair pulling her arms even more tightly against her chest, her brow tightening, struggling to retrieve that name from her reliable memory bank. "You've never talked about him. How, uh, how long have you been dating ... Harry?"

> "Not very long."

> "How 'not very long' is not very long, Sally?"

Another long, painful pause.

Guilt-ridden Sally was now staring down at the table; anything to avoid the icy, probing look of her mother. Gladys's face had turned ashen color.

Detached-Sally to guilt-ridden Sally: "'The bad', little girl you've copped to – now, well, now it's time for the ... 'the ugly'."

Up next, ugly. To be followed by shame and her tag-team partner, humiliation. The answer was going to throw Mom into that state of anguish that both Sallies knew was inevitable.

> "It was a one-night stand, Mom, a stupid mistake. I…"

Now, in a cruel *en connaissance de cause* Gladys recoiled and froze momentarily. Then with an anguished outburst of incredulity:

> "A mistake? A mistake? A one-night stand? What does that even mean? What…? How did …? Did he, did *he*…?"

"No. No Mom, he didn't force me."

"Oh my God, Sally. Who *are* you?"

Gooood question, Gladys: who was Sally? Unfortunately, Sally had nary a clue. After a Baptist upbringing, four years of college culminating in casual coitus with a cad named Harry, for her it was an ongoing, now-unfolding mystery, a dark one. More importantly, she was three months pregnant with no boyfriend or husband in the picture, no job and stuck in Podunkville, Michigan with a very disappointed mom, and soon, dad. What did the future have in store for Sally?

As an old Scottish proverb goes: "Confessed faults are half-mended."

5 Preacher's Children

> "Miss Nancy Ellicott smoked
>
> And danced all the modern dances;
>
> And her aunts were not quite sure how
>   they felt about it,
>
> But they knew that it was modern."
>
> —**T.S. Eliot**, Cousin Nancy

My mother was the youngest of the three Richard and Gladys Martin's begats. She was born and reared in Bad Axe, a town of 3,000 in the thumb region of Michigan. The town's rustic name was originally "Bad Axe Camp," courtesy of its settler Rudolf Papst. Papst was the head surveyor of a crew that broke the first state road through the Huron County wilderness in 1861. On the site where he made camp Papst discovered a well-worn and badly damaged axe. At the time, "Bad Axe Camp" seemed as appropriate as anything to call this frontier stop. For posterity the camp became "Bad Axe."

Sally's brother, Paul, was valedictorian of his high school graduating class with the highest ACT in the history of the high school. He went on to graduate from conservative Wheaton College, outside Chicago and then to seminary. Now at a young age he was a senior pastor at one of the biggest Baptist churches in Dallas, Texas. Her sister Ruth Ann went to Western Michigan University. She became a surgical nurse and married a Baptist missionary named David Livingstone (no joke). Now she was somewhere in West Africa helping him bring Christ to the folks in the Dark Continent. Her Dad had been the First Baptist Church minister in Bad Axe for twenty-five years. There was only one Baptist church in the town so, why "the First"? I don't know.

Sally had fallen a bit farther from the tree than Paul or Ruth Ann – a couple of light years farther. From day-one she was a wild child. She began to mount a valiant, counter-insurgency operation against any and all things "Baptist" by the time she found herself in toddler's Sunday school. In high school she was grounded half of the time for regular bouts of un-Baptist hanky-panky – smoking cigarettes, potty-mouth, immodest attire, sneaking off to dances, coming home past curfew tipsy. Sally was in many ways a typical PK (Preacher's Kid). Every minister's family seems to have at least one – rebellious, antinomian, wild-ass – bound and determined like Samson to grasp the pillars of perdition and pull down the house of shame on the head of Pastor Dad. During her last two high school years, Sally settled down. She hit the books and got a full academic scholarship at Michigan State University. Wild-Sally had always been the yin to the Smart-Sally yang.

Off she went for four years. Now she was back in Bad Axe sitting in the family kitchen watching dear, old mom doing a "Patsy Cline" – falling to pieces. Of course, still in blissful ignorance, was Dad – but not for long. Who was going to relay the glad tidings of great joy to Daddy – Sally or Gladys?

That evening following Sally's midday confession, a deadly quiet dinner ensued with Richard picking up on the nervousness and tension in the air. Sally hastily retreated to her bedroom before the apple pie dessert was put on the table. Gladys cleared off the plates and silverware in silence. Without his asking, Gladys poured second cups of coffee. She placed one of them in front of Richard as he looked up at his grim-faced wife with growing apprehension. Gladys sat down, sat silently for a time looking at Richard wondering how he would react to the details of Sally's predicament. Before she said a word, her husband had figured it out.

Half an hour later there was a gentle tap on Sally's bedroom door.

"Sally, it's Dad. May I come in?"

Sally was red-eyed, sitting on her bed when Dad entered and eased himself down into a chair.

Awkward silence for a bit.

> Sally: "Well Dad, now you know: makes you proud of me, I'll bet."

> Richard finally smiled weakly and said: "Well, Sally, you've always been full of surprises. This one? I'm afraid I'm going to need a bit of time to try to

come to grips with it. I'm not going to go 'preacher' on you. No 'God, sin, prayer, forgiveness, guilt' sermon. That's pointless. It always was. I know it. You know it. But I'm still your father. I love you and want the best for you. But Sally, I fear for your future. I see a self-destructive streak in you. But you're an adult and out of reach for me or your mother."

Sally looked even more glum and continued to dab at her eyes with a soggy Kleenex.

Richard took a deep breath:

"I'm sorry, Sally. I need to ask you this. Your mother and I are wondering what role is, uh, Harry going to play in your 'family way'? I know. Maybe I'm old fashioned. I can't help it. It's not right. Men don't just get to walk away from women they put into this kind of a fix. Is he the kind of man that...?"

"Dad, I don't know what *kind* of man he is. Really, I couldn't tell you. Which makes me even more ashamed of my "fix." I'm ... I don't even know how to describe it. I know it is probably hard for you to understand how differently I look at things than you or mom or even Paul and Ruth Ann. We are in different worlds. Love, marriage, sex, children – for most of us young people, well … all of it is in a flux. Of course, I didn't want this. I just… Harry? From what I know about him, and it's not much, he's not the kind of man you'd want for a son-in-law; not the kind I'd want for a husband, assuming that I even want a husband."

Richard sat for a long while looking intently at his daughter, his eyes tearing up slightly, his lips tightening. Finally:

"No, Sally. I understand, and my understanding of it saddens me more than I can tell you. This world of 'flux' you speak of? I've seen it coming for a long time and to be honest, it frightens me. It's a disintegrating world. I see disaster ahead, not just for you. You've chosen it. I wish it were different but ...."

"Dad, I really am sorry for the anguish this is causing you and Mom. It was a one-night piece of horrible stupidity. You and Mom are disappointed in me for good reasons. I let you down. If you never forgive me, I'll understand. I fear that your congregation will somehow blame you for my whorish ways. They shouldn't. Maybe I should find another place to live until the baby comes. That would be best for the family."

Richard winced, then feebly laughed for a couple of seconds.

"No, Sally. I have a higher estimation of 'my flock' than you do. They'll be ok. Your mother and I will be alright. It looks like, though, from what you're saying, Harry is completely out of the picture. This greatly distresses me, although I don't think that I would want to be around him. I won't say anything more about him. Of course, you must stay with us. You shouldn't have to go through this alone. No matter what, we love you. How could we not? Forgiveness is part of our faith: if it doesn't work in families, what good can it be? After the baby is born we can talk about the next steps."

6 Family Secrets and "Next Steps"

"And because in deliberation, the
appetites and aversions are raised by
foresight of the good and evil conse-
quences, and sequels of the action
whereof we deliberate; the good or evil
effect thereof dependeth on the foresight
of a long chain of consequences, of
which very seldom any man is able to
see to the end."

—Thomas Hobbes, *Leviathan*

I arrived, the first material link in a "long chain of consequences." I came to Bad Axe on December 18, 1969.
My delivery in the Huron Memorial Hospital happened just before a blizzard blew across from Canada
that dropped ten inches of snow. My birthday was the
same as the Soviet dictator and mass-murderer, Joseph Vissarionovich Stalin. The delivery was a tough
one for Sally – thirty hours in labor.

Mom named me Joseph. For the husband of the
Virgin Mary, the Commie butcher, someone else or
nobody? I asked her once. She shook her head and
gave me one of her sphinxlike smiles: "My little secret," she said. Yes, her little secret.

"Secrets, silent, stony sit in the dark
palaces of both our hearts: secrets
weary of their tyranny: tyrants willing
to be dethroned."

—James Joyce, *Ulysses*

Not to belabor my mysterious naming. What's in a name? A cynic by the name of Wyndham Lewis grasped the sheer flukiness of it all. "Bolts from the blue they flop on men and women from nowhere, in their cradles, on each anonymous noodle – all of us worse luck have to be a Something."

For motherhood, Sally was not, at least at this time, well suited or remotely prepared. After six months Mom and the grandparents agreed: it was time for a change, a separation. Sally needed to go somewhere. But where? At first, Sally, Richard and Gladys were pointing me toward adoption. They were warned. "Make the decision quickly!" But they waited too long. I charmed them quickly – "them" being my grandparents mainly. Sally thought I was adorable, but adorable wasn't enough for her to attempt the tribulations of single-motherhood. Gladys and Richard, however, couldn't let themselves part with me. Sally would go. The "love-child" would stay in Bad Axe – for a while.

Sally's major at the university was Political Science. Before her untimely dalliance with Harry, she had planned to go on and study law. She'd taken the LSAT and scored well. That with her magna cum laude grades meant she had a good shot at admission to a top-tier law school. The law was not now in Sally's immediate future.

Instead, Papa Richard, made a reluctant phone call to Sally's uncle, his brother, Daniel who lived in Washington DC. Daniel was a senior legislative aide to John Dingell Jr., the U.S. Representative from Michigan's 16th Congressional District which included Dearborn and the south Detroit suburbs.

Sally had pushed hard on her Dad to make this call. She was desperate. With the family connection, she hoped her uncle might be persuaded to offer her an internship in either the Dearborn or the DC Congressional office. This could be a ticket to bigger and better things for her and maybe a chance at law school someday.

Richard's reluctance to make that call was due to the low esteem in which he held his brother. Daniel's lack of religious piety and his obsession with money and power, Richard believed, made him less than an admirable human being. He was not someone who might help chart a better course for his persistently wayward daughter. But, Sally was unrelenting. Richard finally gave way to her pleading. He could only hope that he was overestimating the seductive power of Daniel's influence and in what unwholesome directions he feared it might lead her.

Family history moves us to the root of Richard's aversion to Daniel. It signals what eventually would unfold from his hesitant complicity in handing his daughter over to his brother's guidance and influence.

Ah, yes, family history. Few families, I'm tempted to think, come up clean when the spotlight turns on the highlights of ancestral "achievements." Poking into family history is too much like dumpster-diving. To extract a few items of value, you must brace yourself. You hold your nose then rummage your way down through layers of fetid, reeking refuse. In the hope of...

Brothers Daniel and Richard grew up near Detroit during the Great Depression. Their father, my great grandfather, Marco LaMare, was born in Italy's Basilicata region sometime in the 1890s. He came to the U.S. with his parents as a young boy. After a short stint in New York City, the family settled in Detroit's Little Italy in an area along Gratiot Avenue and Riopelle Streets near Black Bottom and Paradise Valley east of the downtown.

Marco was probably the smartest kid in the neighborhood, but his inclinations were decidedly and singularly criminal. Though not Sicilian, at a young age he insinuated his way into the *cosca* (clan) of Antonio Giannola, the most powerful of the Mafia crime *la famiglia* in Detroit. Initially, he earned his chops on the streets – gambling, prostitution and commercial hijacking. But as an ambitious and resourceful hoodlum, he was going to go places.

Prohibition unleashed his prodigious managerial and entrepreneurial talents. They made possible his rapid ascent to higher circles of organized crime. By the mid-1920s Detroit was home to more than 25,000 illegal speakeasies. They pushed the demand for liquor to astronomical levels and thus the enticement of financial reward for those willing to engage in the high-risk, criminal work of supply.

Marco's initial success in the booze smuggling business was the result of his organization of a fleet of high-speed boats that moved the hooch brewed in Ontario through southern Lake St. Clair, down the Detroit river in the dead of night to distribution harbors in the Motor City. In the winter, Marco's crew would transport the cases of whiskey across the frozen river from Windsor in small trucks they called "whiskey sixes," so called for their smaller, lighter, six-cylinder engines less likely to break through the ice. When the U.S. Coast Guard muscled up and successfully interdicted the river transportation of the liquid contraband, Marco resorted to small airplanes. This handsome Dago was a problem solver.

By 1929 Marco was heading up one of the most powerful and lucrative bootleg-smuggling operations in the Midwest. He was already a very wealthy man. His spectacular success brought his Italian operation inevitably into direct competition and violent conflict with the Jewish led Detroit Purple Gang. This confederacy of hoodlums controlled many of the highly profitable speakeasies and monopolized its hold on them with deadly force. The Purple Gang was to become infamous for the reign of criminal terror it unleashed in the city during the 1920s. The gang members were a particularly brazen and flamboyant crew, and their escapades became legendary in the annals of American organized-crime lore. The Purple Gang, however, was amenable to working with some of the Italian mobsters. Al Capone became one of their better-known bootlegging partners. Capone's ancestry, like Marco's, was not Sicilian. He defied ethnic solidarity and re-cruited Jews, Irishmen, and Eastern European immi-grants into his ranks. For several years the Purples had a "business" relationship with Scarface. They sup-plied the mobster with Canadian whisky for sale and distribution in Chicago. There were persistent rumors that the Purple Gang had been involved in the infa-mous St. Valentine's Day Massacre on Chicago's south side.

In 1960 "The Purple Gang" starring Barry Sullivan and Robert Blake was released. It was a Hollywood drama that attempted to capture the gang's bootleg-ging, hijacking and murderous marauding. Blake's performance as the most nasty, vicious little thug you'll ever see on a movie screen makes watching this mediocre production worthwhile. In real life, Blake was tried and acquitted for murdering his wife. The Detroit gang even made comic mention in Elvis Pres-ley's rock-n-roll hit, "Jailhouse Rock." "The drummer boy from Illinois went crash, boom, bang. The whole rhythm section was the Purple Gang."

Purple shooters gunned down two of Marco's Si-cilian "soldiers" in 1927. Marco himself narrowly missed assassination. However, by the early 1930s the Mafia took control of the Detroit underworld and put the Purple Gang out of business. Marco had planned the framing of Harry Fleicher, a PG boss, for the kill-ing of a Detroit police detective, a murder carried out by one of Marco's own hitmen at Marco's behest.

With the end of Prohibition in 1933 Marco began planning his separation from the criminal side of the

Mafia operations. By that time, Richard and Daniel were young adolescents. The former crime boss discretely evolved into a "legitimate" business man. He bought commercial real estate. His acquisition of a string of lucrative car dealerships in Wayne and Macomb counties became an auto-sales empire owned and operated by an anglicized "Mark Martin" – "Martin Chevrolet & Oldsmobile." "A deal with Mark is your best car deal" was the jingle that capped his ubiquitous radio commercials and billboard signs. His family residence he moved from Detroit to Grosse Pointe Farms where in a stately mansion his metamorphosis to Waspish-resembling respectability was brought to completion.

Marco was no longer recognized as an Italian-born mobster by the Detroit community. His ample wealth enabled him to manicure his shady past. His shiny suits became pinstriped gray and conservative. His business dealings appeared legitimate, and he anglicized the names of his sons. They grew up as Richard and Daniel Martin. His Italian Catholicism he jettisoned for membership in a Lutheran church. He also shed his Italian-born, first wife, Gina, and married a German-American woman, Giselle – hence his respectable, conservative Lutheran image.

Richard from an early age grasped intuitively the dark and ruthless side of his father's personality and instinctively recoiled from it. Daniel in stark contrast was very much a creature of Marco – ambitious, ethically unencumbered and smart. The brothers' personalities and personal inclinations pushed them in opposite directions and destinations. Richard, introspective and contemplative with deep religious impulses that resembled his mother's, became estranged from his father at an early age. After the divorce he remained with Marco's first wife, Gina. At Baylor University in Waco, Texas – deliberately chosen to be as far as he could from his father – Richard found his professional calling, the ministry. It was the Baptist faith with its message of salvation and redemption and its rather strict rules (then) for personal conduct that became his spiritual locus. The personality difference between Marco and Richard was perhaps an illustration of Newton's "third law": "for every action, there is an equal and opposite reaction."

Four years younger than Richard, Daniel chartered a different course from his older brother and remained with his father after the divorce. He graduated from Kalamazoo College and went directly to the University of Michigan School of Law. Yearning to quickly sharpen his courtroom sparing skills, upon graduation he hung out his shingle as a defense attorney in a modest, one-person office in blue-collar Ypsilanti circa Ann Arbor. There he specialized in the defense of sex-offenders – rapists and pedophiles – in ample supply in Ypsi, as they called it. Daniel must have reasoned: "If I can successfully defend *these* kinds of people, I'll know I'm a damn good lawyer." He was. He was amazingly successful in the courtroom, outdueling city attorneys and county prosecutors. The sex-criminals went back on to the streets to resume their depredations. Daniel was a master legal technician. He had the best jury acquittal rate of all the defense lawyers in the city and was very good on appeals.

His career as a defense attorney was merely a temporary stop for someone of Daniel's prodigious lawyerly abilities. Eventually he moved into a lucrative, private practice with a Detroit law firm whose biggest client was General Motors. His courtroom battles there were for much higher stakes. His successful litigation of a string of lawsuits in favor of this behemoth client attracted the attention of John Dingell Jr. who was known as GM's resident Congressman. Politics was Daniel's true destination. Money was secondary to power, and the offer to align himself with a very powerful man was an offer he could not refuse. He joined Dingell's staff and quickly rose up the ranks to become Dingell's Svengali, largely because his ability to do whatever had to be done closely resembled that of his father. Daniel was results, as well as process, oriented. His success as a feared consigliere to the powerful legislator, and the gratitude of General Motors made him an influential and powerful man in his own right.

As a husband and father, Daniel was not quite as successful as he was in the courtroom and politics. Twice divorced, he was too busy making deals, courting favors and forging useful "relationships" to know his two sons. By their mid-teens, the lads were already quite the connoisseurs of recreational drugs and headed for the deep waters of trouble. The oldest, Daniel Jr., some years later would die of a heroin overdose. The younger brother, Philip, killed a young woman passenger in his car in a crash while driving drunk. Daniel's second wife, Pamela Sue, a planner of high-end weddings for GM executives, went to the Michigan state prison in Marquette for eighteen months for soliciting an undercover-police hitman to kill him. She was planning to collect on a life insurance policy from the divorce settlement. A technicality overturned her conviction. She was released. Her newly-won freedom caused Daniel continuous unease.

Daniel was surprised when his secretary buzzed him to say that his brother, Richard, was on the line. He and Richard had not talked in several years. The last time Daniel had seen his niece, Sally, was at her high school graduation in Bad Axe. His phone conversation with his brother, though not warm, was cordial. It wasn't hard for Richard to sell Daniel on Sally's potential in the Dingell congressional office. She had been an outstanding student and was an excellent prospect. And though the brothers had not been on good terms, Daniel Martin had some of that Demarco Italian disposition of loyalty to family, "*è come se facesse parte della famiglia,*" he said to Richard. "She's quite one of the family." He also sensed that Sally was looking to escape the parochial confines of his brother's making. He was most willing to oblige.

> Daniel: "She sounds great, Richard. I'm so glad you made contact. Have her send me her CV, and I'll arrange for an interview. I'm looking forward to having a family member on the staff."

Richard: "Thank you, Daniel. I'm so grateful to you."

He shouldn't have been. Richard hadn't read Hobbes. He had not considered that "long chain of consequences, of which very seldom any man is able to see to the end."

7 Bad Axe to Babylon

*"We hang the petty thieves. The great
ones we appoint to public office."*

—Aesop

Sally's interview performance with Daniel and the Dingell staff was masterful. She had prepared herself well by spending long days pouring over the *Congressional Record*. She knew the bills, resolutions and motions proposed by the congressman whose office she hoped to join. The staff was amazed at the aplomb of the young woman from Hicksville. How did she acquire such a commanding knowledge of what their guy had been up to for so many years? She was not a jejune, new-university grad hoping for a soft-landing in the Big Leagues, curtesy of an inside connection. They were eager to have her join them.

Thrilled to be able to shake the Bad Axe, Baptist dust off her shoes, Sally headed for Washington DC.

A Puritan in Babylon was the title of a biography of Calvin Coolidge. Puritans were a rare breed in this city, especially at the top. The acerbic H.L. Mencken, who had little good to say about Coolidge during his Presidency, thus eulogized him:

"We suffer most when the White House busts with ideas. With a World Saver preceding him (I count out Harding as a mere hallucination) and a Wonder Boy following him, he begins to seem, in retrospect, an extremely comfortable and even praiseworthy citizen. His failings are forgotten; the country remembers only the grateful fact that he let it alone." High praise from a cynic like Mencken with well-deserved contempt alluded toward Wilson and Hoover.

"Babylon" in a single word captures the decadence and corruption of the capital of the American empire. It's the perfect place for the ambitious careerist who prudently exempts himself from the standards of rectitude he expects from others. To paraphrase a certain writer I admire, "A principled man in Washington DC is someone who objects to anyone else putting his hand in the till." In a single sentence Honoré de Balzac's mordant estimation of post-Napoleonic Paris would accurately describe Washington DC upon Sally's arrival. "No one who knows Paris believes a word that is said there, and not a word is said of what really goes on." Nothing that is said in Babylon matches up with what happens there.

For an astute observer there are certain demarcations – dress, posture, gait, attitude – that set the denizens of Babylon apart from the visitors. Babylonians display a certain mode of being that signals what they are, what they do and, most importantly, what they are after. The most salient feature is an air of sniffy self-importance.

Babylon might also splendidly reprise the lowest of Dante's poetic three divisions of hell – the hell of "the Leopard." He symbolizes fraud. Fraud in Dante's taxonomy of vice was worse than violence because it is a perversion of the higher gift of intellect. A beast can murder, but it takes a rational creature to deceive. Babylon was bursting with rational creatures, professional deceivers who devoted their gifts of intellect to outrageous artifices of self-worship and self-enrichment.

But what to do about Sally's impromptu, cute "begat" with Harry? Grandma and Grandpa were worried about him. Maybe a childhood spent in the fleshpots of Babylon, particularly with Sally's seemingly weaker motherly instincts unchecked, might not be the best place for their grandson. Likely, he would fail to mature. He would grow up unable to resist the destructive seductions of the adult world. Gladys and Richard, as I had mentioned, had become terribly fond of me.

It took little effort for them to convince Sally that I should remain in their tender custody. She would pursue her career in DC unimpeded by the cares and demands of an infant son. Off she went to join Daniel and the Dingell syndicate. Sally was restless. Sally was ready. Sally was determined to make connections and sharpen her elbows. Quickly she acquired the sophistication that brought success, the kind of success, that is, that bore the distinguishing marks of highly ambitious Babylonians.

Then there were the Babylonians who had already risen to the top. This would be the Dingell cabal – Babylonians to the nines – soon to be Sally's new family. The Dingell family was well on its way to becoming Michigan's premier political dynasty – nepotism the way the Good Lord intended. In this case, the "sins of the father" were taken up and further indulged and refined by the son. At the time of Sally's arrival, John Dingell Jr. was in his 8th House Congressional term. His father, John Sr., began his political ascent as a union boss. Elected to the House seat in 1932, he occupied it for eleven terms. He then bequeathed his patrimony to Junior, who went on to complete almost sixty years in the House. He retired as the longest serving member of Congress. Oh, and he ended up the third richest Congressman from Michigan. His net worth was estimated at $6 million. Not bad for a career as a humble "public servant."

Still, with Junior's retirement, the Dingells still weren't done. John Jr. passed his seat off to wife number two, Dame Debbie. He had married her at age fifty-five. She was a mere lassie of twenty-eight at the time. And, thus the trifecta. Dingell-Dingell-Dingell – "three blind mice; see how they run" – for office in perpetuity. "You've never seen such a sight in your life." Not like this multiple-generation of dedicated peculators. "Debbie does Dingell," motivationally and inclination wise, would – considering what the verb "does" in this context suggest – compares closely with the Debbie in "Debbie *does* Dallas." This popular, porno flick was a comedy starring Bambi Woods, who... well... The Dingell-Debbie before her marriage to John Jr. was GM lobbyist-Debbie. This was a line of solicitation-work comparable in its *bare* essentials to that of the Dallas-Debbie. John Jr., I mentioned, was GM's Congressional House water carrier. That corporation's government myrmidons, you'd be shocked to learn, do very well. When Debbie took over Junior's seat in 2014 her net worth was estimated at $3.6 million. You might wonder where it came from – not from producing and selling any kind of useful widgets, not from building or fixing anything. It came not from anything remotely resembling the blue-collar, proletarian work of many of her voting constituents. The median household income of the district she represented was $57,000. *La famiglia* Dingells' wealth was accumulated from the production of "favors" and the selling of influence. Dingell-father-and-son racked up a mind-boggling eighty-two continuous years in their congressional seat snookering the voters of southeastern Michigan before letting Debbie do it. Dynasties are so, you know, undemocratic. So, you might think that the father and son Dingell pocket-lining after eight decades in the same office into which Ms Debbie slipped would not be how "our democracy" is supposed to work. For a large number of the voters in Michigan, that *is* how it "works." Which would suggest that "democracy" for all of its honorific, awe-inspiring power might be a tad overrated. Which also might suggest that Babylon is really the capital of a plutocracy that brazenly calls itself a democracy. Like the Rome watched over by Juvenal: "For what matters infamy if the cash be kept?"

8 Catechumen in Babylon

*"I would not put a thief in my mouth
to steal my brains."*

—William Shakespeare, *Othello*

*"But there's booze in the blender
And soon it will render
That frozen concoction that helps me hang on…"*

—Jimmy Buffett, *Margaritaville*

Daniel put Sally on the Dingell congressional-staff payroll as an intern. He personally mentored her and gave her special attention with a flexible schedule. That enabled her to go to law school at Georgetown University – deep in the heart of Babylon – one of the best. Daniel picked up the expensive tuition tab. Four years later she was able to attach "Juris Doctor" to her name. After graduation and passing the DC bar exam on the first try, Sally joined Dingell's congressional staff full-time doing research and drafting legislation. She was where she wanted to be and doing what she had longed to do. Her hard work made Daniel justifiably proud of his decision to bring his niece on board and pleased with his mentoring. Sally rose quickly to assume a high perch in the DC Congressional office. Her smarts, exceptional good looks and charm made her a natural for liaison work with the many lobbyists that besieged the Congressman hoping to "purchase" his favor.

Soon, Sally was spending long hours schmoozing with lobbyists who were generous with the powerful elixir of compliance, liquor. Whether plying someone for sexual favors or for political favors, booze makes it easier to persuade a reluctant "someone" to come across with the goods. Enticing political favors is a bit more sophisticated and more expensive of a dance than getting casually laid, usually. Alcohol is the lubricant that oils the transmission gears of DC's Lobby-Engine and makes it hum. Without it, the wheelers and dealers – the law-makers and the influence peddlers who vie for their favors – would have to contend with those annoying ethical encumbrances to their transactions.

The tea-totaling ways of Sally's Baptist heritage, as we know from the "fallout" from her date-night at the drive-in movies with Harry, had never taken hold on her. Sally was good at many things including schmoozing. Johnnie Walker Blue at $250 a fifth made her even more effective, less afflicted by pangs of conscience or the constraints of rectitude. She embraced the work and willingly submitted herself to the influence of that costly lubrication. It made "doing business" easier to do. It became a part of who she was – very quickly. The strong affinity Sally acquired for spirits greatly affected the course of her life, particularly her personal life. But… her professional partnership with Scotch, Bourbon & Brandy also tells us something of ominous substance about how the ruling class of Babylon operates.

Alcohol figures markedly in the governing machinations of DC with the kind of *inhibitions* it tamps down among pushers and pullers on the levers of power. You see, politicians with the wrong kind of inhibitions don't make good politicians, "good" meaning getting reelected. By embracing norms that inhibit dishonesty, duplicity and double-dealing, the elected-ones quickly find themselves unelected – out of power, out to pasture. Alcohol's utility is to ensure that good public servants stay "good." It helps to lower and sometimes obliterate those troublesome inhibitions. It makes all that flexible, wink-wink stuff that politicians do on a daily basis – lying, trimming, access-peddling, promise-breaking, bribe-taking, vote-stealing – easier. After a while, it's just second nature. After a while, it just seems, well, normal. "What – me worry?" as Alfred E. Neuman used to say. As long as it doesn't get too brazen or spectacular nobody seems to notice, and the politicians don't worry. Keeping unnoticed is the trick.

> "Barnardine: 'Thou hast committed—
>
> Barabas: 'Fornication? But that was in another country: and besides, the wench is dead.'"

—Christopher Marlowe, *The Jew of Malta*

Once in a while the hijinks do get noticed, and the "wenches" are found alive. As in 1974 when such a spectacle ended the career of one Wilbur Mills of Arkansas. Mills had risen to the heights in Congress as chairman of the House Ways and Means Committee, the revenue-raising and taxation committee – often during his tenure referred to as "the most powerful man in Washington." Then along came Fannie. The married, 65-year-old powerful Committee chairman was discovered by DC police one night in the Tidal Basin romping with 38-year-old Annabell Battistella, aka Fannie Foxe, a busty stripper billed as the "Argentine Firecracker." Both, shall we say, were "under the influence." "Thou hast committed… Fornication, Wilber?" Mills later confessed to a non-Platonic "relationship" with the Firecracker, a much-alive and kicking wench. Who would blame him? He pleaded that "alcoholism," not the Devil, made him do it. That's the standard, fail-safe move of misdirection for politicians and movie stars – "victims" with tearfully expressed regret of their "weaknesses." Or, "mistakes," hobbies that suddenly acquire unfavorable publicity and get the name change that begs forgiveness.

What else could alcoholism "make him do?" For a straight-laced Baptist from the Bible Belt, such a firewater-fueled escapade was just too spectacular of an adventure to be forgiven and forgotten. How about for an Irish Catholic from Boston? Well, now as old Father O'Malley might pause to remind us: there is forgiveness, then there is God's forgiveness that "passes all understanding." Got it, Father. Thanks for that clarification. But for Wilbur? Sorry, God no can do in your case. Mills' fall from grace did provide some comic relief from the usual peculations, misappropriations and fornications that go on unabated in Babylon.

For those curious about how the intersection of alcohol and the exercise of power at the highest regions works, it's worth a look at *Conversations with Stalin*, written by Milovan Ðilas, a Yugoslav communist and a key figure in the Partisan movement during WWII. This highly entertaining book can also be read as a treatise on the "decency-numbing" effects of alcohol on powerful decision-makers. On war decision-making, alcohol, it would seem, brings the worst out *in* people occupying the highest ranks of "the worst" *kind* of people.

Ðilas and his boss Tito, the future dictator, were on numerous occasions summoned by Stalin to Moscow to participate in military-political strategy and planning sessions that would put WWII in the winning column for the USSR. Ðilas's "conversations" were with the General Secretary in his Dacha. Also, there was a pack of hyenas who doubled as Stalin's henchmen. The sessions took place throughout the late evening and early morning hours. As Ðilas relates it, much of Soviet military planning during the war was done by men in ascending stages of drunken revelry under Stalin's demanding supervision. From their mouths through their bladders flowed a steady stream of vodka and Georgian wine that would numb their brains of human impulses. Nocturnal debauches were standard operating procedure for war-planning. The result was cynically calculated betrayal and brutal implementation. Stalin captured the mentality of the schemers in one of his caustic, signature bon mots: "the death of one man is a tragedy; the death of millions is a statistic." Ensconced safely and comfortably in the Dacha with ample food and drink, war for the Kremlin crew was statistics and numbers. "And how many divisions does the Pope have?" Stalin was to have joked on one occasion – well, half-joking. The *Vozhd*, the Boss, held himself off from the heavy hitting of the sauce. Alcohol for him was a tool, a key element for "team-building," for extracting and stimulating the worst impulses – cruelty and treachery – in human beings. It was useful as well to manage opposition and to tamp down the intrusion of those "better angels" – assuming there were any to be found in his underlings.

Let's not, however, just pick on Uncle Joe and his merry band of miscreants. Alcohol's decency-numbing effects also came into play in the conduct of the war with Stalin's comrade in arms, Winston Churchill. Though deified by triumphalist British and American historians, Churchill was by most accounts a prodigious, lifelong alcoholic. That his consumption of spirits was daily and in massive quantities is well documented, though typically downplayed so as not to sully his manufactured sainted image. How much did Churchill's whiskey-soaked brain reduce whatever inhibitions he might have had to unleash the RAF to firebomb Dresden, Cologne and Hamburg – a massive slaughter with no direct military objectives? The results were infernos that incinerated hundreds of thousands of German civilians – women, children and elderly – war crimes of horrific proportions. These crimes, however, were committed by the winners. Winners of wars, as we know, exempt themselves from the moral opprobrium they heap upon the losers and the punishment they inflict on them – for what the winners themselves did – and shamelessly call it "justice."

Washington DC, where my story of Sally's sojourn in Babylon continues, was a binge drinking paradise. From its earliest days, it was home to a veritable rouges' gallery of famous drunkard politicians. Ulysses S. Grant was reputed to be frequently drunk, before, during and after his civil war battles. One might be tempted to draw some unflattering comparisons of Stalin's civilian-slaughtering Red Army with General Sherman unleashed by the whiskey-saturated Grant to reign down his infamous scorched-earth, total war through Georgia. Andrew Jackson distilled his own whiskey and brought it to the White House. Jacob Baer, a well-known whiskey merchant in Washington, DC reported that President James Buchanan made weekly purchases of ten gallons of rye whiskey.

Truman got many of his days started with a shot of bonded Old Granddad. Henry Kissinger related a story about Nixon, who had a low tolerance for alcohol and was reported to be a mean drunk. As Kissinger related it, one evening when Nixon was sloshed, he was trying to decide where in southeast Asia he wanted to "go nuclear." In the Senate, Joe McCarthy,

Lyndon Johnson and Everett Dirksen were hard drinkers. No such inventory is complete without the mention of Ted Kennedy.

As a child, Sally would hear her teetotaler Baptist Dad speak to the subject of booze with a quote from the Old Testament Book of Proverbs: "Wine is a mocker, strong drink is raging and he who is deceived thereof, is not wise." That advice was for Bad Axe. Sally now resided in Babylon, not renowned for its "wisdom," a place where deception is the rule and raging mockery is an esteemed, full-time profession.

All of this points to some intriguing irony with existential implications. Had there been no tipple in the back seat on that one and only date with Harry, there would probably be no me to be writing about her life. Without me, perhaps, Sally's destination might not have been in the worst place for someone imperiled by the domination of strong drink. Who knows? She didn't know it when she arrived in Babylon: I'm not sure she ever did.

9 Arnold Palmer: No, a Different Arnold

"Lay down, Sally, and rest here in my arms

Don't you think you want someone to talk to?

Lay down, Sally, no need to leave so soon

I've been trying all night long just to talk to you."

—**Eric Clapton**, *Lay down Sally*

"I am always looking for meaningful one-night stands."

—**Dudley Moore**

Sally finished law school, and things started going south for her. "South" was in the direction of a well-travelled Babylonian named Arnold Hirshman, a congressional staff member who worked for the Connecticut Senator, Abraham Ribicoff. Abe Ribicoff, an elderly few of you may recall, gained national attention at the raucous 1968 Democratic national convention in

Chicago. During his nominating speech for fellow Senator, George McGovern, Ribicoff veered off-script and poured rhetorical gasoline on the raging political fires inside the convention hall: "And with George McGovern as President of the United States, we wouldn't have to have Gestapo tactics in the streets of Chicago." That was back in the olden days when "Gestapo" wasn't hurled around as an every-day slur. The television cameras then moved close up to the enraged face of Richard Daley in the audience. You didn't need to be an accomplished lip reader to decipher his commentary on Ribicoff's "Gestapo" reproach so pointedly aimed at His Honor, the Chicago Mayor and his police force.

Arnold started courting Sally shortly after she began her full-time work for John Dingell Jr. They met while serving on a conference committee session. The Democrats were drafting trucking regulations and other transportation-related legislation. This was an area specialty of Arnold's. His command of the legislative complexities around the subject and his deft approach to drafting compromise legislation was truly impressive – particularly for Sally.

Not remarkably handsome, nevertheless Arnold had a powerful, ingratiating way with women. Charming, sophisticated and world-travelled, Sally was utterly smitten. Socially and culturally, Sally and Arnold were much the odd-couple. Sally was the smart, but wayward daughter of a small-town Baptist minister from the Midwest, an unwed mother transplanted from the sticks to navigate the treacherous undertow in the waters that flowed through Babylon. She was still testing those waters hoping to swim on her own. Arnold was a Jew, secular and non-practicing. He grew up in the east end of Long Island in the Hamptons, the only child of a mathematics professor at Stony Brook University. His mother was a musician, a concert violinist who taught at the Juilliard Conservatory in the Big Apple. Arnold was educated in private schools. A graduate of Cornell University, he took his law degree at the University of Pennsylvania. He had run unsuccessfully for a Connecticut House seat before joining Ribicoff's congressional staff as his chief legislative aide. Arnold was ten-years older than Sally. His personal portfolio was composed of two failed marriages, numerous affairs, no children and a large ego.

How did Baptist Bad Axe and the Jewish Hamptons come to harmonize? Arnold was a sophisticate who knew the navigation routes in and around Babylon. Sally was an aspiring sophisticate, a tenderfoot in search of an experienced guide. Arnold, she believed, was the one to teach her how to read the navigational maps. Arnold, enchanted with her beauty and smarts, shared her belief and was up for the challenge. Two believers, fellow travelers, in what they saw in and for each other. Too bad they hadn't read Hobbes: "much less can all men consent in the desire of almost any one and the same object."

Sally headed "south" with her dating of Arnold. Then she went "deep south" – with her decision to marry him. She was about to ascend – or would it be, descend? – to a trophy-wife class. Which one that would be? Either way, she was not remotely prepared.

With wife number three Arnold decided a new, innovative approach to making a marriage successful might be in order. Actually, the approach wasn't new. Neither was it innovative. Nor was it likely to be successful. Its appeal was a more sophisticated, contemporary packaging. He had been reading and pondering *Open Marriage: A New Life Style for Couples* by Nena O'Neill and George O'Neill. Published in 1972, the book was on the *New York Times* best-seller list for 40 weeks. It sold more than 35 million copies worldwide and eventually was translated into 14 languages. Former anthropologists, the O'Neills became the world's greatest salesforce promoting the demolition of monogamous marriage as a "lifestyle" option. One person's "lifestyle" is another person's hang up. "Lifestyle" is the perfect modern trope to capture the moral nihilism of the time, a euphemism to *normalize* deviance.

Along came the intellectual house boys as the O'Neills' fan club. These were the professional thinkers who dispensed their imprimaturs in the pages of the *New York Times.* They oohed and aahed over the greatest married-couple, progressive minds since the illustrious Fabians, Sidney and Beatrice Webb. By the way, Sid and Bea, during their hey-day as England's shining-light intellectuals in 1930s, turned themselves upside down oohing and aahing over the "new civilization" General Secretary Stalin was building for the workers in the Soviet Union.

In the "lifestyle" department, monogamy was not where Arnold wanted to be heading – from the get-go. George's and Nena's "contemporary" approach to marital fidelity, you might say, gave Sally's new husband the cover of phony sophistication and pop psychology to justify the wanton womanizing that had plunged his previous two marriages into the divorce courts. After her fateful tryst on movie-night with Harry, linking herself to another conquistador of amour might not have been the smartest move – unintended consequences, you know. It was six months after the nuptials with Sally. Inspired by the prose of George and Nena, Arnold proposed that Sally and he should "explore" outside intimate relationships. "Exploration?" Not exactly. He was thinking more in transactional terms, "wife-swapping," to be more precise, and well, perfectly blunt about it. Think of it as "human trafficking" among jaded, affluent victims of mid-life boredom. "Intimate relationships" did not quite capture what might more accurately be described as "sport-fucking."

Arnold had discovered the whereabouts of a well-heeled band of bed-hoppers in the shady lanes of upscale Bethesda. These sophisticated but randy DC suburbanites were themselves always on the lookout for novitiates to initiate in the ways of lubricious-oriented social clubbing. They were choosy, however. Hey, no problem. This was a handsome couple that offered ... Well, I don't need to get more specific. Reluctantly, very reluctantly, Sally followed Bwana, I mean, Arnold, on his safari into the Bethesda bedroom jungles.

*"I got this story from someone who had
no business in the telling of it."*

—**Edgar Rice Burroughs**, *Tarzan of
the Apes*

I pause here to note that in her youth my mother was, as the expression goes, "easy on the eyes." With thick, auburn hair, luminous blue eyes and a stunning physique, when she entered a room she was a cynosure – heads turned. Was she beautiful? Honoré de Balzac wrote of one of the women in his novel, *Père Goriot*: "if she would have been happy, she would have been beautiful: happiness is the inner poetry of women, just as fine clothes are the mask of beauty." Sally was not a happy woman. Her inner-being was a lugubrious prose that had long ago obliterated her inner poetry. But she had perfected the Babylonian dress-code for successful professional women in the power-broker set. She wore her raiment well as the mask on her external beauty.

Arnold and Sally joined the exclusive club of Bethesda lechery. I don't even try to imagine how grotesque it must have been for this renegade Baptist beauty from the backwoods of Bad Axe.

You'll be shocked, shocked to learn that for my mother the "intimate relationships" offered in this sleazy guild did not lead to the "personal growth" and "self-discovery" envisioned and promoted by O'Neill & O'Neill. Maybe it was more compelling when you read it in the Serbo-Croatian translation – *osobni rast* (personal growth*) samootkrivanje* (self-discovery).

After several unfulfilling "experiments," Sally pulled out. She upped her antidepressant "medication" from her favorite "pharmacy," Chevy Chase Wine & Spirits. It offered an ample inventory in liquid rather than tablet form, and those "pharmacists" delivered the goods to her doorstep by the case at a discount. She was quickly learning that marriage to Arnold was about managing expectations – realistically, as in lowering them. Arnold, of course, was having the time of his life on his lubricous jungle safari. And, as you might be able to predict, Sally's drinking and the resentment it stoked in her, collided most unpleasantly with Arnold's astonishing incapacity to comprehend why his wife was beginning to detest him.

10 From Bad Axe to Bad...

*"Whereof there be almost as many
kinds as of the passions themselves.
Sometimes the extraordinary and extravagant passion proceedeth from the
evil constitution of the organs of the
body, or harm done them; and sometimes the hurt, and indisposition of the
organs, is caused by the vehemence, or
long continuance of the passion. But in
both cases the madness is of one and
the same nature."*

—Thomas Hobbes, *The Leviathan*

*"Welcome to my nightmare
Welcome to my breakdown
I hope I didn't scare you."*

—Alice Cooper, *Welcome to My
Nightmare*

Speaking now of "extravagant passion," "madness"
and "harm." It was during this season of her discon-
tent that Sally came to think that it would be a good
time to "connect" with her son who was now five years
old. Joseph might be the magic cure for "the blues."

This happy, charming little shaver would rescue her floundering marriage. Sally was smart in many ways – this calculation was no less than delusional stupidity. As it turned out, it pushed her toward a decision that some might say led to an unfolding of child cruelty.

Richard and Gladys had had several conversations with Sally over the years about formally adopting me. Sally discouraged them. They followed her wishes. This they came deeply to regret.

My grandparents were my parents for the first five years of my life. As parents they were unsurpassed. They doted on me. They loved and cared for me in a way that would be the envy of many grownups in a glance back at their early childhood. Sally would visit for short periods of time. I was always happy to see her but felt no strong attachment to her. To her chagrin and against her urging, I called her "Sally" instead of "Mom." She clearly understood that her Mom was my real Mom – so much mutual affection. This weighed upon her. It moved her to ruin my idyllic childhood. Of course, that was not her intention. Many Babylonians aren't intentionally cruel. It's just that Washington DC is a place where strong impulses toward human decency are a social and occupational liability. If you arrive with them, you will have to shed or at least diminish them if you hope to move upward. Sally was upward bound and a fast learner. Arnold had at least helped her with this.

A year after her marriage to Arnold, Sally arrived in Bad Axe for what Richard and Gladys thought would be a typically short visit. It was at this time that she dropped another "bomb" on them. She wanted her son, now! That is, she wanted to take her son to live with her and her husband, Arnold, *permanently* in Washington DC.

Sally must not have imagined the kind of emotion, the vehemence, that would explode from her normally staid and composed parents when she told them what she intended. First came anger. Then came resistance followed by recrimination. How could she be doing this? Did she understand what this would do to *me*? Did she *really* care for me? But they had no legal means to stop her. Finally came desperation, pleading and tears. "He belongs here. We love him dearly. Please don't take him from us! Would you take more time to think about this? Maybe it would be better to wait until he is older." To no avail. From Bad Axe, Michigan I flew with her to Washington DC via Detroit. My first ride on an airplane. I cried non-stop through the whole trip and pretty much for the next couple of weeks after my arrival. Welcome to my nightmare.

Try to imagine what this was like for me. Don't bother. Leave it at somewhere between wretched and awful. Left behind were my broken-hearted grandparents who were smitten with me from the beginning. They watched over and separated me from the harder edges of the world and allowed me to remain in a protected state of childhood. My grandmother fussed over me when I was sick, made me great sandwiches, laughed at my childish antics, admired my scribbled artwork and taught me how to read – the most important thing, probably, anyone in my life ever taught me. My grandfather took me fishing, swimming, ice-skating, to baseball games and trick or treating. When I misbehaved he firmly but gently corrected me. His bedtime stories were masterpieces of humor and imagination. A kind and generous man, he was also wise. He hadn't bothered to read the O'Neills' *Open Marriage*. "Lifestyle" was not in his vocabulary. He hadn't been to Bethesda. He treated his wife like men are supposed to treat women. I took notice.

In Babylon the man who stumbled into the role my grandfather had played was Arnold, who on his best days regarded me as a minor annoyance. Comparing him to my grandfather as a man and as a decent human being was like comparing, as talented, musical performers, Sid Vicious to the Cleveland Orchestra.

> "That's the way it goes
> This city is so cold
> And I'm, I'm so sold
> That's why I know…
> Oh baby, I'm born to lose."

> —**Sid Vicious**, *Born to Lose*

> "Music is a labyrinth with no beginning
>   and no end,
> full of new paths to discover,
> where mystery remains eternal."

> —**Pierre Boulez**, Cleveland Orchestra Musical Director

The city of Babylon was cold in more ways than temperature, and in it I felt like I was "born to lose" in a primal five-year old way. My mother now wanted me in her life, but for what reasons? After my painful extraction from my grandparents they were never obvious to me. I didn't see much of her. She worked long hours and was often tired or irritable when she was around me. I hated the expensive private school she put me in. Bad as it was, it was an improvement over the domesticity offered by team Sally-and-Arnold. When Arnold wasn't dispensing his sarcasms on me, he would be berating Sally for her failure to "understand" him – due as he saw it to her hick, repressive, Baptist upbringing. His wife had spurned his noble efforts to extract her from the stifling, moralistic morass of backwoods Bad Axe. She had never been able to escape, to unshackle herself from her prudish inhibitions and complete the metamorphosis to a fully liberated woman, complete with the finer Babylonian nuanced sensibilities. Sally, increasingly, was finding it hard to stomach Arnold's "open marriage" pursuits. The humiliations kept accumulating. She drank. She sulked. He drank. He raged. They quarreled. They stormed apart. They made up and drank. Then they resumed and repeated this cyclical, punishing ritual of mutual loathing and bitter recrimination. I observed. I wondered. I learned. I concluded: the only adult in the house was seven-year-old Joseph, named for...? I keep wondering … and worrying.

This sordid drama show dragged on and on in reruns for years – and years. They would separate. Sally would go "on the wagon." They would reunite, then she'd go off – Arnold's presence being the "off ramp." Each time my hopes were dashed. Finally, yes, all-merciful-God finally, they divorced. Sally then increased her daily "intake," to deaden the pain of the split. Still, this was, relatively speaking, an improvement in my daily life. Post-Arnold, her misery she anesthetized and subdued; mine was lightened just a bit.

Not for long. Don't forget where we were living – Babylon, where the customary recourse to a bad situation is an unwavering determination to make it far worse and pretend otherwise. Don't let this surprise you. "Worse" was out there. "Worse" was a 6'3", 220-pound idiot-child even less suitable as a husband for Sally than Arnold. Mr. Worse was polished, poised and impatiently waiting for that "someone" whose parade he could rain down on. Sally wasted little time in finding the Rain Man and insanely attached herself to another Babylonian blackguard who would make her even more unhappy – me too.

> "Oh, I asked her for water, oh, she brought
> me gasoline
>
> That's the troublingest woman
>
> That I ever seen."
>
> —**Howlin' Wolf**, *I Asked Her for Water
> (She Brought Me Gasoline)*

Are you laughing yet, Reader? I'm sorry. I can't help it. It was too absurd. Into Sally's life stepped Dave

Nowaki, a can of gasoline – another buttoned down, Brooks Brothers sleaze ball she met at work. Dave was a bagman, I mean a lobbyist for, are you ready? The National Trial Lawyers, three words that combine to form a euphemism for "powerfully organized sleaze." GM wasn't Dingell's only Sugar Daddy. Defense, Big Pharma, insurance, commercial investment banking, and, yes, trial lawyers – from wherever the gushing rivers of mazuma flowed, John Jr. always had time to listen, "reach out" and experience the exuberance of knowing his election campaign chest was even fatter. "Can't buy me love." No. But influence? Well, now that's a whole different story with a cast of characters whose souls the devil would refuse. The economist, John Maynard Keynes understood how this worked: "By this means the government may secretly and unobserved, confiscate the wealth of the people, and not one man in a million will detect the theft." Babylon, you could say, was a crowded den of undetected thieves.

11 Psycho Dave and Me

*"If the human heart finds time to rest as
it scales the heights of love, it rarely
pauses in its headlong slide into hatred."*

—Honoré de Balzac

Dave crawled in the same fetid swamp as Arnold, although in the stupider end of it. He was a different, more primitive sort of swamp-lounging critter. He lacked Arnold's sophistication and charm, which he made up for in his habits of bewildering and utterly pointless moments self-assertion. Such as his annoying habit of slowly elevating his chin and scrunching together his eyebrows to mark his disdain for what, to those around him, seemed like a complete mystery. Heavy sighs of exasperation would erupt from him at a 4 to 1 ratio to smiles.

Religion-wise, Dave was Polish Catholic. The "Catholic" part of him, however, was a merely a vestigial appendage from his family's country of origin. It had no discernable bearing on what passed for his scruples. One of his uncles, Leszek Kowalski, was a parish priest in Kraków during a very unfortunate period of history. When the communists were in the throes of mangling what was left of Poland after WWII, they snatched this poor cleric out of hiding and stood him before a firing squad.

"*Gotowy, cel, ogień!*" Bam!

The smoke cleared. In his hands had been clutched a wooden cross when the fusillade cut him down. A faded photo of him placed over the fireplace mantle in the Nowaki family home commemorated his Catholic martyrdom by Stalin's Polish Reds.

Like Sally, Dave grew up in Michigan. He was the youngest of five children. His Dad, a highly successful restaurateur, amassed sufficient wealth to make an escape from his original confines of blue-collar Hamtramck near Detroit and install his family in suburban Troy, an upper-middle class destination for Michigan's Polish-Americans.

Academically, Dave was a step above the average high school student and would have been successful as a regional bank branch manager, an assistant middle school principal or an author/editor of physical education instruction manuals. But Dave was a high school All American football player. Fast added to a big, muscular physique enabled him to set the Michigan high school record for touchdowns scored by a fullback. One of them I saw on a video recording showed Dave dragging two would-be tacklers over ten yards before crashing into the end zone. His end-zone seeking prowess made him a highly sought-after commodity nation-wide by universities with Division I programs. Notre Dame awarded this fleet-footed lummox an athletic scholarship. Beneath the watchful gaze of Touchdown Jesus in South Bend, Indiana, Dave played tight end on its national championship team under coaching great, Ara Parseghian, the first non-Catholic coach at Notre Dame since Knute Rockne. Rockne, it should be noted, did convert in 1925 – probably after one of his "miracle" wins. Who would blame him?

Dave's next migration was from the gridiron to Notre Dame's law school where he graduated some-where in the middle rankings of his class. His high-profile college athletic career and his Notre Dame con-nections, however, opened the doors for him on K-Street in Babylon. Neither on a football field nor in a classroom now, with his usual undeserved good luck, he had landed in the perfect place. Absent any ethical standards, subliminally aggressive and with cunning, reptilian instincts, he rose up in the ranks of the Na-tional Trial Lawyers as one of their high-paid road warriors.

K-Street lobbying work takes a ferocious toll on marriages: long hours, high-pressure, boozeorama schmoozing, and lots of extra-curricular temptations make for unhappy, bitter spouses, who take their sweet revenge in the fullness of time. By the time Sally met Dave, like Arnold, he had unsuccessfully battled a couple of justifiably vindictive wives in the divorce courts. Both were curvaceous blondes. Each of Dave's exes had her high-priced attorney run a pole through him in the divorce settlements. Poor Dave. Then along came Sally. Then along came Dave – to us, a swagger-ing reject, as current psychobabble puts it, "with is-sues." Yes, "issues", as in depleted assets and a severely eviscerated personality, the latter shortcoming his ex-wives' divorce lawyers had nothing to do with.

You may be thinking: "He must have brought something worth making him welcome to Sally." Certainly, in the looks-department Dave had it all over Arnold. He resembled the blond actor, Dolph Lundgren, Sylvester Stallone's boxing opponent in "Rocky IV". Though physically imposing and still bearing the remnants of a gladiator physique, he had a somewhat tamer libido than his predecessor. He was very "possessive" of Sally. This, I suppose, had to be some kind of compensation for her. He didn't spend his spare time chasing choice tail. Unfortunately, the benign absence of that tawdry hobby was overwhelmed by salient attributes that made him less than an ideal husband – jealous fits of rage and an obnoxious, domineering approach to women. Oh yes, and especially endearing, he was a *Besserwisser*. That's German for a know-it-all.

Initially, I think, Sally must have found Dave's inordinate possessiveness and bossing her around appealing – in an understandable, albeit pathological sense. Harry, of course, and Arnold did not seem to want to "possess" her in a way that showed she was uniquely desirable or worthwhile. Arnold had many flaws. Jealousy was not one of them. With Dave, initially, this seemed to work for her. But after a while, not so much. After a while longer, not at all.

Sally dated Dave for about six months during which she attempted –and failed miserably – to sell him to me. From the get-go, I knew he was incurably bad news. "When he tried to be amiable, he usually only succeeded in being ominous," as Wyndham Lewis described a character in one of his novels. These futile attempts did give me some preliminary, unpleasant glimpses into the depths of his dark but utterly shallow soul. Dave was going to disappoint her in new and even more painful ways. No matter. She shackled herself in marriage to this morally misshapen mutton head in spite of my urgent warnings. He moved in. Off they went: Sally's second marriage; his third. Sally's talent in the realm of matrimony seemed to be making three-time losers of the loser-men she chose to hitch herself to.

> "Looking in the eyes of love I can see forever
>
> I can see you and me walking in this old world together…"
>
> —**Alison Krauss**, *Looking in the Eyes of Love*

Cataracts were clouding Sally's "eyes of love." "Forever" and "together" were destined to come up short – not "in this old world." Not in any world.

For Arnold, I was a minor distraction and an occasional irritation. Once in a while he pretended to like me, though. One time he even took me to a Washington Bullets basketball game with good seats. They were playing the Boston Celtics. Arnold knew someone high up in the Bullets management, and after the game we were admitted to the locker room. I met

Elvin Hayes and Wes Unseld, both future Hall of Famers. It was a fine outing for us both. Arnold was, I think, trying to worm his way back into Sally's good graces after a particularly nasty knock-down and drag-out quarrel.

For Dave, I was competition, a threat. Intimidation would be the ticket. He never had kids of his own. Maybe he thought being a Dad was like being Knute Rockne. He moved in and shortly thereafter concluded that I was a spoiled brat and needed "discipline." He was probably right about that. But administering successful discipline requires character: Dave *was* a "character," but he was severely lacking *in* character. Maybe you can guess what followed. Maybe not. The only thing between me and some corrective spankings was my mother. *That* was a line she was unwilling to let him step over. Dave ran a brutal, "command-guy" operation. "Do your homework." "Go to bed." "Don't interrupt me." "Quiet down." "Pick up your bedroom." "Go outside and play." Yup, that was pretty much his warm-fuzzy repertoire. No wasting of words or syllables – minimalist affect in child rearing. Kindness signaled weakness. Gentleness was, well, not a winning strategy. Following his orders was supposed to make me a better person, just like him. He must have been thinking: "With my approach, like me, someday Joey will be a well-heeled, do-whatever-it-takes Babylonian with a hot wife, a German car and a Chevy Chase home address." No, not really: he was never thinking that far ahead of what I was going to be.

I was living with a drill sergeant who was sleeping with my mother. My life was permanent basic training

– "Hut, hut, hut. About face. March!" He spoke to me only in short imperatives, and he barked out orders that pointed toward what hoop I was supposed to jump through at that particular moment. Whether it was time to go to bed or I had any homework or it was cold outside – all were irrelevant to him. His whims were my commands. I had to understand: he was the big boss of little me. One day, I recall, he barked at me after breakfast: "Clear off the table!" I responded: "What do you say, Dave?" "Now!" he bellowed. You get the picture.

At the time, I was reading books on the French-Algerian war. From these I discovered tactics of passive resistance and grasped the concept of "weapons of the weak." Sabotage was my weak-weapon of choice. Dave was a bit OCDC, a compulsive neatnik, which gave me some vulnerabilities to surreptitiously exploit. I would shift his personal things around. For example, I'd reverse the relative positions of his car keys, glasses case and wallet where he always laid them on the side table next to the door in the order that made him feel in control and "comfortable." Sometimes I'd take a twenty-dollar bill out of Sally's wallet and put it in Dave's. That would throw him into a high-anxiety state. "Where did this extra money come from?" With secretive relish I'd observe his frustration, twisting his memory of recent expenditures trying to account for that twenty dollars. In the bathroom, I'd put his toiletry articles in different places and swap out his favorite soap for the cheaper brand Sally bought for the two of us. It was little, chicken-shit stuff, but it drove him crazy, a sweet revenge for me. I would disrupt his routines by changing the time on the clocks by a few minutes. He'd reset them. A few days later, I'd be back at it. Then he'd replace the clocks. I got good at Dave-sabotage, and though he was suspicious of me, I usually avoided apprehension. To his commands I responded with: "Yes, Sir David," which he especially disliked. Even cavemen can grasp sarcasm. Behind his back, I called him, "the Polack Pussy." Sally would scold me for that, but only perfunctorily. I could see that she thought it was funny.

The current of amiability in our household was vulnerable to long periods of interruption analogous to electrical outages in third world slums. Periods of moral darkness ensued with no kindness; no succor we offered to each other.

It took a while, but Dave's fits of jealousy for Sally began to exhibit, shall we say, some ugly, physical manifestations. To put it in the rough vernacular: he began smacking her around. At first, Sally's response was that of the typical "battered wife" – blaming herself, covering up for him, believing his "never again" promises – the whole, dismal, predictable scenario you might see dramatized on a Lifetime Movie of the Week. A couple of times I had jumped into the fray to try to rescue Sally from his abuse. I wasn't big enough to mount a serious assault on the ex-Notre Dame tight end that would save her from the effects of his aggression. He was big and still, very strong.

She resisted for a time, but with my encouragement, Sally came to realize that with Dave in the picture, sooner or later she would be hospital or morgue bound, and maybe me too. For such an incurably dangerous rascal, no miracles of pacification or reform could be performed. She pulled herself together, threw him out, got a restraining order and filed for divorce – *numero dos*.

Dave had been in exile for about a month. However, he had been leaving some abusive and threatening telephone messages on Sally's answering machine. Which, of course, scared the bejesus out of her and pushed her to up her "intake" of liquid medication.

Sally then went out against the stern advice of a couple of her friends – "Don't be stupid. Let the police handle him," they scolded her – and bought a 357 Magnum revolver. A Smith & Wesson J-frame; it was a double action with seven rounds. It could blow a hole through an engine block. You see, Sally had recently taken notice of how Nate Silvermaster, a Dave-like boyfriend of one of her other lady friends, crashed through a court restraining order. By the time the police arrived to "handle him," her friend was headed for intensive care, and Nate was speeding away in his Porsche on his way to another state. It took three months and an extradition order to "retrieve" this dirtbag – a Congressional aide for a well-known New York House Representative – and stand him before a judge who promptly released him on time-served with six-months of "supervised" probation. His congressman-boss pulled some strings, and Silvermaster even got his job back. In a sane society, he would have been tethered to a pole, flogged till he passed out, then warned: "do it again and you'll be dangling from the end of a rope." Very little recidivism with this approach I am guessing – better behaved men; fewer bruises on the ladies – such an obvious, practical solution. But in our modern age of "enlightenment" the wise men in charge seem content to let the women be turned into punching bags.

Sally wisely decided to seek another source of "confidence" in addition to a restraining order and the police. Why not a gun loaded with hollow point bullets to "handle" Dave should he decide to get frisky? Dave full of holes is a better ending to this sorry saga than Sally with broken bones. That makes perfect sense, which is why the gun-solution gets such vehement opposition from those in the smart set. Why is that? Maybe it's because members of the managerial class don't like solutions they don't get to manage.

Late one weekend afternoon, Sally had gotten a jump start on her "happy hour" with a "few" glasses of spritzer and her favorite white wine. I think it was Gewürztraminer. She'd been fuming about Dave's scary phone calls and was not in a good mood. Even with the copious infusions of her Gewürztraminer prescription, the hour was unfolding in the opposite direction of "happy" – her disposition was moving toward "ugly." To put it in precise psychological terms, she was pissed.

I glanced out the window and saw Dave's silver BMW convertible parked across the street. Dave was standing in our driveway with his arms folded. He was staring at the house.

"Speaking of the devil," I said, "Dave is
   out there standing in our driveway."

"What?" Sally gasped.

"Dave's outside the house." I headed for
   the door.

"Don't go out," Sally yelled.

I ignored her. I stepped out onto the porch, off the
steps and then strolled down the driveway in a cocky
sort of way and pulled up about five feet away from
him.

Sally went to the window to watch instead of calling the police, which I think she might have done had
she not been soaking up the Gewürztraminer.

Stupid of me, perhaps, but I wasn't afraid of Dave.
He was fixated on Sally, and Sally was now afraid,
armed and, uh, in her cups, the combination of which
spelled "extreme danger" and had me worried – Dave
as target practice; Sally as an inebriated Annie Oakley
with seven rounds and a hefty grudge.

All I could expect from Dave, I was certain, was
verbal abuse which I had learned over the years to ignore. But I didn't want Sally to shoot him.

When I finally got close to him:

"What do you think you're doing?" Dave
   snarled at me.

"I live here, Dave. I guess you don't remember – and the restraining order?
   It looks like that slipped your mind as

well. You're breaking the law in case that means anything to you. Oh, that's right, I forgot. You're a lawyer. But, I just came out here to tell you that Sally (I never called her, 'Mom') is in the house drinking up a storm."

"So, what else is new?"

"Soooo ... What else is new is that she listened to the friendly messages you left on her answering machine last week. Then she bought a pistol and paid some guy to show her how to use it. Sally's been practicing a lot and is itching to shoot someone with it and not just anybody. From the way she talks about you, I think she'd particularly like it to be some guy she used to know named Dave. In case you're thinking about coming in the house, uh, Dave, my advice is, don't tempt her. Wine, you might remember, turns her trigger into a hair trigger. I'm saying this not because I give a damn about you. With you dead the world would be a better place, at least for Sally and me. But I still need my mother, and she won't do me much good rotting away in prison. I'm thinking that she's probably at the window right now. She might even be drawing a bead on you as we're standing here. Think Dave, think – like about your future."

I raised my arm as a make-believe gun and pointed my finger at him, then … "BAM!"

I confess: this was a crude way for a thirteen-year old kid to talk and behave. But I was precocious. Even at that age I was a hardened realist with a sophisticated vocabulary of sarcasm to match. Sarcasm was my mother's milk. It seemed to be the best language to get through to a blockhead like Dave. I can't imagine how he got through law school.

I relished watching the astonishment roll over his face and then the frisson that came from seeing the fear creeping into his eyes. He hadn't figured on this development. He was probably thinking: "Hmm … Sally plus wine plus gun. Didn't think she'd go *that* route … the gun part." He stood there slowly massaging his simian jaw for a few seconds, his face twisted into an angry grimace. I had put the most extreme, smart-ass look on my face I could muster. It said: "Ha ha. Beat it, knucklehead!"

Then he said to me: "Ok, fine. Tell Sally I stopped by."

"I'm not telling her anything. You're not Sergeant Schultz around here anymore barking out orders. Besides, coming from you, she just might decide to shoot *me* as a consolation."

On that driveway Dave's gridiron bulk hovered menacingly over me for a lingering moment as he digested my sarcasm. No visible signs appeared that he fully comprehended the extent and futility of his stubborn stupidity. Finally:

> "Fuck you, you little dork." Dave then turned and headed for his car.

> I waited. Just when he was opening the door: I yelled, "Hey Dave."

He turned.

> "Ass...HOLE!" I bellowed out at the top of my voice. "And I *really* mean it."

Dave slammed the door and started walking back across the street toward me. At that moment, Sally stepped out on the porch holding the revolver at her side.

> "Keep coming, Dave," she called out, "give me an excuse."

> I yelled, "I warned you Dave. It's a 357. Seven bullets with your name on them. Big holes, you prick!"

Dave put a prudent curb on his aggressive imbecility, executed a quick about-face, dropped his threatening mass into the driver seat of his car and sped off.

> "Thanks, Sally. I hate the sonofabitch, but I'm glad you didn't shoot him."

"I would have."

"Yeah, I know."

That was the last we ever saw of Dave.

Simple solutions when problems get complex – Smith & Wesson makes life simpler… and safer.

12 Goodbye Gladys, Goodbye Richard

"The meaning of life is that it stops."

—Franz Kafka

Dave's overdue ejection meant better times for Sally and me. I was thirteen when she shed the loathsome lunkhead. I then refused to go to school. We battled. Sally surrendered. She went the home-school route and hired a tutor who took me through mathematics over the next several years, enough to get a decent score on the ACTs. The rest of my time I spent reading the Greek playwrights – Sophocles, Euripides and Aeschylus – and the 20th century Oxford language philosophers like J. L. Austin and John Searle. I ploughed through Plato's Dialogues and a bit of Aristotle – *De Anima, Politics* and the *Nicomachean Ethics*. To have eluded the grasp of the Babylonian educational establishment was great, good fortune for me. I was better off not being programmed to resist the constraints of reality if it displeased me in some way. I refused to wear the educational establishment's designer-brand outfit that signaled I was fit to be absorbed into a "system" that would either turn me into a thin, brittle husk of a human being or eat me alive.

The summer I turned fourteen Sally sent me to stay with my grandparents in Bad Axe. My weeks there were a mix of a good time and not so much. Richard and Gladys had aged and seemed sad. They seldom saw any of their children or grandchildren. Long gone was the faun like gait of that boy whom they had nourished for his first five years of his life. Now, I now moved cautiously and with the assumption that my "betters" always covered themselves with practiced deceit. Life in Babylon with Sally, Arnold and Dave had contracted my childhood and turned me into a cynic. I had become a sullen, reclusive survivalist. For my amusement I had compiled my own internal dictionary of insults. From it I retrieved barbed words and fanged phrases of scorn for the interlopers I saw coming into and out of Sally's life. My grandparents were appalled when they would burst out of me, but I think they sadly grasped that I was lost to them. They never stopped reaching out, however. Resisting their kind and gentle warmth was not easy. I found some consolation. I went back to Babylon in the Fall with a lighter load.

A month after my return Sally got a late-night phone call from Bad Axe. Gladys was driving home early in the evening from a visit with a friend when a drunk with a suspended driver's license and four previous DUIs blew through a red traffic light in his Ford Bronco at 70 miles an hour. He t-boned Gladys's Chevrolet Impala on the driver's side. The funeral was closed-casket. There are limits to the skills of the best undertaker.

Richard soldiered through the funeral – it was huge, much of the town was in attendance – and the immediate aftermath. He was composed and manly as I had always known him. He held his grief off on the edges for a time. I stayed with him for a month after the burial. His grief moved from the edges to his core. There is no emotion purer and more intense than grief. It poured out of him and into me.

A year later Richard was diagnosed with pancreatic cancer. Six months later he was dead at 58. Gone were the two fixtures in my life. My family was Sally. Most of the time I felt numb. It was then that I came to realize that my life was a losing race against time.

> "*Remember*, Time is greedy at the game
>
> And wins on every roll! Perfectly legal.
>
> The day runs down; the night comes on;
> *remember*!
>
> The water-clock bleeds into the abyss."

—Charles Baudelaire, *The Clock*

Sally's father was the only decent man close up in her life. Yet, she never seemed to understand him. She never realized how good he was. Richard lived his life fixed on a transcendental, something beyond himself and the material satisfactions and transient preoccupations that most of us devote ourselves to.

Sally's life in contrast was immersion in a degenerate culture that worships one-dimensional idols who shrink and disappear when examined closely. Her pursuits were built on fleeting abstractions – legalese, ideological claptrap, mindless political slogans, corporate hype, pop-culture banalities, self-help, faddish lingo.

Into and out of her life stepped the hollow men.

> "We are the hollow men
>
> We are the stuffed men
>
> Leaning together
>
> Headpiece filled with straw. Alas!"

—T.S. Eliot, Hollow Men

Alas! Washington DC was the worst place for her to be – "a marsh of ruined souls." It was crawling, infested with the hollow men, the stuffed men. Babylon is an elaborate edifice of those pernicious abstractions she wasted her life on – as evidenced by the scurrilous, sordid, venal elites there who cover their breath-taking corruption with rhapsodies to "public service," "our democracy," "we the people," and "bringing us together." Poised just below them are the careerist, power-worshiping, ass-kissing underlings, biding their time, hoping someday to plunge their snouts deep into the hog trough at which with enough longevity, they might emerge with the net worth exceeding that of the Dingell Duo.

> "This is the dead land
>
> This is cactus land

Here the stone images

Are raised, here they receive

The supplication of a dead man's hand

Under the twinkle of a fading star."

Living in the dead land among the stone images, Sally gave up on the hollow men for a time. Well, at least marrying the worst ones that bubbled up through the slime and bobbed along the surface.

Through my early-teens Sally and I lived together in a state of peaceful co-existence. I was coming to understand her and the demons against which she was fighting a losing battle. She worked hard, made lots of money, drank and attempted as best she could to help me get over the loss of Richard and Gladys. Which mostly involved leaving me alone. I was grateful for it. It took me a long time.

At sixteen I went off to the University of Texas at Austin. I was young, but I was ready and wanted to be as far away as I could from Washington DC and the sorts of people Sally seemed to attract and attach herself to. Austin was the perfect retreat. All I did was study. For much of my time there I was *en marge*, a fringe guy, not a typical late-teenaged university student. I had little interest in socializing – fraternities, parties, dating. I engaged in no adolescent debaucheries that out of vanity I would later in my maturity magnify.

I was trying to immerse myself in inquiries and pursuits that might help me understand why the rich, powerful people I observed growing up, seemed so desperate and so empty. Literature, history, philosophy, biology were areas I plunged into. I was deeply intrigued by Hobbes and his clear-eyed view of the human condition – "Man to man is a wolf." I settled on psychology and moved fast. By the time I was twenty-three I had a Ph.D. in clinical psychology, had married and divorced and was ready to get out of Austin and take up "fixing the broken," like Sally. Somewhere along the line I had missed one of the basics: "Physician, heal thyself."

13 Roger and She

"There is yet another fault in the discourses of some men; which may also be numbered amongst the sorts of madness; namely, that abuse of words, whereof … by the name of absurdity … when men speak such words, as put together, have in them no signification at all; but are fallen upon by some, through misunderstanding of the words they have received, and repeat by rote; by others, from intention to deceive by obscurity."

—Thomas Hobbes, *Leviathan*

Sally must have been waiting for me to leave for college before she went off on a serious search for yet another man, one she hoped, might finally be "the one." "Love is the triumph of hope over experience," as the old saw goes. Or perhaps, "love is the triumph of imagination over intelligence." Two different ways to express it, but both are the recognition of a singularly unfortunate feature of the way romance and sex often seem to confound each other. For women, sex flows downstream from the turbulent head-waters of romance;

for men, the river currents of love rush in the other direction. For men, dreams of romance unfold upon the success of gaining "admission" to the promise land in the bedroom. Observing those opposing motions may help one appreciate the wit behind H. L. Mencken's quip, "adultery is the application of democracy to love." Democracies are collective, hopeless exercises propped up by the delusion that their promises are reliable. Two kinds of disillusion result: the romantic kind and the election kind. The demos are perennially unhappy with their unfulfilling relationships, rife with broken promises – from their fickle lovers and from their perfidious politicians – and always in quest of more exciting and attractive "alternatives" who regularly disappoint and betray.

It took about a year, but Sally, imaginative and full of hope, found Hubby *numero tres*, Roger Hatch. Into abeyance went the punishing lessons of her conjugal experience of serial infidelity and physical assault. Her otherwise formidable intelligence was enveloped by a miasma of intellectual charlatanism perfumed with the love of wine.

Sally discovered Roger on a wine tasting tour that wended its way through the Bordeaux region of France. Sally's tag-along on this pricey Bordeaux bender was her latest, best boyfriend, Jim Blanchard. She had selected Jim for his looks, and his looks alone. Mr. Blanchard was a switch-hitter from Iowa – not baseball "switch-hitting." His political assent in Babylon began with a seamy debut as a House intern for the justly-named Gerry Studds, the first openly gay member of the House of Representatives from, where else? Massachusetts. With Studds's encouragement Jim moonlighted as a catamite – willing and eager to be passed around by the not surprisingly large number of House members who gravitated toward the "kinky" stuff. The "mature" Jim was now a campaign advisor for the most bribable politician in the Hawkeye state. His nickname was "Open your Checkbook." Otherwise, he went by Nolan Kaiser. Nolan coveted the House seat in northeast Iowa. He had not yet risen to his highest level of incompetence. A former utilities commissioner for the state and once mayor of Waterloo, Kaiser had befouled every office he had occupied, which meant that his assent to the House was assured.

When Jim wasn't playing pitchman for sleaze balls, he devoted his spare time to fancying himself. Even more revolting, he had an appallingly unbridled appetite for applause, and he expected admiration to flow unabated from those gathered around him as well. Which meant that he was unbelievably arrogant. I say "unbelievably" because he had so little to offer – charm, wit, learning, insight – any redeeming or even mitigating qualities that would make his insufferable arrogance sufferable. He was also blissfully unaware that he would be quickly dumped post-home-coming. Jimmy-the-Great was also slow on the uptake. He had never encountered the venerable Roman philosopher, Pliny the Elder: "Wine moderately taken maketh men joyful. *In vino veritas*: drunkards tell all, and sometimes more then all." Yes, *in vino veritas*. He had been occupying himself too much with his mirror. *"Veritas"* was what Jim was in the business of circumventing. Mr. Wonderful was not paying attention to what the mutual "joy" of Sally and Roger at the tastings was telling him about his future. The "moderately taken" part of it, though, was probably questionable.

Roger's consort on this excursion was his third wife, one Christine Keeler. Unfortunately for her, she had the same name as the English showgirl and prostitute whose seduction of the Secretary of State for War, John Dennis Profumo, 5th Baron Profumo, brought down the Conservative government of Harold MacMillan. Single handedly, the sexy, 19-year-old Ms. Keeler left in her wake the "Profumo Scandal" that rocked the exclusive, old-boy, UK political establishment in the mid 1960s. Roger's American Christine was older and less sleek than the English temptress at the time of her demolition work. Still, she was sufficiently endowed to provoke not inconsiderable male admiration. Unlike her seductress namesake, however, she was chaste and an unlikely impetus of scandal.

On this pricey excursion, Christine, not Roger, was picking up the tab for them both. Because? I'll get into that shortly. The Christine-Roger communion of affection was yet another instructive specimen of the "triumph of imagination over intelligence" – at least on the part of Christine.

Roger knew a lot about wine. Sally drank a lot of wine – a lively match, as you might be able to imagine. In France, they found each other around many bottles of *Château Batailley* – drinking and talking about wine

– a perfect circle of spiritual, or is it, "spirited" delight? Two months after the tour, Christine's slumbering intelligence suddenly awakened and put "imagination" in its proper place. She divorced Roger for reasons that would make perfect sense to almost anyone who spent much time around this enologist buccaneer, anyone, that is, who tried to navigate the dense fog of his conversations when they weren't concentrated on wine. Sally was an exception.

What a "triumph" Roger turned out to be for Sally. To be fair to her: maybe Roger represented not so much the triumph of hope as the revenge of low expectations. And, to continue with fair, he was a notch above Dave or Arnold, which I admit was not saying much. But you pick up the cards as they lay on the table. Unlike Dave, Roger did not slap Sally around for recreation. Unlike Arnold, he did not, for some surgically-enhanced, blond-rinsed, suburbanite-in-heat, swap out his lovely wife like a choice piece of sirloin.

Roger came in at 6' 2" and 150 pounds with a grey beard and a greasy pony-tail, the quintessential stereotype of an effete, middle aged "save-the-worlder". His choice of black turtle-neck sweaters and tweed sports jackets bearing leather patches on the elbows for fashion was the lesser of his more notable shortcomings. For starters was his louche, effeminate intellectuality. Then there was the disquieting business of ambition – his appalling lack of it. With that unfortunate combination came the crowning piece at work in Sally's life-long, lousy man-choice apparatus – her willingness to support him at his customary high level of undeserved comfort. In short, for Mr. Right number three, Sally had gone bonkers for a gigolo. From a philander to a wife beater to a deadbeat. There is a trajectory at work here, but its meaning remains to be deciphered.

But to continue with the gigolo. Roger was quite the sophisticate with high standards in wine and cuisine. For *vino* he preferred *Chateau Lafite Rothschild* at $900 a bottle as long as someone else was picking up the tab – a deadbeat with an exquisite palate. This, I believe, was what pushed his darling Christine to take the desperate measure after the wine tour that culminated in his expulsion from her chambers. That he had been paying too much attention to Sally around tasting time during the France excursion was just a minor irritation for her. Among others was the tone of nasal peevishness his voice would take on after ingesting several glasses of wine. Christine had recalculated her estimate of Roger's affordability, and her final decision was a no-brainer. His cost far exceeded his benefit. In fact, she was struggling to remember why she thought his game, such as it was, was ever worth the candle. On her balance sheet, Roger was easily, happily excisable.

What tangible value did Roger offer in exchange for Sally's support? Only "The Shadow" and Sally knew. She stubbornly continued to be "looking for love in all the wrong places." You see – and here is where "love is blind" seems so blindingly real – Roger was a (likely permanently) unemployed professor of "English."

Here I must reluctantly plunge into a topic with piles of manure-ishly tinged details that relate to one of our once sacred institutions – the University. "English Professor" at today's university is shorthand for a "shrill barker of grievance-victimology with an arcane, tortured dialect intelligible to only a select cohort of fellow pretenders." No Ezra Pounds or William Butler Yeatses in this bunch. These effeminate illuminati converse in their secret society mumbo jumbo and publish mountains of unreadable bilge, the source of their mutual admiration. You must experience it to believe it. A short sample straight out of the English department at the illustrious UCLA is a "good" place to start. From a book by Paul Fry, *A Defense of Poetry*.

"It is the moment of non-construction, disclosing the absentation of actuality from the concept in part through its invitation to emphasize, in reading, the helplessness — rather than the will to power — of its fall into conceptuality." This verbal discharge from a professor of Oromo-Igbo. No, wait – of English.

Imagine the punishing headache you'd get having to plow through an entire volume loaded with this verbal ordure before you trip and "fall into conceptuality." How many precious "moments of non-construction" have passed you by? How many times have you been engulfed by the misery of "the absentation of actuality"? Maybe these are things you can't describe, like Supreme Court Justice, Potter Stewart on pornography: "I know it when I see it." Or, maybe Paul was in a deep lament: his coded messages were about how terrible it feels to be banished from the faculty lounge for never uttering a clear, concise sentence. Who knows? Who cares? If poetry has to depend on defenders like "Professor" Fry I'd say: it's time for the bards to run up the white flag of surrender and beg for mercy. Give me the simple prose of some straight-talking, beery-breathed philistine precariously perched on a bar stool. It never dawned on this professorial pretender that he could be doing something more useful than producing bags of word salad – perhaps a Starbucks barista or servicing cars from underneath in the oil pits at Jiffy Lube.

With a Ph.D. in some kind of postmodernist claptrap from Duke University, Roger had shuttled around the halls of ivy for years searching for a permanent watering hole where he could sink into a state of permanently-paid uselessness. Finally, some apparatchik chairing the search committee at Georgetown, probably after a three-martini lunch, seized by a bout of alcoholic amnesia, must have recovered and hired him thinking he was someone, anybody, else.

At Georgetown he got serious, well, as serious as someone like Roger could manage to get, and toiled away hoping to "earn" tenure. The "earning" part of it works this way: you spend six years of compiling a resume of mostly unreadable publications in journals no one reads, on subjects no one cares about before its "thumbs up or down" on whether you get to be exempt from the reasonable standards of employment that apply to most working people. Roger's earning power in this questionable endeavor was significantly under powered. Up he went; down the shoot he came. "No dice Rog. Don't go away mad, just go away."

"Tenure," incidentally, is shorthand for "an undeserved ticket to fuck off for the rest of your life with generous pay and no responsibility." It's the mother of all sinecures. With it, you indulge yourself in scribbling drivel or praising someone else's drivel so that he will approve of yours. You go to Hawaii or Cancun on paid junkets, I mean, scholarly conferences. With your self-infatuated, fake-thinker colleagues, when not drowning in Cadillac margaritas, Tequila Sunrises and looking for "action," you emerge from your over-stuffed mental closet and go for a swim in an ocean of deconstructionist babble – then stage some skit of mind-numbing mystification. You perform rituals that un-couple you from your "symbolic chains." All of us are bound by them: we just don't know it. "The lure of imaginary totality is momentarily frozen before the dialectic of desire hastens on within symbolic chains." So, Reader, how many of your family and friends have complained to you of their struggles to resist the lure of "imaginary totality"? Would Prozac or a stiff shot of Virginia Gentleman help with this? My own "dialectic of desire" desires a non-dialectical explanation of why people who write and talk like this should not be locked away in mental institutions or dismissed as village idiots.

Tenure opens up life-fulfilling opportunities for the self-proclaimed gifted. They get free time to show up at protest rallies toting those hefty, plastic water bottles and bluster about how much they care about those oppressed, those whom they are fortunate enough to live far away from. They are "awarded" year-long vacations, called "sabbaticals" for important labors such as "defending" poetry or lowering their golf handicaps.

If anyone did *not* deserve tenure, that would be Roger. Instead of getting paid to put students to sleep at Georgetown, he found Sally. Yes, Sally was willing to pay just to keep him around and bore her lawyer friends who were no slouches themselves at driving dull, tedious conversation into ditches of inconsequential conclusions.

I must comment, though, on what went wrong with Roger's bid for a sinecure at Georgetown. It seems that he'd bet on the wrong horse. It was his choice of a "victim-group" to champion. I can't remember now which one. Either it was gay jockeys of color or the voiceless transvestites of Cuba. Fidel Castro called them *"maricons"* – especially insensitive for a commie champion of the oppressed. Whichever one it was, its lack of victimhood pizzazz had driven it even closer to the bottom on the list certified by the literati legions of coercive compassion. In any case, not enough of Roger's morally superior peers who were deciding his professional fate gave a rat's hairy ass about any of them. Maybe they thought Fidel was on to something. Who knows? But I'm guessing there's a post-modern doctoral dissertation out there that's going to answer the question – except that you won't know the conclusion even after reading it.

Roger also had limitations that were out of his control. The Senior Professorette who chaired the meeting of the tenure awards committee that ran the pole through him was reported to have concluded the meeting with this succinct summary: "Fuck him. We don't need any more dumb-ass, white guys in this department." "Any more"? Sort of makes you wonder, doesn't it? How much fun was it to be one of those men of non-color and limited cognition in that department? Tenure, perhaps, would make it bearable. Poor, dumb-ass Roger didn't get a chance to find out.

Needless to say, Sally didn't think Roger was "dumb" or an "ass" – quite the opposite. She seemed to be fascinated with him – inexplicably. His sesquipedalian stem-winders on what was wrong with the world, though semi-intelligible and utter fantasy were mildly entertaining in small doses along with large applications of Chivaz Regal. For Sally, he was a misunderstood savant whose genius the mediocrities at Georgetown had failed to comprehend. Were these uppity so-and-sos mediocrities? Most likely, Sally was on target with them. Roger's genius? She was an admiration society of one.

Sally introduced me to Roger after he had moved into her house along with the ugliest, little dog you've ever imagined, his American Hairless Terrier, Rasputin. Rasputin was well-named. Mom called and asked me to fly up from Austin just to meet him, Roger, that is. Which led me to believe that she was deadly serious about him. Most concerning to me after the "serious" part was the "deadly" qualifier. Exactly what I was afraid of. She was. "Serious," alone, is usually curable. With a little patience and a gentle approach, serious can be nudged into casualness, and then insidiously be set adrift into the faraway rapids of faint memory. But no. She was gaga-serious over him. That must have deluded her into thinking that I would find him "acceptable" in any capacity beyond her hairdresser or sommelier. I remember the conversation we had – just the two of us – at the conclusion of an interminable evening the three of us, well the four of us, spent together. Rasputin had attacked my best pair of Gucci designer loafers – gnawing away the tassels and the toes earlier in the evening. I had foolishly slipped them off before dinner. We had disposed of three bottles of *Chateau Clos du Roy* and a small lagoon of Cognac, Frapin VIP XO at $160 a bottle. The consumption was not equally shared.

Roger had discretely escaped to the kitchen to do the cleanup, safely out of listening range of what was going to be an uncomfortable conversation between mother and son. I was working on a tannin-headache and repressing the impulse to kick Rasputin across the dining room.

Sally poured the last few ounces of a Petit Verdot from her $400, Riedel Fatto a Mano decanter into her hand-blown, crystal Bordeaux glass. Expensive glassware enhances all the attributes of the pricey reds, she firmly believed. I wouldn't know. She set it down and clasped her hands together. Amazing. She could down so much wine and appear absolutely sober. She gave me "that look." I braced myself. She was going to hit me with the question I knew was coming and did not want to answer:

"What do you think of Roger?"

"The dog? No wait, he's Rasputin, right?"

"Don't be a smart ass, Joe."

"What do I think of Roger?" I heaved a sigh and asked myself: "Do I go for a brutal, direct approach or seek an evasion that buys me time to think of how to dampen her ardor without arousing her animosity toward me?" The latter:

"It depends. You're not considering marrying him." Long pause. I was rolling my eyes – slightly less an annoyance for her than grinding my teeth. Her face was signaling the bad news.

"Are you?"

"Well, to be honest, we've talked about it."

"I'm happy for 'honest', but *seriously* "talked about it'?"

"Yes."

"And? … And?… And?... Please look at me, Sally."

"It's going to happen" was the unmistakable look I got.

"How many previous marriages?" was my
next question, the answer to which I
knew I didn't want to hear.

Sally was resistant. She flashed me a forced, tight-
lipped smile.

"Come on, Sally: how many divorces?"
I had picked up "ex-wife" references
from Roger during the dinner chit chat.

Silence.

"How many? Three? More?" These were
not far-fetched questions. Not for people who live, couple and uncouple behind the walls of Babylon. One of the
dapper Don Juanitos Sally had dated
for a short time, a hot shot lobbyist for
one of the big pharmaceuticals – I
think it was Pfizer – was married four
times. Just a couple of divorces here
on the banks of the Potomac means
you are practically a virgin.

"I repeat. How many previous marriages?"

Finally, after a stop-irritating-me sigh:
"Three."

Now I switched to brutally direct. "Jesus Christ,
Mom," This was the first time I ever recall calling her

'Mom.' "Are you crazy? Three women gave him the heave ho. Maybe they learned something about him that you have yet to discover and soon will. The guy doesn't have a real job. He talks in run-on, multisyllabic, word-salad sentences. His social machinery is in serious disrepair. His charm is waxing on you now, Sally. But, trust me. It's going to starting waning, and I'm thinking sooner rather than later."

Sally then retreated into a stony, silent snit. She always did this when she could not fend off my arguments. I needed to back up and soften up. "Be nice. Be understanding. Direct never seems to work with her," I told myself.

> "Ok, ok, I'm sorry. What do I know? I just met him. He's cool … in a way – a cerebral, academic type. He's very deep; maybe that will be good – a different social venue for you to meet people who aren't lawyers. No offense. Lawyers are great people, of course. But, you know? Variety? Spice? All that? Whatever. Just promise me this. After you set the marriage date, then you'll tell him you want to delay for six months beyond that. Just six months. Trust me, I'm a psychologist. Ok, stop rolling your eyes at that. Seriously, he won't leave you. After those six months, if he still makes you happy, go for it. Ok… Okaaay?"

"Ok."

"Promise."

"I promise."

"Cross your heart; hope to die?"

"Piss off, psychology-man! I promise."

"What about my Gucci loafers? Is Roger going to pay for them?"

"Relax, Joe. I'll replace the goddamn shoes. I promise."

"Why should Sally pay for them," I thought to myself. But I needed to attend to my headache and had no desire to prolong this conversation.

Sally broke her promise, of course. Not about the loafers. She bought me a nicer, replacement pair. Two months later, she and Roger got hitched. They honeymooned for two weeks at Sally's expense in Mendoza, the heart of the wine region of Argentina. Mendoza was in the foothills of the Andes, famous for its Malbecs and Torrontés. Sally arranged for several cases of Roger's pricey favorites to be shipped to her (their) home in Babylon.

What *did* I know? Roger worked out better for Sally than the first two husbands. I say "better" only in the most cruel, relative sense. The marriage lasted longer than I thought it would. It was after four or five years, post-nuptials, that Roger's ticker went from sort-of-bad to sayonara-bad. With no advanced warning, he up and died from the big one, a myocardial infarction. I was on hand to witness his untimely exodus. We were at Dabney, one of DC's finest restaurants. On this occasion I was picking up the check. Roger had just polished off a large bowl of lobster-bisque. He was headed for the main course of Atlantic Goliath Grouper steamed in parchment with sour orange sauce and Martini relish. Suddenly, he stood up, clutched at his chest and keeled over face first on the table. Most upsetting was that in going down he knocked over and spilled what he had intended to pursue the Grouper with, a nearly full bottle of *Château Lafite Rothschild - Pauillac* 2001 – restaurant price, $1,113.58. I couldn't help but wonder if this was Roger's way of telling me: "If I'm not going to be able to drink it, no one will." When the waiter picked up the empty bottle off the table he gave me an unmistakable "what a pity" look. Ok, that was nasty. To be fair, my Gallo-tuned-palate wouldn't have done it justice anyway. Beyond ten bucks a bottle, they taste all the same to me.

I attempted CPR. Couldn't bring him back. The medics arrived too late for his *Schwanengesang*. He was already wending his way up to join the Three Musketeers of the Postmodern in the afterlife, Michel Foucault, Gilles Deleuze and Jacques Derrida. What a grand opportunity for him! These prolix rascals were planning to subvert the authority of St. Peter, begin the deconstruction of heaven and the defenestration of the patriarch of all patriarchs, God. Best of all for Roger, when you arrive in heaven, I've been told by someone of unquestionable authority, that they award you with tenure – no strings attached. Best part: no word processors there to spew out monstrosities like, "The Replacement of Unitary Power Axes by a Plurality of Power/discourse Formations," or "MAN.i.f.e.s.t.o.: A Poetics of D(EVIL)op(MENTAL) Dis(ABILITY)." It's almost enough to make you believe that, unlike down here, the right folks are in charge up there.

Now, I have to say that Roger worked out better than the first two husbands. This marriage, unlike the previous two, did not end in the pain and humiliation of divorce. Sally, as I had predicted, was getting weary of Roger. It took longer than I thought. This was a better outcome – for her, anyway – and now, finally with tenure, for him.

14 Lone-Star Blues

"The stars at night are big and bright (clap, clap, clap, clap) Deep in the heart of Texas.

The prairie sky is wide and high (clap, clap, clap, clap) deep in the heart of Texas.

The sage in bloom is like perfume (clap, clap, clap, clap) deep in the heart of Texas

Reminds me of the one I love (clap, clap, clap, clap) deep in the heart of Texas..."

"[I] made too many wrong mistakes."

— Yogi Berra

Well, this is going to be awkward... Upon finishing the Ph.D. at UT, I divorced Teri-Lynne six months after our wedding in Austin. Whoa, now, partner! What was this all about?

Full disclosure. Teri-Lynne had been a cheerleader on the squad for the Texas Longhorns football team, the head cheerleader, actually.

"Texas Fight, Texas Fight,

For it's Texas that we love best,

Hail, Hail, the gang's all here,

And it's good-bye to all the rest!"

—University of Texas Fight Song

Good golly, Sweet Jesus! How in the Holy name of Darrell Royal – "Peace be upon him!" – did an un-jock, cerebral type like me manage to snag my navel-gazing self a Longhorn cheerleader? More to the point, *why* would I want to marry one? Good questions. Liaisons with cheerleaders are supposed to be precipitous, short-term deals. Get in quick, then out and on to more serious business.

I must therefore retreat to a brief episode in my youth that remains an embarrassment for me to this day. I'm not diddling about with excuses, sport fans. This is a *mea culpa*. I am confessing. If confession is good for the soul, after coming clean with this stash of my dirty laundry, my soul will be a model of spiritual vitality and moral purity.

Teri-Lynne enrolled in the undergraduate class I was teaching in developmental psychology and sat in the front row, pleased to give me a glimpse of her fulsome décolletage. She fell for me after the first two weeks. My professorial gravitas was the spark, plus my eyes. I have a rare eye condition called heterochromia, a difference in the irises. My irises are completely different colors. The right one is blue; the left, green. A lot, I mean a lot, of women find it … appealing. Teri-

Lynne was one of them the most smitten. The *nom d'amour* she came to bestow on me and would coo in our tender moments was "Dr. Cool Eyes."

I fell for her. It was her … well, I shouldn't have to spell it out for you, should I? The course she took from me was required for an elementary education major – probably the most demanding one in a curriculum that doesn't demand the most, uh, brain power, I think is the kindest way to put it. I didn't date her until after the class was over by the way. Ok, nearly over. I gave her a B+ grade. She wasn't going to get a gift "A" from me, by God.

I know. I hesitate even to mention this. You will think less of me for it – rightly so. I was sorely tempted to omit it. Call it a "trial marriage," a matrimonial miscue – no begats, no hard feelings, some good nights to remember, no lasting trauma for either of us.

A further confession. And this will make you even more disillusioned. The reason I married her, I think I already hinted, was because she was sexy and very good looking – uniquely blonde, deep-in-the-heart of Texas-gorgeous. Longhorn cheerleaders back then didn't come in any other packaging, in case you are wondering. That's it – not money, not personality, not connections. All of my normally reliable instincts, my vitality, my highly refined insight into the human condition? They collapsed into an indistinguishable, cognitively-crippled mass that converted itself into the singularity of sex. Only the logic of sex can explain it, and the logic of sex is invincibly self-referential. It explains nothing beyond itself. I would like to be able to tell you more to help you understand it. You won't. I can't. I won't even try.

> "I'm goin' through the big 'D' and don't
>   mean Dallas…
>
> I got the jeep and she got the palace…"

—Mark Chesnutt, *Goin' Through the Big D*

No jeep. No palace. But, there *is* the follow up question: why the divorce? Come on, seriously? The answer should be obvious – our cruise ship down the river of eternal love had departed with very few long-term provisions. "The fuse got short and the nights got long," as that Country & Western ballad goes.

I was in the Lonestar state with the Lonestar blues.

> "When I got them North Texas blues
>
> Thought, I'd paid all my dues
>
> Then them South Texas blues
>
> Told me, son you ain't through
>
> Had them East Texas blues
>
> And them West Texas too
>
> I've done all I know to do
>
> Tryin' to lose, tryin' to lose these lone star
>   blues."

—Delbert McClinton, *Lonestar Blues*

Well, hold on to your hat, partner. There is this other detail I need to get to. It shines even more unwelcome light on this tawdry episode of my mostly well-spent, well-behaved years in the Lone Star State. That "detail" is Teri-Lynne's "Daddykins," a Mr. Jerry-Joe Heddleston. He went by J.J. J.J. owned and operated the biggest cattle ranch in West Texas and a gusher oil well or two in Midland. He was also on the board of trustees at Texas Tech University in Lubbock, birthplace of the legendary Buddy Holly. Given to self-apostrophizing asides of his great wealth and magnanimity, J.J. was a seven-figure donor to Tech's College of Agriculture. This ten-gallon hat philanthropist had his name attached to a couple of buildings and an endowed professor chair in the Department of Ranch and Livestock Management.

Daddykins's seemingly unbounded wealth also included friends, themselves rich enough to buy people, places and things like they were discarded appliances at a yard sale. Jerry Jones, owner of the Dallas Cowboys was one such compatriot. The Cowboys' bunkhouse chief was tapped to be J.J.'s best man at, I think it was, his third wedding. Mr. Heddleston was a frequent guest in Mr. Jones's private, luxury owner's suite at Texas Stadium. When the team played in their home stadium in Arlington, these two Big Enchilada Jerrys would be perched on high, following the game, observing the bouncing endowments of the cheerleaders and chasing Lone Star beer with shots of Jose Cuervo tequila.

J.J.'s third wedding, I learned from Teri-Lynne, was a modest million-dollar blow-out nuptial affair with Brett Blacklock, Chief Justice of the Texas Supreme Court, conducting the ceremony. El Rancher Supremo had pulled on his best pair of python-skin, cowboy boots and selected his Emerald Valley turquoise bolo tie in preparation to hitch himself to the daughter of Mexico's largest heavy construction conglomerate owner, Juan Domingo Beckmann Legorreta. (Short quiz: How many names do you have to have to be an *hombre importante* in Mexico? Answer: As many as it takes.) Señor Juan begat the lovely señorita Isabel Beckmann Ruíz, the dark-eyed, sinuous knockout for whom J.J. was getting himself all gussied up to make into his third "little-Mrs." The comely Mexican maiden was a mere twenty years his junior. She'd been first-runner up to Miss Mexico a few years back and was a star in one of Mexico's most popular telenovelas. Second place was enough in this case to meet the groom's high standards of female pulchritude. Perched on Spanish-made saddles on twin, white Grand Azteca stallions, they took their solemn vows and went for a short gallop before greeting the admiring guests. The reception facility was big enough to hold half the population of Abilene. The volume of beer that flowed from the kegs could have put out the 1871 Chicago fire. Isabel's wedding present from J.J. was a fire-engine red Ferrari in which he had installed a horn that blasted out a couple of bars of "The Eyes of Texas." After the wedding it was rumored that Isabel could be seen driving her sleek toy at 140 mph on the highways outside of Lubbock.

Needless to say, J.J. was not exactly to my taste in fathers-in-laws and conversationalists. He was a man whose metrics of worldly success were in many respects what I had observed from an early age in Neiman Marcus Babylon. His were just expressed in that out-sized belt-buckle West-Texas sort of way. Every fashion statement he made gave "garish" new dimensions of meaning – more gauche than you'd see in the Babylon crowd. But in hindsight, J.J.'s style was more genuine, virile and a whole lot more entertaining to experience.

That this Emperor of the Llano Estacado mesa didn't care much for me either, you're probably not surprised to learn. In fact, he worked himself into quite a lather when his daughter stuck her thumb in his eye and married some egg-head, pansy-ass shrink, who on top of it was "a fuckun Yankee." He believed that I had hypnotized her. No, really. He thought that. How else could some football-illiterate nerd who didn't know a "wideout cross" pass pattern from a "deep comeback" attract a hot number like his daughter? Psychology, he believed, was on a plane with Voodoo. Perhaps he was more intellectually astute than I realized. "His eyes," he once said to Teri-Lynne when they were alone, "they give me the goddamn creeps." J.J. was planning for the split even before the nuptials. He'd hired a private detective who followed me around for a month before figuring out what a dull, straight-arrow doofus I really was. "God fucking damn it!" I'm guessing he snarled after reading the gumshoe's final report. "Hold on now, cowboy! I'm paying you to tell me that this dipshit professer spill-yer-guts-about-yer-feelings is content with one gal at a time? Why am I not surprised? Well, at least he's not a closet fag."

Six months after the divorce J.J. married Teri-Lynne off to a Texas Tech former All-American tackle, Billy Bob Royal, B-Bobbie, as they called him. Post-university days, B-Bobbie played briefly for the Houston Oilers until he blew out a knee from a vicious chop block in a game against the Oakland Raiders. Rumor was that Raiders owner, Al Davis, had put out a hit on the hulking interior lineman. Everything about B-Bobbie was outsized beginning with, well, his size. Which was twice mine. He went on to own and operate the largest beer distributorship in the entire southwest and live in the biggest mansion in the largest county in Texas, Brewster county. His wife was possibly the best-looking woman in Texas.

Another piece of this confession: I owed my temporary father-in-law. J.J. was a consummate West-Texas *cretino,* but he was no dummy. Teri-Lynne and I were both better off after the quickie, no-fault divorce he paid for. When I made my final adios to J.J. we were standing next to a new black Corvette he'd just bought the day before with some of his pocket change. I was secretly admiring it as we talked. After making my parting gestures, I shook his hand, itself a powerful, crushing instrument of his ostentatious, imperial personality. He then paused for a moment and slowly scratched his ass with his free hand, perhaps a reflex unique to west-Texas titans that preludes either a momentous decree or a thunderbolt of execration. J.J.'s face at this moment ploughed itself up into a look of proud self-assurance and, yes, generosity. Squinting up his eyes and with a deep-fetched tone of kindness I'd never heard before he said: "It's for you, son." He handed me the keys attached to a fob made from the official badge of the Texas Rangers. The Vette was just to show his generous appreciation for how gracefully I had stepped out of the future he'd planned for his ex-cheer leader daughter with the beer distributor goliath. I hoped maybe he was thinking: "That little Yankee piss ant is probably an ok guy, but no way for my Teri-Lynne." Another little piece of shame: I accepted the pay off, err, the car. Teri-Lynne's Dad and my Mom were much happier with the final outcome.

My time in the Lone Star state was over. Happiness was Texas in my rearview mirror.

From:

> "The cowboys cry ki yippee yi (clap, clap, clap, clap) deep in the heart of Texas.
>
> The dawgies bawl and bawl and bawl (clap, clap, clap, clap) deep in the heart of Texas."

To:

> "I wish they all could be California girls."

My years in Texas were good – mostly. Shortly after my divorce, I interviewed for a position at the University of Southern California Department of Psychiatry and Behavioral Sciences. Teri-Lynne's seductive vapors had cleared out of my brain: I was focused and compelling. The Head Shrink there called and offered me a postdoctoral fellowship that would be a quick step-up to a full professorship of Voodoo, I mean psychology. I accepted, jumped into my Corvette and sped off through the desert to the Golden State in grateful hindsight for the foresight of J.J.

Ok, Reader, I know what you're going to say: "All those years of advanced psychology under your belt and some philistine, West-Texas, cattle rancher cowboy could see from the get-go that you were a no-go for his daughter?" I'm sorry. In this case, I'll just have to depart from professional protocol and respond the way W.C. Fields did in that movie when he was being harassed by some irritating, little twerp: "Go away son, you bother me."

15 Boys Will Be Boys

"For man also knoweth not his time: as the fishes that are taken in an evil net, and as the birds that are caught in the snare; so are the sons of men snared in an evil time, when it falleth suddenly upon them."

—Ecclesiastes, 9:12

"Let parents bequeath to their children not riches, but the spirit of reverence."

—Plato

Shortly after I arrived in Los Angeles to assume the fellowship, I became intrigued by a spectacularly gruesome crime story that dominated the news. The details, which were unfolding in the preliminaries to the trials of Lyle and Erik Menendez, soon attracted national interest. Court TV, a crime-themed, cable channel would televise the trial proceedings. Overnight, Lyle and Erik became the focus of a nationwide audience. Court TV not long afterward carried the orchestrated farce that the O. J. Simpson trial would turn into.

The Menendez trials and the story behind them were sensational with all of the ingredients that would turn them into media circuses. Call them "celebrity trials," garish entertainment spectacles curtesy of the rich and/or famous – Hollywood degenerates and louche millionaires who seem surprised to discover that – at least sometimes – they are not exempt from the laws of felony.

Defense attorneys like O. J.'s Johnny Cochran turn these staged tribunals into cartoonish burlesque for the TV-land viewers. The nonchalant Roadrunner, Mr. Cochran "beep-beeps" at the judge and jury and taunts the hapless Wile E. Coyote prosecutors as they chase him around the courtroom. Courtroom Road-runners like Cochran, wear Giorgio Armani suits; the earnest, Coyote prosecutor dorks buy theirs off the racks at JCPenney.

Consider by contrast that other class of defense attorneys, public defenders. These palookas are the lumpen proletariat of the lawyer class. Anonymous and low paid, they represent the Wal-Mart, Dollar General and Value Village clients. The courtrooms they toil in are not cable-TV suitable. The unfortunates they defend – innocent or guilty? They're down-and-out nobodies. Nobody cares about them, their guilt or innocence, their past, present or future – not squat, *nada*. At least, no one out there in TV-land, the only place where "caring" counts in the form of a continuous revenue stream.

The celebrity lawyers are the unseemly aristocrats of the guild – attention grabbing headliners who perform flamboyantly and expertly in front of the cameras, grandstanding live before national audiences. Outside the courtroom they condescend to give ring-kissing interviews to sycophant celebrity-chasers like the reptilian Larry King and oleaginous Barbara Walters. Yet, another entertainment ritual of the modern television world – dialectical disclosures to titillate the millions of couch-potato voyeurs. "Important" *people who need* an audience of "regular" *people*." The latter, I must say, are not all that "lucky."

I played a role in the circus. I'll get into it shortly.

Two things made the trials and the circumstances surrounding them a popular sensation. First, the affluence of the Menendez family. The murdered father, José Menendez, had fled Castro's Cuba as a boy. His rise to become a wealthy and highly successful businessman was phenomenal. In 1980 at the age of 35, he was named RCA executive vice president in charge of the domestic Hertz rent-a-car division. From Hertz he moved to the record division of RCA. There he signed performers of the stature of Menudo, the Eurythmics, and Duran Duran. The two sons grew up in ease and affluence with all the trappings and advantages of great wealth. José had the highest aspirations for his two sons. Both boys attended the exclusive Princeton Day School in Princeton, New Jersey. Upon graduation from high school, Lyle went on to Princeton University. There he was expelled after one semester for cheating in his psychology 101 class. Erik was a star at tennis and rose to the rank of 44th in the nation for 18-year-olds and under. He was considered by some of the in-the-know people in the tennis world to have the talent to rise to the top of the professional ranks. The world was going to be their oyster.

Second, and even more fascinating for me was the trial itself and the conduct of trial by Erik Menendez's lawyer. I was an expert in child-parent psychology, and the defense strategy of his lawyer was in and of itself, you might say, a labor of "abnormal psychology." More on that to come.

These two handsome lads shot their parents, José and Kitty, with Mossberg twelve-gauge shotguns. Mossbergs are not made for hunting; they are made for purposes of self-defense, to kill intruders. In this case the intruders themselves were wielding the shotguns and doing the killing. The brothers bought the weapons shortly before the slayings. To avoid the tracing of the purchase of the weapons to themselves the boys used a driver's license they had stolen from a friend. Case closed, you might think, for "premeditation." Plead guilty and beg for mercy. Dream on, Bumpkin.

The horrific parricide took place on a late evening. The unsuspecting couple had been sitting on a couch in the den of their $5-million-dollar, Spanish-style, Beverly Hills mansion. They were eating strawberries and ice cream. Upon attack, a wounded Kitty managed to escape after the opening volleys but was finished off in the hallway. José took five blasts to the head and body. Kitty was shot nine times in the face and chest. Their bodies were left unrecognizable. Both parents were also shot in the kneecaps in an attempt to make the murders appear connected to organized crime. The autopsy report stated that one of the blasts to the head of José had caused "explosive decapitation with evisceration of the brain." "I have heard of very few murders that were more savage," reported Beverly Hills police chief Marvin Iannone.

With the proceeds from the ample inheritance, the brothers went on a no-holds-barred spending spree shortly after the homicides. José was worth $16 million at the time of his death. Within six months, Lyle and Erik had blown through a portion of his fortune. Between the two of them: Rolex watches, a Porsche Carrera, two restaurants – Chuck's Spring Street Cafe and a Buffalo Wings. Erik, so traumatized by the murder of his parents, hired a full-time tennis coach and flew to Israel to compete in a series of tournaments. Eventually the boys vacated the family mansion and bought adjoining condos in Marina del Rey. All of this, I think most people would conclude, is not exactly how you'd imagine a normal "grieving process" would be unfolding for a recently-orphaned pair, particularly with such a traumatic spectacle of the hideous mutilation that resulted from the slayings.

Of relevance for anyone seeking to form a fuller picture of the personalities and characters of the boys accused of murdering their mother and father is the following. Several years before the killings, Lyle and Erik had gotten into trouble, serious trouble of a criminal nature. They had burgled the homes of two wealthy owners and stolen a combination of over $100,000 in cash and jewels. Thanks to their father, they escaped prosecution. José took care of it. He arranged for the return of the stolen money and jewels. Erik, under-aged at the time, took the fall for Lyle so Lyle would not be barred from entry to Princeton because of a fel-ony arrest record. Erik escaped with probation. Why would the sons of parents so wealthy they could buy most anything they desired be up to burglarizing homes and thus risking their futures? This should be a burning question and highly relevant to the question of their guilt for the murders. The answer suggests pa-thologies consistent with highly disordered, amoral personalities that were firmly in place, highly active and ultimately lethal for the two people who brought them into the world and showered them with "stuff."

Lyle and Erik were twenty-one and eighteen when they committed the grisly murders in 1989 – *fully adults*, it is necessary in this context to stress. In 1990 they were both arrested and charged with premedi-tated homicide. Their separate trials, however, did not begin until 1993. The reason for the delay was that the evidence for the prosecution of the crimes was sus-pended in a legal battle that went all the way to the California Supreme Court.

The disputed evidence was a series of tape-record-ings made by a psychotherapist, Dr. L. Jerome Oziel. He was treating Erik Menendez for depression at the time of his arrest. Erik confessed to the murder of his parents to Oziel who then persuaded Erik and his brother Lyle to record their confessions. Which, inci-dentally, makes you wonder how Lyle was smart enough to get into Princeton. Here is where the story of the aftermath of the murders takes on the wacky features of a full-blown soap opera-ish script. Oziel, then married, was having an "extracurricular" with a prospective patient, Judalon Smyth. He would involve her in his taping of the confession. He arranged for her to be perched outside the door of his office to listen to Erik and Lyle describe the details of the killings. Maybe Dr. Oziel skipped his professional ethics classes. Who knows? In any event, this was, you might say, *highly* irregular. But come on! What good is a confession to a grisly, multiple murder if you can't get your mistress involved to, uh, cement the relationship? Whatever her initial reaction to the confession, in spite of her extracted promise to Oziel not to, Judalon went to the police. The arrest of the brothers followed shortly after.

The three-year court battle was over the admissibility of the confessional tapes as evidence. They were deemed admissible by the court.

16 Flipping the Victim

Aus Opertum erwächst Macht, From
victimhood, power.

"There are no facts anymore, kiddo.
only good or bad fiction."

—William Shatner

The trials began in 1993 with the psychotherapist who had taped the confession testifying for the prosecution. Normally, this would not be permitted for reasons of patient-client privilege. That restriction was removed because Oziel claimed that Lyle threatened to kill him. As a stereotype for a slimy operator posing as a "therapist," L. Jerome would be your choice. He claimed to have an expertise in phobias of various sorts, but the majority of his professional publications dealt with sex-related disorders. And, as he testified, in Beverly Hills there was no shortage of would-be patients.

Dr. L. Jerome Oziel's license to practice was eventually revoked. Now he's "Jerry," some guy who conducts marriage, relationship and sex seminars in Portland, Oregon. According to his website, the seminars are for "single, widowed, or divorced women and mother/daughters. They provide extensive practical advice on how to deal with men in hundreds of situations in which women tend to make major mistakes." This man certainly had a command of "major mistakes."

But on to the legal proceedings. There was no question in the trial as to the material facts: Lyle and Erik killed José and Kitty. The outcome of the trials turned on what the jury would conclude was their motive for the killings. With their parents dead and out of the way, the sons would have millions of dollars to spend however they felt like. And, when you are a young, handsome eighteen to twenty-one-year-old guy there are just so many nice things, places to go and people to spend money on. Which, as I mentioned, they did with reckless abandon. To a careful observer, the post-mortem shopping sprees, their earlier adventures in grand larceny, plus other evidence of pre-mediation would suggest that the motive was greed … open and shut case. If so, José and Kitty were the victims of premeditated, first-degree murder of which Lyle and Erik were stone-cold guilty. Under California law, worst-case for them, execution – barring that, life in prison. Not much fun ahead for those two playboys either way.

Given those facts, you'd have to think that to keep these two lads out of the San Quentin death chamber their lawyer would have to be a magician in front of a jury. There was such a lawyer-magician. She just happened to be available for hire. Her name was Leslie Abramson.

Let's say you were thinking of murdering some-one. Let's also say you planned on getting away scot-free. Leslie Abramson would be at the top of your list as the one to get you past the jury and out free, trip-ping down the sidewalks, feeling like a million bucks. She had rescued twelve people from death row. One of them was a Pakistani-born gynecologist accused of strangling his 11-year old son and chopping him into 200 little pieces. The jury acquitted him.

Magicians like Abramson, it is correct to assume, do not come cheap. You want cheap? Get a public de-fender. Public defenders plea-bargain. Plea-bargain-ing is boring stuff done in the drab, courthouse hall-ways – "Bla bla bla, last offer for your loser client. Ok, just a minute. [Pause.] Yeah, my knuckle head client will take the deal. Let's go grab a beer." No soap opera, entertainment value in these boring, seamy ex-changes. Nothing that would meet the high expecta-tions of Court TV viewers – "People who need peo-ple" voyeurs getting off on the kinky hijinks of the rich and famous. "Plea-bargaining" was not in the vocab-ulary of a courtroom thespian of Abramson's stature. If asked, she couldn't find the word in a legal diction-ary. Fortunately for Eric Menendez, a portion of the $16 million estate of the parents he had killed was at her disposal. It would become the source of Ms. Abramson's retainer.

Abramson's "Eric Menendez magic show" did not involve sawing a beautiful lady assistant in half. Given what her client had done, dismemberment was not the sort of imagery she would want to dangle in front of the jury. Her act consisted in a trick I call "flipping the victim." Here is how it worked. A blood-drenched perpetrator – Eric – stepped behind a curtain. Then Abramson rolled out a tear-jerker drama for the jury. In it, cute, little Eric grew up in a horror show of parental abuse. His childhood was a continuous nightmare. The authentication would come in a polysyllabic smog of psycho-babble from a for-hire crew of chin-stroking experts on "childhood trauma."

Pause and drum roll: Eric then stepped back out from behind the curtain. Eric the, plotting, cold-blooded assassin was now a broken down, sympathy lathered-up victim of savage child abuse. The poor little guy was reduced to seeking consolation from his toy animals. From the *LA Times*: "Menendez, testifying for a third day in his murder trial, said Wednesday that his father was so controlling and his mother so emotionally unstable that he sought comfort in his "own family of stuffed animals." Poor Eric. Only Mr. Cuddle Bear cared about him. Between stepping behind the curtain and stepping back out, the show was spectacular – perfect for normally boring daytime television.

Still, there was the problem of the law and the facts. Lyle and Erik, two big, strong, fully grown men, after careful planning without the encouragement of Mr. Cuddle Bear, blew their parents brains out and pretended that mafia hitmen did it. Abused or not, how could they possibly become the victims? How did Leslie "flip" José and Kitty, the victims, and make them into the guilty parties? This was heavy lifting for any attorney. But Leslie Abramson was not just any attorney. To pave the exit lane for Erik out of the courtroom and back out into that wonderful world of dating, tennis and fast cars, she would have to show the jury that José and Kitty were a monumentally awful couple. How awful? So vile and despicable that Erik and his brother had no option but to kill them.

That said, killing your parents, even if they are exceptionally mean and lousy at parenting you, are still not, legally speaking, justifiable reasons. Especially when you are a grown up and able to get away from them. Proving self-defense, the *old fashion way*, requires showing that for fear of your life you have no other options. But Abramson was going to turn the brothers' shotgun killings of their parents into an act of self-defense a *new-fashioned way*.

Let's face it: you've got to be an indescribably wretched Mom and Dad to reach a point where you have pushed your kids to do what Lyle and Erik did to José and Kitty. What or where, you must be wondering, is "that point"? Abramson had to convince the jury that José and Kitty were monsters in human form, dedicated, full-time sadists who over the years finally drove their sons to such desperate measures. Otherwise, it's: "Hello lads. Sleepy time forever awaits you. Won't you step into my little chamber with the green décor?"

So:

> "They did the mash, they did the monster mash
>
> The monster mash, it was a graveyard smash

They did the mash, it caught on in a flash.

They did the mash, they did the monster
    mash."

—**Bobby Pickett**, *Monster Mash*

Abramson pulled out all the theatrical stops. She
would hit the jury with José and Kitty doing their ren-
dition of the "Mommy-Daddy Monster Mash." She
signaled how she expected it to catch on "in a flash"
with the jury.

> "Look how compelling these abuse cases
> are. I mean, you have these clients who are
> not criminals, but sympathetic, decent peo-
> ple who are in *terrible trouble*. And their *so-*
> *called victims* are *nothing short of monsters*
> who *deserved to be stopped*. Just because
> you're dead doesn't mean you're a victim,
> a saint. *Hitler is dead* too."

"[I]n terrible trouble"? Whose leg was she pulling?
I'm thinking José and Kitty, while eating their ice
cream and strawberries on the couch that fatal night,
were about to experience "terrible trouble," "a grave-
yard smash," beyond the kind that even a connoisseur
of horror like Stephen King could dream up for one of
his novels. But one person's trouble is another person's just desserts. Parsing this little gem does rather
put your head spinning around like Linda Blair's in
"The Exorcist." The "so-called victims," "monsters" in
human form, "deserved to be stopped"? That's right,

they "deserved" what they got. Brutal – but hey! Sometimes "decent people" gotta, you know, make a statement – "explosive decapitation with evisceration of the brain." Now, I'd say, *that's* being "stopped."

So now you see how this excrement-flinging lady lawyer works her magic of victim-conversion. By smearing the dead with – what else? – the old stand-by, "Hitler" imagery. Not original, but you go with what works. José and Kitty, those "so-called victims"? No, dummy. You stupidly thought they were just an exceptionally mean old Mom and Dad? No, again. They were just the sort of parental Hitlers you could only find goose-stepping around their Beverly Hills mansions, torturing their kids with private schools and a lifetime inundation of expensive stuff. Which naturally turned Lyle and Eric into Churchill and Eisenhower and that Friday evening pair of murders a Normandie invasion. After all, someone had to "stop" this tag-team of Fuhrers before, before, before... Before what, exactly?

These two "monsters" of Abrahams's conjuring, however, did seem to do a masterful job of keeping their "monsterhood" a secret over the years from everyone. It took Leslie to help Eric figure it out just in the nick of time: when he was looking at his future in San Quentin.

> "The scene was rockin', all were digging the sounds
>
> Igor on chains, backed by his baying hounds

The coffin-bangers were about to arrive

With their vocal group, 'The Crypt-Kicker Five'

They played the mash, they played the monster mash."

The trial was pretty much a performance of the "monster mash" with Leslie "digging the sounds" of the "baying hounds." The spectacularly brutal physical annihilation of José and Kitty by their sons in the mansion they shared would be followed by a brutal, post-mortem assassination of their characters in a courtroom – kicking their crypt and banging the coffins – so to speak. This hit job would be carried out expertly by a lawyer financed by the wealth left to the killers. All the pieces were coming together. Abramson got $755,000 from the estate to defend Erik. He was, in Abramson's words, "adorable." Which shows the power of that kind of inducement to turn a guy who should be memorialized in Madame Tussaud's wax museum, the Chamber of Horrors in London into a teddy bear, more lovable than Mr. Cuddle Bear.

For the deceased José and Kitty, the one-two punch. Nothing would be left of them – their bodies or the memories of them – that wasn't savagely mangled, first by their sons, then by their high-priced hireling. José was the primary target, a father who, it was alleged, sexually molested Erik continuously from a young age including rape, sodomy, forced oral copulation and beatings. Kitty went along and contributed in her own sadistic way to pile on to the daily horror.

These accounts were alleged, never proven. They produced many skeptics.

You might expect, and you'd be right: there was a lot of "psychology" involved in the kind of defense that this defiler of dead bodies was mounting. That psychology turned heavily on the trial judge's ruling that the "battered women's" unique legal remedy of self-defense extended to abused children and was admissible under California law. Battered women's syndrome made its way into the courts beginning in the late 1970s. It was then expanded into "battered person syndrome." Eventually it was established as a sub-category of Post-Traumatic Stress Disorder in the American Psychiatric Society's *Diagnostic and Statistical Manual of Mental Disorders* (*DSM*), a massive tomb of hieroglyphics compiled by modern-day sorcerers for use in the conduct of their shaming rituals. Its inclusion in the *DSM* gave a veneer of medical credibility to a legal defense of homicide based on long-established patterns of abuse.

The "battered-person" concept in the courtroom expands the meaning, and thus the legal application of self-defense for homicide. The use of lethal force against someone attempting to inflict immediate, serious bodily harm upon you is legally-justified self-defense, long-established and readily acceptable to judges, prosecutors and juries. Rules for its proof are clear and understandable. However, to seize upon or create an opportunity to kill someone in a defenseless posture who has been abusing you, even long term, is legally speaking, a horse of a different color. To convince a jury that killing your unsuspecting parents while they are sitting on a couch eating ice cream is an act of "self-defense" is going to be a tall order that would have to overcome centuries of legal theorizing and precedent. Its efforts would be strenuously resisted by a rational mind. To make it work requires the theorizing of experts outside the legal profession, psychologist-experts. They would have to convince the jury, non-experts strongly disposed to think otherwise.

The prosecution team for the Menendez trial knew where Abramson was going with this. They approached the head of the Department of Psychiatry and Behavioral Sciences at USC where I had my appointment. He pointed them in my direction. For three days, they put me and two of my colleagues with an expertise in the psychology of parent-child conflict through a series of interviews. The questioning was probing and intense. The prosecution was trying to determine if any of us had the technical expertise to testify and counter the defense. Would we be willing to do so? I was interested in the preliminaries to the trial and had followed the case closely. I had many professional and theoretical reservations about the validity of "battered person syndrome" as justification for a self-defense slaying, particularly for adult children. This is not to say that I am unsympathetic with abuse victims and not loathing of abusers. I saw it up close with Sally and Dave.

The Assistant Prosecutor, Lester Kuriyama thought I would be the best one in the group they interviewed to testify for the prosecution. My colleagues concurred. Given my youth and trial inexperience, however, I was reluctant. Kuriyama convinced me that his team could protect me on the cross-examination. We rehearsed my direct testimony as well as some role-playing of my cross-examination. I was called to testify as a prosecution expert witness.

17 Invitation to Humiliation

"A celebrated people lose dignity upon a closer view."

—Napoleon Bonaparte

"Never try to bullshit a bullshitter."

—Anonymous

The judge for the Erik Menendez trial was Stanley M. Weisberg. Weisberg had presided over the first Rodney King trial. That case ended with the acquittal of the Los Angeles police officers charged with beating Mr. King. The LA riots followed shortly after the announcement of the verdict. During the Menendez trial Weisberg was parodied on *Saturday Night Live*, portrayed by Phil Hartman who had impersonated many famous personalities including Ronald Reagan and Bill Clinton. Ironically, the comedian himself was murdered in a domestic dispute at the age of forty-nine.

On the day of my appearance at the trial, I was understandably nervous. Leslie Abramson was regarded as one of the most ferocious, coruscating cross-examiners in the business, the Madame Defarge of defense attorneys. She took no prisoners. Behind her was littered a trail of witnesses she had handily broken down before juries over her career. Taking the stand to face her was an invitation to experience a weapon of humiliation drawn from her ample arsenal. Witness, take the oath, then take your choice: Kleenex-soaked blubbering, impotent fury or stammering incoherence. One of those was what you most likely would be in for when she had you trapped on the stand, pretzel-twisting what you thought made perfect sense into an outburst of monumental stupidity. Leslie had perfected a broad array of courtroom personas to present for the jury, each one calculated to move her prey to dismemberment. She could be scathingly sarcastic, wildly histrionic, cautiously insinuating, bullying and insulting – sometimes even nice. Whichever one she deployed, she was merciless. For the judges, holding the reins in on her was a challenge.

As I took the witness stand, I imagined I was prepared to take her broadsides and come away with my manhood at least partially intact. Seated on the stand, as I was taking the oath, I looked out and saw her sitting next to Erik Menendez with a slightly amused look on her tanned, fortyish face. Her head was encircled by a wild, frizzy mass of blonde Orphan Annie-style hair. Her coiffure was selected, I suspect, to draw rapt attention to herself as a one-person spectacle. She was wearing a tight, knee length, fire engine red suit-dress over a black, turtle neck sweater and long dangling earrings. Although only 4' 11", there was nothing subtle or understated about her. She wasn't what I had envisioned as an eat-you-alive, courtroom barracuda. No. She looked more like a television game show host. Or a Beverly Hills, upper echelon real estate agent, a fast-talker who could schmooze the high rollers on the hunt for that special mansion and stroke their bloated egos. But when I saw the set of her jaw as she slowly arose from her defense table and the way she sauntered toward the witness stand with a calculating gotcha-look in yellowish eyes that resembled those of a bird of prey – I knew I was going to suffer. I was the fat mouse; she was the cat. As my great grandmother, Gina, might exclaim: "*Madonna mia*!"

Thus, it began.

> Abramson: "Dr. Martin. It is *Doctor* Martin, correct?"
>
> Me: "That's correct."
>
> "How old are you, Dr. Martin?"
>
> Prosecution: "Objection, your Honor. Irrelevant."
>
> Abramson: "Relevant to expertise and experience, your Honor."
>
> Judge: "Overruled. Answer the question, witness."
>
> Me: "Twenty-six."
>
> Abramson: "Twenty-six." Long pause. "Alright. You were called to testify before this court at the behest of the

prosecution as an expert witness, were you not?"

"Yes."

"An expert at the age of twenty-six?"

"Yes."

Another long pause as she shakes her head ever-so-slightly as a gesture of incredulity.

"In your direct testimony to the court this morning you stated your professional credentials. Would you please repeat for this court what your expertise consists in?"

"I have a doctorate degree in clinical psychology from the University of Texas at Austin with a specialty in the psychogenesis of child-parent violent behavior. My doctoral dissertation on adolescent-familial violence won the Federation of Associations in Behavioral and Brain Science 'Outstanding Dissertation Award.' Currently, I am a postdoctoral fellow with a ranking of Associate Professor at the University of Southern California Department of Psychiatry and Behavioral Sciences where I direct clinical-practicums, teach graduate seminars and supervise doctoral dissertations on the subjects of parent-child conflict and domestic violence. I have guest lectured at numerous universities including Princeton, the University of Wisconsin and Vanderbilt University School of Law. I have published research extensively in peer-review professional journals in that area. I have developed predictive models of aggression and depression-related behavior in adolescent males widely cited in research literature. My clinical experience involves the creation of psychological profiles of adolescents who act aggressively, sometimes violently against their parents."

Sounds good, doesn't it? So, why would she ask me this? I made this recitation for the prosecution in my direct testimony only hours before. Why remind the jury members what an expert I was? It was her first move in setting me up for the take down.

"Very impressive, Dr. Martin. I'm sure the jury members would love to sit in on one of your lectures and be able to review your publications. But this young man sitting before you is on trial for his life. [Nice move, no? Great misdirection with the sympathy angle.] We don't have that luxury of time. [It had been four years since the slayings.] I am more interested in your experience in actual trial observation and providing expert testimony in a court of law. As you must know [of course I did], a courtroom is not a lecture hall or a seminar room. So, would you please tell the jury members how many homicide trials you have observed professionally and at which you have testified in a courtroom as an expert witness?"

"This is the first trial I have appeared as an expert witness."

'So, the answer to my question, Dr. Martin, is, aside from your appearance right now, 'none.' Correct? 'None'?"

"Yes, none."

"And ... at a *young* age [pause], with *no* [pause] such previous experience as an expert witness you have unshakable confidence in the opinions you've stated in your direct testimony?"

"Yes, I am confident."

"How confident, young man?"

Prosecutor, angrily: "Objection!"

Judge: "Sustained! Ms. Abramson, watch your step."

"I'm sorry, Your Honor. May I rephrase the question?"

"Yes, proceed."

"How confident are you, given your relative lack of courtroom experience?"

"As confident, I suppose, as anyone with an expertise in a highly theoretical and complex field of study can be, particularly one that applies scientifically to the behavior of human subjects."

The "I suppose" was a stupid slip up on my part. Experts don't "suppose."

She seized upon it.

"You suppose?"

"Yes."

Abramson reacted with a look of faux shock that she shifted back and forth from me to the jury. Finally:

"Well, I'll accept your 'suppose' for the moment."

Abramson turned abruptly and walked back to the defense table. She paused and picked up what appeared to me to be a document of some sort. She returned with it to resume her cross examination.

"I want to move on to your doctoral degree which I assume is a major source of your expertise and your 'supposed' confidence in the direct testimony you gave. I have here in my hand a report from the American Psychological Association, the national accrediting authority for professional education and training in psychology. The APA lists the rankings of the doctoral programs in clinical psychology in the United States published at or around the time you would have been submitting your application for admission to such a program. This I'll submit to the court as evidence. Let me see where the University of Texas is ranked." She looked at it as if she were inspecting it for the first time and made a long pause for dramatic effect.

"Well, congratulations, Dr. Martin. It comes in at 10th. Were you aware of these rankings at that time?"

"Yes, I was."

"Then let me ask: did you apply to any doctoral programs other than the University of Texas?"

I hesitated.

"Dr. Martin, I repeat the question: did you apply to any doctoral programs besides the University of Texas?"

"Yes, I did."

"Were any of those other programs that you applied to ranked near the top? Let's say, UCLA, number one or Indiana University, number five? Let me remind you that you are under oath. We can subpoena the application records of any of these institutions."

"I applied to the University of California-Berkeley."

"You applied to UC-Berkeley?"

"Yes, I did."

"Can you tell the members of the jury what was the ranking of the UC-Berkeley doctoral program at your time of application?"

"At the time I applied, I believe, it was number three or four?"

"And … your application to the third or fourth-ranked program was …?"

"Rejected."

Feigned shock and a long pause to let "rejected" resonate with the jury.

"I want to be certain the members of the jury heard you correctly. Your application for the University of California-Berkeley doctoral program in clinical psychology was *rejected*?"

"Yes. But..."

"No, that's fine. No explanation needed.
Not *confident* enough to apply to number
one. Rejected by number three.
Well, don't feel *too* badly, Dr. Martin.
You were good enough to crack the 10th
rated one. What was the motto of the
program – 'We try harder'?"

Rumblings of laughter through the jury box. I am
light complected. My face was burning red.

Prosecution, angrily, "Objection, your Honor.
Council is insulting the witness."

Judge: "Sustained. Strike those comments
from the record. I know it's hard for
you, but *please* restrain yourself Ms.
Abramson. Let me remind you of the
conduct I expect from lawyers in *my*
courtroom. Your job is to *question* witnesses, not demean them. Remember?
We've had this conversation before. I
don't want to have it again. Am I
making myself clear on this?"

Abramson with feigned contrition: "Of
course, your Honor. I apologize to Dr.
Martin. I'm sure the University of
Texas at, where is it? ... oh yes, Austin is a fine institution."

Nice move on her part. I looked even more like a
helpless little boy who needs Dad to step in.

Judge, deep sigh: "Proceed. Proceed."

"Dr. Martin, I have read several of your publications. One that I found particularly interesting contained conclusions that are critical of the work of Dr. Jerold R. Wasserman, a highly-regarded clinical psychologist, a pioneer in the same field as yourself.

"This is the article." Abramson then waved a copy she had been holding in her hand for the jury to see, then gave it to me.

"Do you recall writing this article?"

"Yes. I do."

"Then, would you explain as succinctly as possible the basis for your criticism of Dr. Wasserman?"

Prosecution: "Objection, your Honor. This is all irrelevant."

"Abramson: "I can show the relevance, your Honor."

Judge: "Overruled. Proceed."

Abramson: "The basis for your criticism of Dr. Wasserman, Dr. Martin?"

"I believe that there are flaws in his methodology, observational techniques and the conclusions he draws. You see…"

"That's sufficient for the jury."

Cutting off witnesses in mid-sentence was one of her techniques to set up for the kill. She had an uncanny ability to know exactly how far to go with an answer before it would work against her. She was able to get away with it much of the time. Weisberg let her get away with it this time. Leslie was the speeding MAC-truck; Dr. Martin was now the possum in the middle of the highway. I was about to become an expert-witness patch of gooey-guts roadkill.

> "Now, Dr. Martin, Dr. Wasserman, you obviously must know, is a distinguished *full* [pause] professor of clinical psychology in UCLA's department of psychology – the number *one rated* [pause] Ph. D. program in clinical psychology in the country, by the way. Professor Wasserman, who also possesses a law degree from Stanford University, according to my records, is 58 years old. He has 30 years of experience in the field and world-wide recognition. He has been a visiting professor at the University of Edinburgh's Medical College and the University of Vienna's Institute of Psychiatry, among other prestigious institutions. He has been President of the California Psychological Association and on the editorial boards of many prestigious professional journals.

He is considered one of the top bridge builders of the discipline of psychology to the fields of forensic psychiatry and criminal law. And you also must know, he has written extensively on parental-inflicted, childhood trauma and its potential to ignite overly-compensatory defensive responses on the part of the child. From my reading of your recent publication, his basic perspective on psycho-genetic triggers of adolescent violence appears to conflict directly with some of the key elements of your direct testimony this morning. Would you say that is a reasonably accurate assessment, as a lay reader on my part?"

"Yes, I would, for the most part."

"For the most part? Fine. I will take that as a qualified yes."

I mistakenly believed at that moment that her next question would open up an opportunity to make some telling criticism of the psychology behind "battered person syndrome" and expose some of Wasserman's methodological flaws. Instead, the next and last question put the dagger through my expert-witness heart.

"So then: let's say you were a lay jury member. Based on a comparison of a number of factors including quality of credentials, breadth and length of professional experience, peer recognition and international reputation, and range of achievement – Dr. Martin's or Dr. Wasserman's – whose expert opinion would you be more inclined to accept?"

Prosecution angrily cries out: "Objection, objection your Honor!"

Abramson: "I withdraw the question. No further questions for this 'expert,' I mean, witness."

I glanced over at the prosecution team. The looks on their faces resembled those of the losing players on the sidelines at the end of a 42-0 Super Bowl route. "I'm sorry, guys."

What a debut! The triumph of a tongue-tied dummy. Some "expert" I turned out to be. Evisceration total and complete. I was the star of a law school instructional video: "How to impeach the testimony of an expert witness."

I had hoped to exit the witness stand with a swagger; instead I skulked off like I'd been caught stealing chickens.

18 Abstractions

*"But yet they that have no science are
in better and nobler condition with
their natural prudence than men, that
by mis-reasoning, or by trusting them
that reason wrong, fall upon false and
absurd general rules."*

—Thomas Hobbes, *The Leviathan*

*"There is another task I must undertake
first. I must try and educate myself."*

—Nora Helmer in Henrik Ibsen's
Doll House

The humiliating thrashing administered by Leslie
Abramson had left me, as the French say, *désemparé*. I
spent the next month licking my wounds. How, I kept
wondering, had I let myself get set up for such a devastating takedown? I was like Dante's "miser" in the
"*Divine Comedy*": "eager in acquisition" of professional reputation and acclaim; "but desperate in self-
reproach when Fortune's wheel turned to the hour of
his loss – all tears and attrition."

Attending to my injuries led to an inquisition of my life, my professional career and my plans on how to live out the rest of my days. My encounter with Leslie Abramson that afternoon in the Los Angeles courtroom was fateful. The humiliation at her hands: what did it mean? What would come of it? It was one of the most fortunate things that had ever happened to me. As the "Uninvited Guest" instructed a distraught Edward Chamberlayne in T.S. Eliot's play, "The Cocktail Party": "You will find that you survive humiliation. And that's an experience of incalculable value." I did survive, and...

The Abramson demolition of my professional pretension was the stone which broke open my understanding of how the modern world works. Voila! The confusion, the conflicting doubts and diffidence began to dissipate, and I emerged from the *selva oscura*, "the dark wilderness" as Dante described his own moral confusion at the beginning of the *Inferno*. My vision came into a sharp focus. I had been a lost soul adrift. Seduced by this world's many comforts and entertaining distractions, I had been oblivious to all of its futilities and absurdities – and yes, so many of its contradictions. Why had I failed on that witness stand? How did that failure connect with what was wrong was the world? This sounds like pointless navel gazing, but forgive what sounds like self-dramatization and stay with me for a while longer. I promise you: some illumination will emerge. Your patience will be rewarded, and you will thank me.

In spite of its technical-scientific-medical triumphs over so many limitations of past centuries, the modern world was for me an empty vessel. The modern world: A "blind, deaf machine, fertile in cruelties." These were the words of Baudelaire. The source of my alienation? A simple answer. I was living in, and occupying myself increasingly with, an accumulation of abstractions. Worse, for all of their sophistication and power, they had tenuous connections to things that linked people together in physical and emotional ways that made them better for each other. Abstractions – systematized, stylized, professionalized and commercialized – drive people apart. Our bodies live longer; our souls die sooner.

The modern world rules with abstract systems, tangentially related. Each one moves independently, autonomously with no purpose, logic or standards for success other than consistency with its own standards – removed from and indifferent to the damaging effects on the people caught up in it. Moreover, these systems move relentlessly toward increased specialization. Specialization by its nature marks an increase in power. Every specialization creates specialists with enlarged authority who exert that authority and its power over those dependent on their specialized knowledge.

I pondered Abramson's masterful performance. The façade cracked open. A naked, modern world popped up and laughed at me. It then gave me the finger.

It was thinking about "the law" as an abstract system that got me started and how the trial I had participated in had unfolded. The trial itself, I realized, captured the essence of this self-contained system that functions as a show, as entertainment, a circus. Leslie

Abramson was the star in a "happening" staged largely for the benefit – the enjoyment – of the onlookers. What made it so fascinating and attention grabbing was the audacity of the star performer.

The trial in its basic form was analogous to any sporting event that is played according to a set of arbitrary rules, monitored by referees – the winner determined by a combination of skill and luck – the skill a purchased commodity. Money buys the best athletes; it buys the best lawyers. "Best," can only mean "the winningest," which completes the circle in which each piece refers to another piece within the system. Apart from its entertainment value, the game has no intrinsic relevance to anything outside of its own internal standards for excellence and success. The winner is the winner of the game. The winner is unconnected to anything apart from the game that is good or bad. Would you trust the "winner" to be your friend, to comfort your child, to keep a promise, to hold firm against corrupting enticements? To answer those questions, you must step away from the game. That's impossible: we live inside "the game" as either participants or spectators. The trial I observed and participated in was completely detached from the moral fundamentals by which human beings over the millennia have used to hold themselves to account for their actions and to separate out and punish wrong doers.

Law, as a body of rules and procedures came into being, not by conscious design, but as a structure emerging from organic growth. Its origins could be understood as a spontaneous force that would lead people to, as Hobbes put it, avoid "a great deal of grief in keeping company where there is no power able to overawe them all." Law was about keeping peaceful company, for people to associate in ways that protected the weaker from the depredations of the stronger. Law provided an escape from the "state of nature," from "the war of all against all."

Law, manners, custom and religion in their origins were the constraints a civilized order used to reign in aggressive human impulses and put boundaries and limitations, on our conduct.

> *"What is it that distinguishes honesty from knavery, but the hard and wiry line of rectitude and certainty in the actions and intentions? Leave out this line and you leave out life itself; all is chaos again…"*

—William Blake, *A Third Testament*

The modern order has subverted these constraints. It conducts a relentless assault on lines and boundaries of actions and intentions and moves toward chaos guided by abstract ideology. In the Great Leap Forward, Mao's "modernizing" of China, it was the "Four Olds" – "Old Ideas, Old Culture, Old Habits, and Old Customs" that were abolished and plunged China into anarchy and terror. The guiding ideology was Marxism; the goal, *real* equality.

In the west, we purge our "olds" in order to make our lives endlessly entertaining. The guiding ideology is progressive-utilitarianism. The goal is to forget our mortality. Mortality is the "limit" that stamps itself on our cradles and stalks us into our dotage. Entertainment ceases to entertain and turns stale when it's not dismantling boundaries, removing those limits. Boredom. It's the modern world's worst enemy. Breaking things makes it go away. Breakage makes "progress" possible and sustains the illusion that life is limitless, pleasure is forever, all wants can be fulfilled. Which is why "ground-breaking" is the word of highest praise for professional critics who comment on cultural productions and social actions like movies, plays, works of art, literature, music and liturgical rituals.

"Ground-breaking" also aims at the "equality," prized by Mao's Red Guard. It breaks down hierarchies such as patriarchy. Its goal is the atomization of individuals – each and every one of us to be interchangeable.

The modern world has perverted law and turned it into a highly complex, abstract system detached from its origins in meeting concrete human needs – protecting the weak, enforcing promises and punishing rule breakers. Instead, these systems have become ends in themselves, their success measured by their self-reflexive internal standards – increasingly elaborate and complex rules and procedures that produce outcomes irrelevant to tangible standards of human goodness and welfare.

By the standards of an abstract legal system, my great uncle Daniel was a spectacular success – successfully defending his sex-criminal clients – a vindication and affirmation of "the system." The system "works." His rewards? Professional acclaim and respect; upward mobility in the profession and, of course, wealth and power. His "success" as a lawyer in tangible, physical terms meant more depredation, more pain, more human suffering for the victims of his clients. Think about the experience of the woman raped by one of the repeat-offenders successfully defended by Daniel. With his technical mastery, Daniel, knowing him to be guilty, nevertheless was proud to put him back out on the street. Daniel was a superior player of "the game," the winner. Therein you see a glaring illustration of the contradictions produced by the growth of a modern abstract system like law. The criminal-justice system has become all system, no justice. It has become a parody of the original aspirations of law and justice.

The proliferation of lawyers in modern America signals the triumph of the systematic, destructive force of law's abstracted essence. They complicate and contaminate every aspect of human associations. Families? Divorce and family practice law firms feast on the misery of failed marriages. The workplace? The vast sea of arcane employment and labor law burdens the employers and employees with the cost of compliance and the encouragement of opportunistic, retaliatory lawsuits. The modern workplace must endure ever more laws made by the lawyers in Congress. For what purpose? To make more work for lawyers. The benefit of these laws for employers and workers? More non-productive compliance costs for organizations and employers that require the oversight of lawyers.

Thus, to contemplate: one more abstract circle of self-interest that operates under a cloak of fairness and equity. In America, the well-tested, informal, lower-cost means of easing and diminishing human conflict – custom, manners, tradition, *our* "three olds" – had given way to the high-cost adversarial arena of modern law with its reliance on experts to navigate the "system," to reduce our "exposure" to ever increasing "risk." The more experts, the more the dependency on *their* mastery of the arcane rules of the "systems" in which they navigate. Dependency is the order of the day. Its trajectory is steadily upward.

Here was the conclusion I drew. It changed my view of the world.

> *The modern world is a world of hostages to the complexity of abstract systems and their designers.*

Leslie Abramson's measure of success as a lawyer illustrates even more spectacularly the perversion of the original purpose of law. Abraham's defense of Erik Menendez drew into its orbit another cadre of experts. Operating within the boundaries of their theoretical system, they would assist her efforts to turn Erik Menendez, the worst form of a degenerate human being, into what any resident in a non-abstract-theoretical realm would view as absurd, into a victim. Not pleasant to do, but think of it: a grown man who bends over his mortally wounded, helpless mother and blows her face away with a shotgun. A "system" that attempts such a "conversion" is utterly, hopelessly perverse and completely detached from the real world, from real human relationships and how they should be understood.

Abramson employed a cluster of defense experts, psychologists who asserted their authority with a language that would inject confusion and doubt into the minds of the jurors, a highly sophisticated form of gaslighting. Gaslighting manipulates its target (jurors in this case) into turning against their cognition, their emotions and who they fundamentally are as human beings.

The moral concepts of agency and legal concepts of motive, opportunity, premeditation had to give way to the medicalized concept of compulsion. Strict scientific causality would eliminate moral and legal culpability. The experts spoke in terms of "interrelated symptom clusters" and "sequela," "consequences" in normal English. In order to take the jurors off their cognitive course, medicalized language *had* to be injected in order to subvert the language of morality and law and negate the concepts and perceptions of moral guilt and legal accountability. Experts for the defense asserted the functional equivalence of "battered-person syndrome" with "battered-woman syndrome," a strategic move necessary to set up Eric as a victim.

It wasn't all smooth sailing for Ms. Abramson's magical mystery tour. One of the defense experts under cross-examination was forced to concede that there was no such thing as a formal diagnosis of "battered-person syndrome." Nor could any of the experts produce a precise definition of it in the scientific literature.

Although I was destroyed as a witness, the prosecution sought another expert to testify. University of Michigan psychology professor, Melvin Guyer, a lawyer, research psychologist and professor of Forensic Law in the Department of Psychiatry took the stand. He fared much better under Leslie's grilling than I did. "Battered-person syndrome," he insisted, was a "catch-all for impressionistic clinical judgments.... Being sexually abused is not a diagnosis," he argued. "It is an event."

I kept thinking about the trial and the implications of the defense strategy. The jury system? It was now akin to a vestigial social organ, an increasingly obsolete, pre-modern approach to determining the guilt or innocence of a person accused of a crime. In its original conception a jury was an impartial body of *peers* assembled to determine the guilt or innocence of the accused. Their deliberations were to be guided by their experience, common sense and the rules of evidence. A "peer" is by definition: "a person who is equal to another in abilities, qualifications, age, background, etc. ..." An "expert" stands above the peers. His abilities, qualifications, knowledge and training are what make him stand apart.

The interposition of "experts" into a jury trial profoundly changes it. Guilt-determination becomes a process highly mediated by their expertise and knowledge, knowledge inaccessible to the non-expert. The experts are the stars; the jury, the supporting cast. The Menendez trial, predictably, turned into a battle of the experts – those hired by the defense; those the prosecution used to poke holes in the theoretical pretensions of the defense witnesses. When the experts disagree, who gets to say who is right, who is wrong?

More experts. Where does this leads us? Into a meta-theoretical, infinite regress in a search for the holy grail of credibility. Juries of non-experts are simply suspended in the purgatory of self-doubt. They have to make their best guess at which expert to believe. At some point, when logic prevails, we must let the experts decide and forego the farce of the jury.

Leslie Abramson's attempt to "flip" Erik – perpetrator to victim – was only partially successful. His trial resulted in a hung jury. Erik's brother Lyle, was tried separately. His lawyer attempted the same defense. This trial as well resulted in a hung jury. Enough of the jury members from both trials resisted the "theorists." The brothers were retried together in a courtroom absent of TV cameras presided over by Judge Weisberg. It was less of a circus. In the second go around Weisberg imposed stricter limitations on defense testimony use of sexual abuse claims and refused the jury the option to vote on manslaughter charges instead of murder charges. The brothers were found guilty of first-degree murder and conspiracy to commit murder. They were sentenced to life in prison with no possibility of parole. Ms. Abramson had managed to save the lives of the Menendez brothers. Their convictions and sentences, she has continued to assert over the years, were a gross miscarriage of justice.

19 Abstractions as Distractions

*"Abuse of speech: [W]hen [men] use
words metaphorically; that is, in other
sense than that they are ordained for;
and thereby deceive others."*

—Thomas Hobbes, *Leviathan*

*"Beware intellectuals…. Not only
should they be kept well away from the
levers of power, they should also be
objects of particular suspicion when
they seek to offer collective advice."*

—Paul Johnson, *Intellectuals*

The Menendez brothers trial brought me to the crux
of my problem with the domination of the modern
world by abstraction systems. The source of that problem is not with the use of abstractions per se, but with
their abuse.

Abstractions are tools of thought. Properly used,
they generalize over our experience and apply our intelligence beyond our immediate physical boundaries.
To treat abstractions as *things* that can be confronted,

managed or manipulated is to court disaster. An egregious example is "the war on terrorism," the legacy of President George W. Bush, a man whose cognitive limitations and puppet-like usefulness to dark, oligarchic forces are well-established. Terrorism is an abstraction: you cannot kill or destroy an abstraction. You can kill a terrorist. You can destroy a community of terrorists, but you cannot kill or destroy the abstraction, "terrorism," ever. To announce a "war on terrorism" is to commit, what the philosopher, Gilbert Ryle, called, "a category mistake." Terrorism is not the kind of *thing* that can ever be killed – whether in a war or any other way the way an insect or a human being can be killed. The Bush-Cheney "war on terrorism" is the paradigm for the kind of "modern warfare" the ruling class has been conducting for several generations to extend their usurpations of power and control over every facet of our lives.

Likewise, you can arrest, detain, punish and deter *criminals*. They are the sorts of *things* that can be arrested, etc. But you can never rid the world of the abstraction, "criminality." You can punish wicked people, but you cannot rid the world of "wickedness." You can alleviate the suffering of the *poor*, but you cannot eliminate "poverty."

No one should even *try* to eliminate these or any abstractions. Why? "Criminality," "wickedness" and "poverty" are useful tools of language that point us to permanent defects and limitations in the human condition. Criminality is the perversion, the misuse of desire and ambition. To eliminate criminality, you would have to eliminate both of them. Wickedness is a corruption of love. To rid the world of wickedness you would have to eliminate love. Poverty is always and everywhere a relative condition. The poor in Chicago are well off compared to the poor in Kolkata. Kings in 16th-century France are poor compared to today's middle class in Grand Rapids, Michigan and Fort Worth, Texas. To eliminate "poverty" you would have to eliminate human beings.

The modern world has increasingly preoccupied itself with abstractions, abstractions misconstrued as "things" that can be confronted and eliminated. And, since they cannot, continued efforts to do so have produced a collective psychosis. A psychosis is defined as *a severe mental disorder in which thought and emotions are so impaired that contact is lost with external reality.*

I'm reluctant to say this, but that's where we are – collectively impaired with remote connections to reality. Nasty Don Quixotes – the kind you wouldn't trust around your little sister – are running the show. They use us to make war on their invented abstractions. A war on an abstraction – the war on terror, the war on poverty, the war on drugs, the elimination of racism, the elimination of hatred – any and all of these elaborate fantasies proceed with impaired thinking that play upon the emotions of fear and vulnerability – your fears and your vulnerabilities, that is. Demagogues manufacture and exploit them: they promise to "fix" what is unfixable, to rid us of what is un-ridable. These are "mental disorders" of colossal proportions.

These attempts to "defeat" abstractions plunge us into a continuous cycle of frustration and failure. A system that is stupid, perverse and illogical we are supposed to embrace and support. The criminal dishonesty of the ruling class mandarins combines with hubris. They try to convince us that with sufficient power and resources they will be able to do what they cannot possibly do. Instead, they use that power to insulate themselves from the intrusion of "external reality," the evidence of their failure. Those stubborn abstractions they battle, however, never submit to defeat. Abstractions do not negotiate. They do not surrender. Those who point this out are scapegoated as heretics and traitors. The propaganda organs sniff them out, then manufacture their guilt. The Big Lie, the manipulation and distortion of information, comes in wave after wave of moralistic bombast to convince people that the world is not what it really is. All "wars" to eliminate abstractions are exercises in mass psychosis. They become endless wars against imaginary enemies to achieve what is unachievable – interminable, rolling waves of collective insanity.

The Menendez trial convinced me: I was a misfit in this modern world of abstract systems. Having made that determination, I realized that my life could not continue as I had planned. Briefly, I considered seppuku, ritual suicide favored by the Japanese warrior code, Bushidō. It's an extremely painful and slow means of making your final exit chosen to demonstrate your possession of courage, self-control and strong resolve. Seppuku would signal redemption from my pathetic, unwarrior-like collapse under the assault of a four-foot eleven, lady pettifogger wearing dangling earrings. Too messy, too gruesome. For better or worse, my psychologist side kicked in. I concluded that, perhaps, suicide as a response to this personal failure was an overreaction. Which meant that I was at a loss to know how I could continue. This realization, however, plunged me into a deep depression, for a time immobilized. No one was permitted to detract from the darkness of my despair.

> Knock, knock.
>
> Whose there?
>
> Nobody who?
>
> Nobody home.
>
> But thank you for stopping by.

I stopped working. Sally sued the doctor who treated her deceased father for cancer for malpractice – early diagnosis failure and negligent treatment – and won a substantial settlement from his insurance company. Most of the cash proceeds of that settlement she gave to me in the form of a trust fund. It enabled me to live modestly while unemployed. The irony: the death of my grandfather – a man who worked his entire life – would enable his young grandson to live without working. I think, I know, that he would have disapproved. "Buck up, grandson. The world is a mess. Don't take it personally. Do some kind of work, even the humblest kind. Wash dishes, clean bathrooms, bag groceries. That will help you find yourself." That would be his version of "pastoral counseling."

Finally, I channeled that advice from the spirit of my Grandfather and stepped back into the modern world. Well I should say, from my head I cleared the delusion that I had ever been outside of it. There was no way out other than... I was not going to take that way out.

20 Life in the "Cave"

"The creatures outside looked from pig to man, and from man to pig, and from pig to man again; but already it was impossible to say which was which."

—George Orwell, *Nineteen Eighty-Four*

Plato's "Allegory of the Cave."

> "Socrates: 'Imagine this: People live under the earth in a cave like dwelling. Stretching a long way up toward the daylight is its entrance, toward which the entire cave is gathered. The people have been in this dwelling since childhood, shackled by the legs and neck. Thus, they stay in the same place so that there is only one thing for them to look at: whatever they encounter in front of their faces. But because they are shackled, they are unable to turn their heads around.'"

A fire is behind them, and there is a wall between the fire and the prisoners.

Socrates: 'Some light, of course, is allowed them, namely from a fire that casts its glow toward them from behind them, being above and at some distance. Between the fire and those who are shackled [i.e., behind their backs] there runs a walkway at a certain height.' Imagine that a low wall has been built the length of the walkway, like the low curtain that puppeteers put up, over which they show their puppets."

—**Plato**, *The Republic*

How then did I escape the depression that had locked me into this self-indulgent, malignant stupor for so long? The short answer is: I didn't. I learned to "manage" it, just as Sally moved through her life as a "functional alcoholic." The waves of pessimism that had rolled over me were corrective. I turned depression into a functional way of life. I channeled it into a muscular cynicism with moral power. I'll expand upon it shortly. I had come to possess the vision of a saint but with no connection to saintliness.

I could continue to make my way in the modern world only by refusing to believe in it. Its promises were false. My newly galvanized cynicism gave me a feeling of epistemological superiority. I knew what those around me fail to grasp. Everyone searches for superiority in their own way. The feeling of epistemological superiority may be the purest and sweetest superior feeling of them all. That fundamental truth also was the premise for my new calling as a prophet decrying the "progress" of the modern world.

As I arose to launch my confrontation with the modern word, I found myself, of all places, in California. Here was the epicenter, the glittering triumph of the modern world. What good fortune! California, the magic kingdom. Its fame and allure have come from its vast power to entertain, to transform solid substance into fleeting appearance, to substitute imagery for reality. Rising to the top here are empty suits who levitate themselves on the vapors of self-help bromides, mindless clichés and faddish spirituality. The royalty of this kingdom are costumed mortals of modest cognitive powers whose imitative talents before cameras transform them into omniscient Gods who demand adoration and obeisance.

California's crown jewel is the entertainment industry with Hollywood as its pinnacle. The entertainment industry is, perhaps, the most insidious and dangerous of all the modern abstract systems. Its power overturns the material and spiritual constraints of external reality – pathologizing what is normal; normalizing what is pathological. Hollywood is a modern abstract system of subversive perfection – producing propaganda masked as innocent diversion from *Lebenserfahrung,* life-experience. Its vast creative power has made for us a modern, "Plato's Cave" in which we dwell and delude ourselves permanently.

In Plato's famous allegory, chained prisoners observe the shadows projected on the wall from objects passing in front of a fire behind them. They name the shadows, take them for reality and believe them to be what they are not. Those "objects passing in front of a fire" come to us non-stop from Netflix, Amazon, Hulu and the rest of the organs of diversion and distraction. This includes the "news," a subsidiary of the entertainment complex. A child born today from her earliest hours grows up immersed in "the shadows," a world dominated by the vast, inescapable entertainment-web of modern life – TV, movies, sports, video games, music videos, YouTube videos, social media, the cable channels, talking heads – a world of imaging disconnected from the physical, organic experience of life. Adolescent boys in Japan – at puberty, nebbish wimps – have forsaken real girls; they prefer "virtual" dates – sexual solipsism.

Only in California could the Governor of that state be someone who ascends from the ranks of famous professional pretenders – actors, and not even the best ones. Mr. Reagan's acting fame? "Bedtime for Bonzo" in which he pretended to teach human morals to a chimpanzee. Consider that irony. Mr. Schwarzenegger's? A muscled-up, robot assassin from outer space. So, a pretend monkey trainer and a pretend killer robot – perfect credentials for the modern leader from the most beguiling of our systems – professional purveyors of fantasy. Their role was to sustain and augment the collective delusions, to convince the "prisoners" that the shadows are real.

If only I could escape from California, I thought. Then I realized: there is no escape from it. California, Plato's Cave, is everywhere.

This realization descended upon me, and I grasped that I was alone and was lonely. It was the kind of desperate "alone" I came to think that the succor of a woman might ease. Men and women, of course, need each other in the most basic physical, spiritual ways, even to share their misery. Which bespeaks to one of Balzac's most memorable epigrams: "Nothing in the world creates so much understanding as shared pain." My testosterone-tinged misery needed estrogen-assisted company. But men and women approach each other with different, often incompatible agendas. They hugely complicate the possibility for, shall we say, friendly, affectionate, long-term togetherness and mutual support to cope with "shared pain." These complications come in droves with modern-manufactured complexities. Modern complexities, however, are no one's fault. Well, they are not supposed to be. Voila! *No-fault* divorce. Divorce of a no-fault species makes marital dissolution convenient, easy and, well, just downright modern.

Where, you wonder, was no-fault divorce conceived, birthed and so appropriately named? California, of course. Where else was the resolve to obliterate obstacles to *self*-fulfillment so powerful and so much the way of the future? Who else but an actor to make it happen. *Acting* as governor, Governor Ronald Reagan, on his way to becoming the first divorced American President, signed the "It's been nice knowing you" divorce into law in 1969. Perfect timing. Nineteen sixty-nine, the end of a decade that smashed through many boundaries. Marriage was soon to be "Californicated" nation-wide.

"I do?" Well, now it's "I don't, Life Partner. Don't cry, little Jennifer and Jason. Mommy and Daddy still love you very much." Marriage in modern America? Once an institutional bulwark of civilized society; now a "lifestyle" choice.

The modern world is all about agendas. Many of them are woven out of abstractions that provide no foundation or support for what men and women need in order to be faithful to each other. In fact, these agendas are often about the destruction of fidelity, euphemized as "lifestyle" choices that enhance our Oprahesque feelings of "self-worth." The movement toward the atomized living of modern people "celebrating" themselves continues unabated. No-fault divorce was another milestone in the march of modernity, breaking through boundaries, creating and advancing new agendas – helping *you* discover the new "you".

Modern marriages fail for modern reasons. Consider what rocky shores breakup and sink the ships of so many marriages – the rocky shores of that darkest of abstractions, unhappiness. An unhappy marriage is the modern world's perfect definition of a failed marriage. Marriage partners must make each other happy, or else – very tricky and very iffy. How did that come to be?

To make happiness your life's goal is a newish thing, a couple of hundred years old. It is the product of the European Enlightenment, technically expressed as "maximizing utility." "Happiness" is a thoroughly modernized, mathematized abstraction. It is what you are told from an early age should be your quest. It is the *sine qua non* for a successful marriage and the measure of your life.

So much is wrong with this that it is hard to know where to begin. No one can make anyone else happy. Most people don't know how to make themselves happy, and if they figure it out, it's a temporary fix as in a shopping spree. We need Hobbes, again, to help us grasp this point: "Because the constitution of a man's body is in continual mutation; it is impossible that all the same things should always cause in him the same appetites, and aversions: much less can all men consent in the desire of almost any one and the same object." Happiness is, of all human goods, the most elusive, the most undefined, the most difficult to hold on to. H. L. Mencken captured the illusiveness of happiness: "My belief is that happiness is necessarily transient. The natural state of a reflective man is one of depression." Thus, it is.

Yet, we persist in making happiness the measure of our lives and the test of our marriages.

Here then, is the cynical and irrefutable take on it. "Happiness" as the goal of modern life, including marriage, makes possible a vast number of flourishing service industries. The merchants who run them dangle happiness before us as the goal of existence. They make happiness "accessible" and affordable" – for everyone. Couples think they need it to stay married. Single people believe that marriage will make them happy. Your job is supposed to make you happy.

Think of the vast unemployment that would result if overnight happiness disappeared from our collective aspirations for marriage and other important life pursuits. Many churches would fold. No more "Lifetime" cable channel. Self-help writers would become waiters, medical technicians or morgue assistants. Publishing houses for romance novels would wither away. Goodbye romantic comedies, thus fewer actors. The movie industry would contract. Divorce lawyers would file for bankruptcy. Marriage counselors would retire or become travel agents or investment advisors. A reduction in wedding planners would result as there would be fewer second and third marriages.

Back to my quest for a lady-partner to share my pain. I was *à bout de force*. My brief, failed marriage was a frivolous, impulsive act. Older and wiser, perhaps I could launch a more valiant try. I needed to find a serious woman to wed – a formidable challenge. I lived alone. I wasn't working, didn't go to church, didn't go to the gym, didn't socialize. A singles bar was not the place to meet the kind of women I was hoping to find. I couldn't think of a *place* to look. I spotted a beautiful young woman once on one of my outings to Albertson's grocery store as I wandered down the frozen food aisle in front of the Häagen-Dazs ice cream section. As I moved in for a closer look, her beauty suddenly vanished – Poof! It was the message on her tee-shirt: "If you like my mountains, you'll love my Busch." Recoiling, I struggled to imagine what collusive, nefarious, modern forces had produced the kind of mentality that would lead a young woman to turn herself into a walking beer commercial and publicly present herself brazenly in such a crude, degrading fashion.

But:

> "Here, another Saturday night
> And I ain't got nobody…
> Now, how I wish I had someone to talk to
> I'm in an awful way."

> **— Sam Cooke**, *Another Saturday Night*

An awful way, indeed. Time to go in a modern direction, online dating. Yes, I know, Reader. You are laughing at me. You should. Here I am railing against modern, abstract systems. And now I confess that I was going to resort to the most modern of them all, an impersonal, computerized system that attempts to link men and women struggling with the most uniquely human aspirations of their lives, the pursuit of intimacy, love and companionship. Remember Dupont's advertisement slogan years ago: "Better living through chemistry?" Now: "Falling in love through algorithms."

"Tempt not a desperate man," as Shakespeare said. I was a desperate man who had to yield reluctantly to temptation. Online I found my second wife. Her name was Karen Carpenter, same name as the singer who died young from *anorexia nervosa*. I should have recognized that as a bad omen.

Finding Karen, however, was not easy.

21 Trials of an Un-modern Man

"Everything I want the world to be

Is now comin' true especially for me

And the reason is clear, it's because you
are here

You're the nearest thing to heaven that
I've seen."

— The Carpenters, *Top of the World*

"If music be the food of love, play on,

Give me excess of it; that surfeiting,

The appetite may sicken, and so die."

— William Shakespeare, *Twelfth Night*

An online dating service presented serious obstacles to an unobstructed vision of "the nearest thing to heaven." The first one was almost insurmountable. To get myself set up in "the system," I had to create an online "profile." The profile is your description of "you," your personality deceitfully represented in flattering, cutesy, picturesque fluff so as to attract a buyer – someone for whom your "specs" will meet their product expectations. "Can't buy me love!" Says who? This pretend-game of "Who am I" has to be rigged so the outcome makes "you" into a salable commodity, fake charm that warbles "true love" to entice someone perhaps even more unstable than you. I worried that I might be heading toward a product liability tort. I could be liable for damages if the product (me) turned out to be defective or unsafe in the estimation of the buyer (her). Think of what "defective" and "unsafe" could be tortured to mean in today's battle of the sexes by some skilled, devious divorce lawyer with an expertise in the injury of "feelings." More consulting opportunities for psychologists as "expert" witnesses. There are torts. And *then* there are torts – close encounters of a weird kind. Now you can understand my anxiety, comrades. Sometimes "diamonds are [not] forever," *Heer* De Beer.

I was determined, but utterly helpless and stuck. How would I construct this frothy "Song of Myself" sales pitch stocked with enough empty slogans and contemporary buzzwords to sell it to someone who herself was confused, demented or worse? How would whatever it ended up saying attract the kind of woman I wasn't sure I wanted to attract? I knew what I didn't want – some needy, insecure babbling brook of banalities toting her catalogue of complexes and her Aqua Deco water bottle. But I wasn't sure I knew what I did want. I continued to flounder desperately in an endeavor that looked like a long shot at best. Then I stumbled across a website where I found advice from a woman on how to create an online profile that would get me that special woman I wasn't sure I really wanted.

"Think of specific aspects of your personality that you want to highlight. Then, don't just state them — demonstrate them. Instead of, 'I enjoy Stanley Kubrick films,' say, 'The other night I was watching A Clockwork Orange, and I found myself thinking it would be a lot more fun to watch and discuss it with someone else.' Humor is especially important. Not everyone shares the same sense of humor, so saying 'I'm a funny person' isn't sufficient. 'I love quoting lines from Monty Python sketches and Simpsons episodes' gives other users a better grasp of your personality."

Apart from the condescending tone and annoying style of a high school English teacher lady doing her didactic duty, this counsel was wrong-headed and lame from the start. The first sentence should have read: "Think of specific aspects of your personality that you want to *hide*," like your susceptibility to gimmicky, online marketing ploys. Or, "I slip into a deep melancholy a couple of hours after reading Kierkegaard."

The more I strained to extract something useful from this useless pep talk, the more I realized that it was the perfect expression of modern American culture *reductio ad excrementum*. I asked myself: "What kind of tranquilized, hermetic world must a person who wrote something like this live in?" My conclusion: it was one that would be most comfortable and appealing for congenitally anxious unfortunates, ideal candidates for transorbital lobotomies. Or maybe a recent, purple-haired graduate of Oberlin College armed with a cinema studies major and a nose ring – and with no clue about the source of a hundred thousand dollars to retire her tuition debt. This would be just the right someone to dispense tips about romance, someone who assembled her "personality" from randomly chosen plots of romantic comedies and repartee from Simpson cartoons.

How to pull off this "personality profile" scam? I, a resolutely anti-modern man, would have to pretend to be a hip, breezy sort of ultra-modern dude, decked out in a Jerry Garcia tee-shirt, sensitive and needy, conversant in all things reeking of pop-culture. How many plots from "Seinfeld" can I regurgitate? Where is the best Sushi bar? Where can I get tickets for "Lion King?" Do you like Jimmy Buffett? Let me croon a couple of verses of "Margaritaville" for you.

> "Nibblin' on sponge cake
>
> Watchin' the sun bake
>
> All of those tourists covered with oil…
>
> Wastin' away again in Margaritaville
>
> Searchin' for my lost shaker of salt."

Ok, one is plenty.

Yeah, I was definitely "wastin' away," but not on sponge cake. I was sober and in a grimmer region than Margaritaville. I was "searchin'" – not for a salt shaker, but something, someone with a cheerful but sober personality and with breasts. A woman is what I had in mind. But how am I going to attract a woman, any woman with my brutally honest personality profile that reads like this: "30-something, massively cynical, completely nihilistic, profoundly disillusioned guy in revolt against the modern world is in quest of a resentful, but stunningly beautiful woman who would consider joining me on an elephant hunt, doesn't recycle, despises romantic comedies, sit-coms, Tom Brokaw and soccer, and has *zero* interest in 'saving the planet'?" A resurrected, jack-booted Benito Mussolini strutting in full regalia topped off with his black fez would likely spark more interest from romance-starved, American ladies of the 1990s than me. Get real! No room for irony in the world of online dating.

By going the modern-man route – what choice did I have? – what species of alien invertebrate would be drawn into my orbit? A devotee of Mötley Crüe? A karaoke party animal trying to sound like Sheryl Crow?

> "If it makes you happy
> It can't be that bad
> If it makes you happy
> Then why the hell are you so sad?"

Well, it just might be "that bad," Sheryl. No. Worse. It would make me "happier" if the singing Crow would develop permanent laryngitis, fly away and take up dirt bike racing or lady wrestling.

With no encouragement at any moment my true love harvested from online, I feared, would decide to get "serious" and launch into a screechy, hair-raising version of "We are the World," a disgusting avalanche of feeble-minded sentimentality.

> "We are the world
>
> We are the children
>
> We are the ones who make a brighter day,
> so let's start giving."

How many shekels do I have to shell out to make you stop singing this?

> "We can't go on
>
> Pretending day-by-day
>
> That someone, somewhere will soon make
> a change."

Change or no change, I refuse to go on pretending that someone, anyone, anywhere who likes this assault on intelligence is not incurably obnoxious or disastrously defective.

> "We're all a part of God's great big family
>
> And the truth, you know, love is all we
> need."

I think we've heard this upchuck-inducing inspirational guidance before from, who else? The celebrity-duo of the reality-averse set, John and Yoko. What's missing in "God's great big family," are the words, "permanently and highly dysfunctional." "And the truth"? Completely out of reach for the "We are the World" crooners. I'm still trying to figure out how the "love is all we need" part works with Jeffry Dahmer, Mike Tyson and the NFL playoffs. I suspect that Iron Mike and the Milwaukee Cannibal were never family members in good standing with God. Iron Mike's understanding of "the truth" was what you would call "fact-based": "Everyone has a plan until they get punched in the mouth. Then, like a rat, they stop in fear and freeze." "Love," by the way, doesn't get you into the Super Bowl. It doesn't pay off your student loans. Divorce lawyers don't do pro bono.

What then might be the upside of throwing in with such a hedonistic study in arrested development?

She could fill in my gaps on "Friends," or "Sex in the City" episodes. Our conversation would unfold in a dreadful dialect of hybrid drivel hammered out in the DMZ's war between the sexes. She'd theorize about the flaws of her "exes" and enthuse over the results of her workout routines at LA Fitness. Life with such an imperfectly formed psychical entity would immerse me in a continuous flux of popular trends attached to a miasmic slew of trivia. Our understanding of the world would reach back about at least half a decade. It would be an Oprah-world of insipid "feelgoods" and her signature, jaw-dropping non sequiturs. This one from Her Wisdomness is a keeper: "True forgiveness is when you can say, 'Thank you for that experience.'" I'm reserving that one for the next time I'm getting mugged on the Capitol Mall. Nothing like an old-fashioned, jaw-fracturing mugging to unlock the forgiveness stowed away in your cold, stony heart. "Thank you for 'that experience' of getting punched in the face and separated from my wallet. Please don't max out my VISA card. Oh, sorry, I forgot. Thank you, too, for not killing me while you were at it. Maybe 'that experience' for the next time we meet. Thank you for that in advance, for obvious reasons, Amigo. No hard feelings, of course."

> "But, [you'll] never break, never break
>
> Never break, never break this heart of
>   stone
>
> Oh, no, no, this heart of stone…"

That won't fly with Oprah.

At this point, I considered tossing in the towel with perhaps a retreat to a hermit's cave in quest of Brahman while clutching a volume of the *Upanishads*. I was also thinking about something H. L. Mencken said about the quest for love: "Women are also the cause of the worst kind of unhappiness." But what did he know? And, who needs "happiness", whatever that is? My heart was set on a woman. She had to be the right one, however, one who could speak to me in a language that I understood – not in the ubiquitous, stylized inanities of contemporary pop-culture. The only way to proceed, I decided, was to ignore the received "wisdom" and craft a personality profile short, mysterious and off-putting enough to entice only a daring few. Maybe there'd be a mysterious Madonna out there who could read between the lines and see a wounded, kindred spirit lurking in the shadows. Well, "lurking" probably doesn't have the right ring in this context of making romance come alive. Here it was: "Original and contrary-thinking 30-something guy who drives a black corvette, but otherwise lives like a Trappist monk, seeks a modest, introspective and thoughtful woman prepared to understand and appreciate him and do a slow reading with him of T.S. Eliot's 'The Wasteland' or the 'Malatesta Cantos' of Ezra Pound. Her choice."

You can guess. It took a long time. I got few takers with this – two to be precise. The first one, Charlotte Rampling – same name as my favorite English actress from the 1970s – showed tentative interest. That made my heart beat faster. I responded. We agreed to rendezvous at a posh restaurant, the Mission Inn in Riverside. It was her choice. I had serious misgivings about Charlotte even before we met. How could she live up to her name? Also, her personality profile was on the order of someone following the advice I scoffed at above. What subliminal blunders had I made with mine that might be misleading? But the harvest from mine, as I noted, was light. Go with the flow; on with the show, Kemosabe.

Charlotte arrived stylishly late, and she came very well assembled. She was also appropriately decked out – contemporary California *coutre* – a denim button-down Western shirt underneath a trim, black leather jacket with shoulder pads, and tight, dark green Victoria Beckham drain pipe jeans. On her feet, a pricey pair of Dr. Martens Combat Boots. She had put serious effort into the presentation. I was appreciative. But worried.

We quickly launched into that awkward tango that moves to the lyrics of: "Are you worth an entire evening of my time?" She seemed slightly embarrassed to tell me that she'd grown up in Dayton, Ohio and graduated from the University of Akron. What do you think of when you think of Akron? Rubber tires, probably. Of Dayton, Ohio? Well, nothing that would entice you to visit unless you are researching urban decay, rust belt *mise en scène* and endemic obesity. I was understanding, of course. In so many words spoken *sotto voce*, "You're not to blame," I assured her in my best therapist pose – though uncertain of whom else to put it on. How did she get to California and why? We never got that far. She looked to me frighteningly too much like Cyndi Lauper. I think it might have been the spikey, platinum-blond *chevelure*. And, I suspected that she had fibbed about her age – more like forty than mid-thirties.

I had accoutered myself in a wool, three-piece Bill Blass, grey, pinstripe suit. The white shirt with a conservative navy-blue, knit tie and a black pair of Cheltenham Brogue shoes completed this sartorial ensemble. My hair was short, and I was clean-shaven with some expensive men's cologne, Creed Viking from Saks Fifth Avenue. Looking and smelling like a high-priced, Manhattan ambulance chaser, I was amused to see the double take when she saw how I was dressed – very un-California and not *comme il faut* for this kind of mating dance. Which was what I was aiming for.

"This does not bode well" is the vibe I picked up from her when she surveyed the "un-hipness" of my duds and sniffed the fumes of my toilet water.

We introduced ourselves and did the obligatory LA hug. Is there anyone in California who *doesn't* "hug?" Do the guards at the county jail hug the prisoners before "lights out"? Does the "last meal" in San Quentin's death row come with bear hugs from the warden and the padre?

Off we went.

> "Getting to know you
>
> Getting to know all about you
>
> Getting to like you
>
> Getting to hope you like me."

Sally loved Julie Andrews. Me too, though with less gusto. But it was the third line in that cheerful ditty that put a hitch in my get-along that evening. "Getting to like you" more than often does *not* follow from "Getting to know you." For this occasion, it was a non sequitur.

To my dismay, Ms. Rampling, I quickly got to know, was a full professor in the department of teacher education at Cal State San Bernardino. She made a point to tell me that she had just gotten tenure, not knowing, of course, how much less that made me think of her. More troubling: she taught California's future public-school teachers, that is, set up young people to be absorbed into the State's "educational system" to do what modern systems are designed to do – needlessly complicate the lives of people who are sucked into the maw, obliterate any flickers in them of spiritual awakening, and vomit them out as an undifferentiated mass of yes-folks, trained robots.

After a half-an-hour conversation with her I knew that the future of the Golden State was certain doom. After another half-hour of "sharing" I observed a slight shudder ripple across her shapely frame and sensed the feeling of horror that was descending over her. Whatever she imagined that I was trying to say with my profile, suddenly the realization hit her: she had been "dangerously" misled. Those subliminal signals I had fretted about. Not my fault! I squirmed a bit, seeing myself, again, as a walking product liability tort. What would Sally advise? Hmm… Probably not the best source of advice in matters like this.

> "Getting to know you
>
> Getting to feel free and easy
>
> When I am with you
>
> Getting to know what to say"

Another wince-making non sequitur. The feelings of "free and easy" were not appearing on the horizon for either one of us either. I had flunked the "Getting to know what to say" part of this excruciating oral exam in the company of a professional Teacher Ed lady. What to say?

> "Trying to keep up with you
>
> And I don't know if I can do it

> Oh no, I've said too much
>
> I haven't said enough..."

—REM, *Losing my Religion*

From the breezy bonhomie of Julie Andrews to the introspective angst of REM in about the time it took to bring the ghastly lyrics of "Jumpin' Jack Flash" into my head.

> "I was drowned, I was washed up and left
>   for dead
>
> I fell down to my feet and I saw they
>   bled..."

Had I said not enough or too much? God, I wish I knew. I was washed up. This date had been dead on arrival.

After a hasty, obviously concocted excuse, Charlotte quickly drained the last ounce of her second glass of non-oaked Chardonnay. She jumped up, dug into her purse and threw a couple of Andrew Jacksons on the table. "Here's looking at you, Kid," I guess was what she was saying. Her plate of pepper crusted tuna she left untouched. Off to the parking lot she fled and escaped in her cute, little Audi TT with those four, intersecting rings on the grill. Audi's slogan, by the way, is "*Vorsprung durch Technik.*" It means, "Being Ahead through Technology." I guess you have to be a German engineer to get it. Perhaps something got lost in translation, although I like the active-sound of the German better than the passive English – "*Vorsprung,*" more energy than "being ahead," whatever that means. In any case, what a disaster technology had been for Charlotte that evening at the Mission Inn. It had been an unpleasant detour on her highway to love. Her abrupt departure was a trifle rude, but really, I couldn't blame her. I felt bad about her disappointment, genuinely so. The modern "mystery man" she was hoping to entice had turned out to be a reactionary refusenik. Wasn't her fault. I don't think she would ever have been up for "The Wasteland," much less the "Cantos."

> "A heap of broken images, where the sun beats,
>
> And the dead tree gives no shelter, the cricket no relief…"

—T.S. Eliot, *Burial of the Dead*

That evening brought out so many "broken images" on my horizon. I sighed and settled back into my chair. From the restaurant window I calmly followed Charlotte's harried departure. Behind the wheel of her red convertible she floored the gas-pedal and peeled out onto the highway. Her abrupt, unceremonious leave-taking aside, not having stiffed me for the tab left me thinking rather kindly of Charlotte Rampling. Her next outing, I hoped, would be more rewarding. I stayed put long enough to polish off my goat cheese croquettes with spiced membrillo with an after dinner single malt Scotch. Then, back to my lonely casa and Shostakovich on the stereo, Symphony no. 7, the Leningrad – a musical reflection on the city's 900 days under siege by the German army. 800,000 dead just to put my blues in perspective. Charlotte's pepper crusted tuna? Why throw it away? I brought it home in a box for my two Rottweilers, Abbott and Costello.

22 If I Were a Carpenter

"From the Intense Inane to the Inane Intense

My soul took flight upon the wings of
sense.

But very soon my soul flew back again

From Inane Intense to the Intense Inane."

—Wyndham Lewis, *Self-Condemned*

Date number two was Karen Carpenter. Four months after our first encounter she became my second wife.

"We've only just begun to live

White lace and promises

A kiss for luck and we're on our way…"

Some sad irony in those lines written by Paul Wil-
liams and sung by a lovely voice that fell silent at 32 years old. Should I have been thinking: in the quest for love, like mother, like son? Here's how *my* Karen's online profile read: "I'm an angry, frustrated, fairly good-looking mid-30s brunette, disappointed in love, looking for a taciturn, mid-30s man who will *not* dis-appoint this time around." That was it. No sales job,

no pop culture crap, no bullshit – completely, uniquely weird and definitely off-putting. Angst and alienation in spades. It was likely I was going to be in love with her. So, I was hoping that "fairly good-looking" was her bow to modesty. Could be the other way. I was willing to risk it. She did, however, get more hits than I did. Does that mean guys are more desperate than gals or less discriminating?

In our initial communication Karen said she did not want to meet at a restaurant. Her preference was for something more "on the edges," as she put it. I puzzled a while with "on the edges." Far away from contemporary California fashionable pretensions or pursuits, I guessed, was where she was going. Which pushed the right buttons with me. I guessed right. I proposed for our first romantic encounter a bowling alley in slightly-seedy, blue-collar Reseda, just west of Burbank – so close, yet so far from Hollywood. She jumped all over it. For the occasion, I bought a used bowling shirt at Value Village for six dollars. It was short-sleeve, lime-green with a black collar and black ribbing – 20 percent cotton, 80 percent polyester the product tag read. Its logo: "Cal-central Pipe-fitters League." I was a little hesitant about what washing might do to it, so I didn't.

It's worth mentioning that my "shopping" venture at Value Village in quest of the bowling shirt took me to East Los Angeles, a microcosm of America's "slumification" of the big cities. East LA has all those interchangeable features of the many U.S. skid row, third-world cities: liquor stores, smoke shops, check cashing places, hair extension parlors, pawnshops and crummy fast-food joints. You could be anywhere, Detroit, St. Louis, Baltimore, Newark, Oakland, parts of DC – whatever few trees and bushes that might be in place would be the only tip off as to what part of the country you are in.

Karen, attired sans frou-frou, arrived at the bowling alley ahead of me. We didn't hug – healthy reticence. She and I were on the same page for this initial meet, however. She showed up in a shiny, solid pink bowling shirt with the logo, "Reseda First Baptist Ladies League." That night we were doing a hipster sort of thing without knowing it. No matter. The sparkling stars of romantic bliss had converged directly above us. We rented our shoes below. We smiled goofily at each other as we tried not to think about all those feet that had slipped into that leathery foot ware before ours. Our evening was launched with a *haute cuisine* of corn dogs and fried pickle chips. We chased them down with ice-cold, long neck bottles of Budweiser. Dessert was an ice cream sandwich. The bowling ball I grabbed was macho black and well used. Karen chose one with pyramid path teal and a brand-new gleam. Then we gutter-ball bowled our way through the evening with the league veterans good-naturedly cheering us on. They could tell: it was love at first frame. And, she was far above "fairly good-looking." Bingo.

> "My heart began to tell my body and my
> soul,

That it had gotten in the mood to lose
    control...

If I'm not in love I'm on the verge."

—**Collin Raye**, *On the Verge*

23 Karen's Breaks

"No navigator has yet traced the lines
of latitude and longitude on the conjugal
sea."

—Honoré de Balzac

Karen was a year or so my senior. She was born in San Francisco on June 6th, 1968, the same day the Palestinian, Sirhan Sirhan shot Bobby Kennedy in a kitchen hallway of the Ambassador Hotel in Los Angles.

Karen's parents were hippies. She showed me a picture of them taken around the time she was born. All I could see were eyes and mouths. Everything else was hair.

"Hair, hair, hair, hair, hair, hair, hair, hair

Flow it, show it, long as God can grow it,
   my hair…"

—The Cowsills, *Hair*

You have to feel sorry for the barbers back then when God himself was working against them. I think it was the men of the tonsorial arts who were first on board with the curse words, "fucking hippies."

For the first year of Karen's life her parents migrated through the communes in and around the Bay area, smoking lots of hashish and experimenting with whatever hallucinogenic substances that came their way. During one of their few lucid days, they dimly grasped that *their* parenting of their baby daughter was not going to be in her best, long-term interest. The hippie mom and dad decided to hand Karen off to her maternal grandmother, Alice Reynolds, for safe-keeping. "We'll be back," they told Alice. They then split for the New Buffalo commune in Arroyo Hondo, north of Taos, New Mexico. New Buffalo was the inspiration for the commune scenes in the movie, "Easy Rider." Whatever few, fully functional brain cells that remained in the heads of Karen's mom and dad were in peril and at some point, likely perished. The events of their lives written up properly could be cast into a fascinating case study and preserved in the archives of a psychiatry library for future investigations into late-twentieth-century social pathology – nihilist, primitive-style rebellion against soulless, modern mechanisms – a Cornelian dilemma.

Alice, a widow, lived in San Jose. Her husband, Burt, an infantry soldier, was wounded and captured in the first wave by the Chinese communist troops when they poured south across the Yalu River to fight General Douglas MacArthur's forces in the Korean peninsula in 1950. Burt was declared MIA until his remains were repatriated in 1954. Karen's mother was four years old when her dad went missing in combat.

Widow Alice was a strict, devout, pre-Vatican II Roman Catholic, but a gentle kind-hearted woman.

No longer young, and arthritic in her knees and ankles, she stepped up to the task of surrogate mother for her granddaughter left to her by her derelict daughter, Rhonda, and Harold Ware, the tag along, ne'er-do-well boyfriend and father of Karen.

Alice lived on a small pension from Burt's military service. She worked as a legal secretary for a lone attorney, Howard Wolpe, who did DUIs and quickie divorces. Karen grew up learning the Latin mass and how to pray novenas. As a teenager, she was devout – caused no problems for her loving grandmother. Much to her good fortune, Alice sent her to a Catholic school and subjected Karen to those nuns who knew how to teach and what to teach to young children. It worked out well. Karen was an exceptionally good student, serious and disciplined. At fifteen, she won a Bay Area spelling bee.

After her first year at Loyola Marymount University, Karen had enough of the Jesuits and Catholic education. They had served her reasonably well. She transferred to UC Berkeley and graduated with a major in physics and a minor in mathematics, eschewing the bacchanalia and the vandalism surrounding her. She then got a job with a law firm researching and evaluating patents. It was there she decided to go to law school. Karen completed the three-year program at UCLA in two-and-half and graduated near the top of her class. The biggest, most prestigious corporate law firm in Los Angles, Gibson Gunn & Crutcher recruited her. She signed on as associate and for several years did antitrust litigation with a staggering workload, cranking out the billable hours. That firm chewed up and spit out their hard-toiling, 80 hour-work-week associates by the car load. Despite her efforts, she failed to make senior partner and was dropped by the firm. Shortly after she suffered a nervous breakdown.

After she pulled herself together she enrolled in and completed a teaching-mathematics masters- degree program at California State University, Dominguez Hills in Long Beach. For several years she taught math to high school kids in Burbank. Then came her second nervous breakdown. This one was courtesy of a guy named Ross Barnett, her husband at that time. She had met him through a mutual friend. Ross was a stunt man for Warner Brothers studios. His sister was married to Evel Knievel, the famous daredevil who tried to jump the Snake River Canyon on his rocket engineered motorcycle.

Ross's specialty was motion stunts – getting knocked off horses, jumping off speeding trains, car chases, that sort of dangerous stuff. He also did fist-fights and bar brawls. Ross had broken most of the major bones in his body and a lot of the minor ones. His hands were an impressive configuration of boney knots, out of place knuckles and crooked fingers. I met him after their divorce and liked him a lot. In some ways I envied him. His life was densely physical.

Ross was everything those soft-hands, lawyer guys that Karen had spent so many of her working and off-hours with were not. Which was, no doubt, a great part of his appeal to a woman too long ensconced in a world populated with manicured-up, professional pettifoggers who couldn't change a flat tire, drive a semi-tractor-trailer or gut a deer. Tough? Are you kidding me? Ross had been a Green Beret in the Army's Special Forces. He could kill a man with his bare hands. Hell, he could do it with just one. He had a couple of black belts – big, physical and soft-spoken, he was a man of action, not words, especially words in the long, tangled sentences of the legalese that lawyers make their living producing and inflicting on uncomprehending clients. "In witness where of the parties hereunto have set their hands to those present as a deed on the day month and year hereinbefore mentioned." Karen had choked on too much of that bilge, and Ross was refreshingly direct and minimalist in his assemblage of syllables. "You better not mess with *this* U.S. male, my friend." Ten words; twelve syllables and crystal clarity.

What Ross wasn't was what eventually drove Karen off her normal course of stability and into her second stop-over in the "Town without Pity" – breakdown number two.

"Stable" was not the best word to describe Ross. He seemed to have a lot of Evel Knievel in him. How should I say this? Ross's personality fragments, though individually impressive, were not assembled quite right, which probably had something to do with him being a good stunt man. He was exceedingly reckless, for one, physically and in other ways. A compulsive gambler, he often found himself in debt for large sums of money, occasionally to people who were not very "understanding" when he failed to cover his drops in a timely fashion. In a single evening he could win, then lose huge amounts of jack. His gambling miscues had resulted in alterations of his dental work, sometimes a broken bone or two. He drove fast and recklessly in his Shelby Mustang and was often in risk of losing his driver's license. He'd been in several serious *real* car crashes. While he always treated Karen with affection and understanding, he had an extremely short-fuse of a temper with most everyone else. That cost him – jobs, friends and opportunities.

Ross also was subject to a strange, verbal tic known as Spoonerism. Sponnerism happens when a speaker accidentally transposes the initial sound or letters of two or more words which sometimes produces comical results. "It is kisstumary to cuss the bride," for example. That one came from William Archibald Spooner, the nineteenth-century Londoner for whom this weird tic is named. Harry von Zell, an American radio announcer and movie actor, was prone to it as well. Von Zell, who was the basso-voiced announcer for the George Burns and Gracie Allen television show, once on his radio program referred to President Herbert Hoover as "Hoobert Heever." Ross was deliberately Spoonerist for comic effect on occasion. "A blushing crow" ("crushing blow"), "a lack of pies" ("a pack of lies"), "Wave the sails" ("Save the whales") and "It's roaring pain" ("It's pouring rain") were some of Ross's Spoonerisms Karen remembered from the better times. This strange man was the rarest, appealing medley of scary, quirky, kind and supremely cool. Karen deeply loved him. I could see why.

All true, but Ross was too much of a problem-guy to sustain a marriage for the long haul. Between his gambling, his driving and his temper, he had finally rendered himself into an unfit, life companion. He divorced Karen. That's right. *He* terminated the marriage. He dearly loved her, but his excesses had driven her into a deep depression. He could not reach her, and he could not change. He stepped out of her life.

> "As the soul leaves the body torn and bruised
>
> As the mind deserts the body it has used…
>
> Simple and faithless as a smile and a shake of the hand."

—**T.S. Eliot**, *La Figlia Che Piange*

He blamed himself for which he was right. She blamed herself, though it was not her fault. Karen blamed herself for not being able to change him, to make Ross into that better person she knew he was capable of being. Which he wasn't. But this was Karen. She suffered from a "disease." I discovered it. Eventually I gave it a name – "*orexia moralia*." It's not yet in the *DSM*.

24 Orexia Moralia

"The mind of guilt is full of scorpions."

—William Shakespeare

Anorexia nervosa (AN): "an emotional disorder characterized by an obsessive desire to be thin, and a compulsion to lose weight by refusing to eat." Celebrity-victim – Karen Carpenter, famous singer. "We've Only Just Begun."

Orexia moralia (OM): "an emotional disorder characterized by an obsessive desire to be morally perfect, and a compulsive embrace of the guilt that results when the perfection is not attained." This can be translated to mean, "blame yourself for never being good enough to make the world better for others." In sum: The world's failings are "my failings." OM is a kind of poisonous moral solipsism that fuels excessive altruism. Non-celebrity victim – Karen Carpenter, my future wife.

"*Orexia*" is the Greek word for "appetite"

or "desire." "*Anorexia*" literally means "no desire" – "*an-orexia*." "*Anorexia nervosa*" is the loss of desire for food caused by psychopathology.

"*Orexia moralia*" is an excess desire for moral perfection.

Two Karen Carpenters; two *orexias*. Could this be just a coincidence?

"*Winners do not believe in coincidence.*"

—Frederick Nietzsche

I'm a winner – I think.

OM like AN afflicts mostly women. For AN it's young women who are most at risk. For OM it is a much broader range of age. In fact, *orexia moralia* seems to feast more on women when they get into their 30s and beyond. AN comes with a distorted "body image." You are thin, skinny, skeletal even. Still, you always see yourself as fat. With OM you carry a distorted "moral image" of yourself. You are good, caring, dutiful, accomplished – flat out wonderful as others see you. But you see yourself as morally deficient – never good enough, not caring or selfless enough. AN means you can never be thin enough. That ideal weight is forever out of reach. Which drives you to eat less, so much less you face starvation before you can arrive at that destination. OM means you can never be good enough. You never reach that state of moral perfection, and your life descends into the misery of unrelieved guilt as you continue trying and falling short. You've programmed yourself to fail... at life, at being that good person you want more than anything to be. OM does not respond to perceived failure at perfection by deprivation the way AN does, but by excess, an excess of altruism. You can never give enough of yourself. When others fail, it's because you have not given enough, tried hard enough, done enough. Moral perfection remains forever out of reach, but you never stop blaming, and giving even more of yourself.

This was Karen, a poster child for *orexia moralia*. Her life was a perpetually frustrated quest to create a morally perfect self by achieving selflessness. Her imperfection, she believed, was why she had failed to save Ross from the effects of his own moral and character shortcomings.

After Ross divorced her, through an effort of sheer will and determination she pulled herself together and went back to work. This brought a remission of sorts. She found herself alone and for a time that was good. Then she began looking for someone new, someone with lots of baggage, someone to rescue.

Then I came along.

25 A Not-So-Happy Genius

"If when my wife is sleeping
and the baby and Kathleen
are sleeping
and the sun is a flame-white disc
in silken mists
above shining trees, --
if I in my north room
dance naked, grotesquely
before my mirror
waving my shirt round my head
and singing softly to myself:
'I am lonely, lonely.
I was born to be lonely,
I am best so!'
If I admire my arms, my face,
my shoulders, flanks, buttocks
against the yellow drawn shades, --
Who shall say I am not
the happy genius of my household?"

—William Carlos Williams, *Danse Russe*

Karen had big, round eyes, green lakes that invited my troubled soul to fall into them. We married four months after our bowling excursion. It was a civil ceremony in Burbank before a morbidly obese judge with a batrachian mien encased in a navy-blue robe. Sally came for it and to meet Karen. She stayed for three days. It had been a long time since we had been together. She and Karen seem to ... well ... click.

Shortly after Sally left to go back to DC, I asked Karen what her impressions were of Sally. It was a question that clearly made her uncomfortable. She attempted an evasion.

> "What do you think of my Mom?" I asked her.

> "Your 'Mom?' That's curious, Joe. You never called her 'Mom' when she was here – it was always 'Sally.' So, maybe there are two questions: 'What do I think of your Mom?' And 'What do I think of Sally?' Different questions; different answers. Which one would you like me to answer?"

This was very "Karen," but it took me back. Maybe it shouldn't have. After all, it was just the kind of analytically-charged probe that any old therapist in a counseling session might have used to attempt to untie knotted up emotions and complex, troubled relationships.

I recovered: "Ok, let's start with the easier one, with Sally."

Karen: "She's lovely, charming, quite beautiful, actually, and loaded with intelligence. I can see why she's been so successful in the political big leagues. She's warm, perceptive, a careful listener. When you are talking to her she gives you the impression that you're the only one in the room. She's really funny and witty too. I see a lot of you in her."

"Me?"

"Yes." Long pause.

"Do you think she is a phony?"

"No. Where did that come from? You're looking for something in what I said that wasn't there. I think she is genuine. Do you think she is a phony?"

"Maybe. I'm inclined to think so. She's been highly successful in a line of work that makes 'phony' an asset. How about my Mom? What do you think of my Mom?"

I'm seeing hesitation and discomfort and am thinking; "Karen doesn't want to go there."

"Maybe for a later time?"

"No. I'll say it now. I think she is a woman who is waiting."

"Waiting for what?"

"Waiting for her son to forgive her."

There was another long pause. I wasn't sure if I wanted to continue with this. Finally:

"To forgive her for what?"

"For taking you away from Richard and Gladys, for taking up the life she has chosen and been successful in. I could tell. She feels your resentment."

Of course, she did. Karen's moral, emotional "antennas" were acutely sensitive. So, that's how we left it that evening. The ball, as Karen saw it, was in my court as far as my mother was concerned. It had been in my court for many years. How would I return it?

We didn't know it at that time. From the beginning Karen and I were on a collision course. Karen perceived the world as good. She was driven to make herself better in order to make it better. Her future, *orexia moralia*. My world was decadent and corrupt. I would become worse by embracing it, by approving of it. My future was cynical revenge on the modern world. It came in the form of moral disapproval nourished by the courage to confront reality. I would relish my sense of epistemological superiority. "The only thing that is going to get better is the jokes," a smart-aleck guy named Jim Joad once quipped. "I was born to be lonely. I am best so!"

26 The Defender and the Prophet

*"If the rule you followed brought you
to this, of what use was the rule?"*

—**Anton Chigurh**, *No Country for
Old Men*

Karen owned a small condo in Burbank. We married.
I moved in. We were both battling our own nasty, little
demons. Karen had gone back to teaching mathematics to high school kids after she had pulled herself together, post-breakdown with the departure of Ross
from her life. But she was restless and uncertain. She
needed to find another way to assert herself, that is, to
give *more* of herself. You can guess where this is going.

Unemployed for a couple of years, I had been trying to restructure my depression to accommodate the
modern world in some way so that I could retain my
sanity, self-respect and my principled opposition to
the deceptions that kept raining down from on high. I
needed to work. Epistemological superiority alone
was not going to pay the bills. It was not going to get
me up at a reasonable hour in the morning and ready
to move through the day un-zombie-like.

What could I do to make money? I decided to start
a private practice as a licensed clinical psychologist.

Hmm... Reader, you're thinking: "It's not going to work, Mr. Anti-Modern Man." As always, you're way ahead of me. After a year I had enough patients to cover my overhead and generate a modest profit. But I was having problems, rather serious ones. The biggest one? I was not helping them. They came. I counseled. They paid. They left – in distress, unhealed. It struggled to understand why. Then it suddenly hit me. And, why did it take so long? I'd been through this before.

My patients were struggling with the problems created by the modern world they lived in and believed in. The therapeutic solutions I could offer them were modern world solutions. But I no longer had confidence in them. Thus, the questions I could no longer ignore: Were the illnesses of the patients I counseled illnesses *within a system*, a system that worked more or less in a good way? Or, was the *system itself* one massive manifestation of illness? The German-Jewish philosopher, Erich Fromm was on to this long before Harry met Sally. From his ironically titled *The Sane Society* published in 1955:

> *"The fact that millions of people share*
> *the same vices does not make these*
> *vices virtues, the fact that they share so*
> *many errors does not make the errors*
> *to be truths, and the fact that millions*
> *of people share the same forms of*
> *mental pathology does not make*
> *these people sane."*

Who was crazy, me or the system?

It was the latter. The system was sick. I was no longer a physician. Physicians don't "heal" systems. I was a prophet. A prophet speaks the truth without revealing it: only in retrospect can his words be tested. No one pays attention to prophets until it's too late, until after they are dead. "A prophet hath no honour in his own country."

Weary of beglamoring the impossible, I closed my practice.

No more teaching Euclid to kids. Karen decided to go back to lawyering. Not corporate law, mind you, but a legal calling perfectly suited for a woman prone to the affliction of *orexia moralia*. She joined a public defender practice in Los Angeles County, one of the largest of its kind in the country. This was noblesse oblige work. It was, of course, a perfect combination – low paying with explosive pathological potential for those strongly inclined toward "giving of themselves."

The problem Karen discovered is that she could never give enough of herself. The stream of broken, needy people in trouble with the law on their way to prison and/or back to prison is wide, deep and endless. Many if not most are irretrievably maleficent, permanently lost souls. They are cogs in a simulacrum of a legal system. Regularly and routinely they recycle themselves through a Kafkaesque asylum that is all the more baffling for its enormous costs, its staggering inefficiencies and the willful blindness to its utter perversity. No matter. Karen's life was a relentless determination to multiply her social responsibilities, to assume morally purifying burdens. Representing the poor was not a job. It was a religious calling. It was about changing the moral imbalance in the world, an imbalance that she saw tilting unfairly toward herself. She was privileged – undeservedly, she believed. Her privilege was the source of her punishing guilt. A victory for a downtrodden client was a small correction of movement in the cosmic balance scales. A loss was her failure to move the world toward a proper balance.

I once posed a question for her: "Your privilege – it's luck. You feel you don't *deserve* it, and that makes you feel bad, guilty. I understand. But, you don't *not* deserve it either. It just happened – deserving or not deserving had nothing to do with it. So why the self-laceration?" She never answered me. I concluded that the notion of "privilege" used as an abstraction to describe a person's, any person's, station in life was a pernicious superstition.

When I failed the patients in my practice, I blamed the system they were immersed in. It sucked. They didn't realize it. For Karen, the system, ideally, was supposed to work in favor of her clients. Her job was to make it work. When it didn't, she blamed herself for not moving the system closer to its ideal. This was *orexia moralia* in high gear.

From our attempts to provide each other solace and comfort, three years into our marriage a child was born to us, a boy. We called him "Richard Thomas." "Richard" was for my grandfather; "Thomas" was for Thomas Hobbes. As I found myself together with our newborn Richard and Karen, no one could say that I was "not the happy genius of my household."

As I sat holding my week-old Richard late one night, thoughts and emotions ran through me I had never before experienced. Karen and I together had made a baby, another human being. Life doesn't get more organic, more physically concrete, more removed from abstraction than that. Beyond that intense feeling, what struck me was this: In spite of what I said at the beginning about spawning an offspring being a frightening, genetic crap-shoot, making babies is the most important thing we ever do. Everything else is secondary to that. If and when we stop doing it, we die. "We" being "us" collectively. Then it occurred to me: there are "we's" all over the planet who have given up on making babies – Italians, French, Spanish, Germans, Scandinavians, Japanese and European-descendent Americans have set other "higher" priorities for themselves than the making of babies. The modern world makes babies, our existential future, no longer a given, but an option. Options get sorted into higher and lower. They compete for position. There are winners and losers. Babies have been a losing option for some time for some of us. In the not-to-far future, many of those "we's" will be gone. *Arrivederci* Italians, *adios* Spaniards, *auf Wiedersehen* Germans and goodbye to the rest of those "we's." For them, for us, it was great fun while it lasted. Soon it will be a different "we." Whether a world with no Swedes or Japanese, etc. is going to be good or bad, who dares to say? You can get into serious trouble for attempting to answer that question. Unquestionable is that it will not resemble what it replaced. What is certain is that, barring some interplanetary catastrophe or nuclear war, it is a certainty. With all the leisure, entertainment options, creature comforts and freedoms at our disposal, the people of the Western world are quietly embracing their own death.

> "I sat upon the shore
>
> Fishing, with the arid plains behind me
>
> Shall I at least set my lands in order?"

—**T.S. Eliot**, *What the Thunder Said*

27 Rats' Alley

*"Whenever a husband and wife begin
to discuss their marriage they are giving
evidence at a coroner's inquest."*

—H. L. Mencken

No longer in the business of broken-psyche repair, I moved toward a more modest endeavor, that of a house-husband. I took up the care of Richard – changed his diapers, did laundry, some basic cooking, trips to the grocery store and the pediatrician's office. All of these pedestrian chores added up to an important "something" like nothing I had ever done in my life. They connected me with my young son in ways that I could not have imagined. With Karen, however, things began to get complicated – in ways that should have been obvious if I had been paying closer attention from the start.

Karen worked long, exhausting hours as a public defender. She was a good one, as I knew she would be. She had the best jury acquittal rate in the practice. But for her it was never quite good enough. That said, she was a good mother to Richard and was deeply appreciative for the devotion I was giving to our domestic maintenance.

The complication was that the time I spent with my child had accelerated the movement of my alienation from the modern world. My once moderate extroversion took me inexorably toward introversion. I became saturnine, increasingly caught up in a Puritanical ritual of self, consumed by a darkened view of almost everything around me. I was content to retreat into a world of reading, writing and contemplating current events with the perspective of a Juvenal, a Gibbon or a Balzac. That retreat did not agree with Karen. It created friction – lots of it.

> "What are you thinking of? What think-
> ing? What?
>
> I never know what you are thinking. Think.
>
> I think we are in rats' alley
>
> Where the dead men lost their bones."
>
> —**T.S. Eliot**, *The Wasteland*

Yes, we were gnawing at each other in "rats" alley. Karen's approach to ordering her life was altruism – more giving of herself. Which is fine. But, it would always cross over a line and turn into severe austerity, self-abnegation and a fractured soul – manifestations of OM pathology. My approach was to order my thoughts from which followed a daily existence that embraced only the people and things I cared about. I had limited them to a select few. My life was my family and its demands. Karen's life was the world and its needs. It demanded that she save as much of it as she could. She could never save enough of it. There we were, the Scylla and Charybdis from Greek mythology, two immortal and irresistible monsters who beset the narrow waters traversed by the wandering Odysseus described in Homer's Odyssey. Only we were poised on the opposite shores of the narrowing waters of a disintegrating marriage. Karen was Scylla – "I hate myself." I was Charybdis – "I hate the world." We were two haters, intense emotion rooted in moral revulsion. Nothing in between could pass through the narrow straits and reach the port of marital felicity.

As you can imagine, it became increasingly difficult to pursue a "conversation" on any matters beyond, "Is it trash day?" Or, "Do you think we need to clean out the garage this weekend?"

> "Try to see it my way
>
> Do I have to keep on talking 'til I can't go on?
>
> While you see it your way
>
> Run the risk of knowing that our love may soon be gone
>
> We can work it out…"
>
> —**Beatles**, *We Can Work It Out*

No. I stopped talking. I could not go on. How could she see it other than her way? We could not "work it out."

I was a man with a blue guitar.

"They said, you have a blue guitar,
You do not play things as they are.

The man replied, Things as they are
Are changed upon the blue guitar."

—**Wallace, Stevens**, The Man with the
Blue Guitar

"Please, Joe," Karen pleaded with me. "For
me, for a day climb down from your
hermit's immaculate pedestal of philosophical petulance. You've converted
your innate grumpiness into a monk-
like rejection of normality. You've embraced an unsatisfying salvation in
your suffering. Take a brief time out
from magnifying your exhaustion with
these horrors of your 'modern' world.
Just for a moment, please, please, please,
stop nurturing your disgust for these
vultures you see everywhere picking at
our bones."

Our marriage was the culmination of a high-speed
head on collision – the Blue Guitar-SUV colliding with
the Altruist-pickup truck. That said, we were both dutiful parents, which created even more complications.
Who was going to get custody of Richard? It may
sound absurd, but it's absurdly true: the dissolution of
our marriage proceeded not from infidelity, financial

disorder, substance abuse or anger management problems. It was from a clash of philosophical premises. Or was its demise the ravage of mental illness? And whose?

Custody of Richard? Karen was a hard-working lawyer and a responsible mother. I was a realist and an unemployed father – *nolo contendere*. I moved out of the house into an apartment. Karen took legal custody of our son. My access to him was at her discretion. She was generous, of course. She could not be otherwise. I was obediently grateful. Still, it was not the same.

I then lived off the funds from the trust set up for me by Sally. Once I pulled myself together after the split, for a year I diverted my agitations to writing a book about the Menendez brothers' trial. It was a highly critical appraisal of Leslie Abramson's huckster-like efforts to turn the brothers into victims. It also raised the broader philosophical conundrum of moral responsibility versus scientific causality.

The topic, my Menendez trial experience and my academic and professional credentials were sufficient to persuade Oxford University Press to publish my book. It came out under the title, *Make Me Your Victim: The Reincarnation of Eric Menendez*. The book got some praise, but for the most part it was savagely reviewed. Many of the attacks were ad hominem. I was on the side, it seemed, of men who beat their wives and fathers who raped their children.

The criticism was unfair and outrageous, particularly given my personal experiences, my childhood with Sally and the pathologies of her marriages. However, I was swimming upstream against the ethos of modern culture and the medicalization of morality – immorality transformed into sickness. Sickness requires sympathy and treatment, not condemnation and punishment. Eric's trial in a spectacular, epical way was an illustration of the "medicalization of crime." Crime as a causally determined event that reflects psychological suffering is no longer a delict. A legal text book will tell you that the five elements that compose a delict are: conduct, wrongfulness, fault, causation and damage. Medicalization removes the first three and thus takes the legal processes that judge conduct (agency), wrongfulness and fault out of the picture. The outcome of legal proceedings a determination of guilt or innocence. There is no guilt in medicine – only suffering and the alleviation of it.

With no wrongfulness there can be no punishment. To punish suffering is a benighted impulse from a pre-modern era. Decades ago the world-famous psychiatrist, Karl Menninger, laid out the case for this thinking. *The Crime of Punishment* was a bestseller. *All* punishment, he argued, was useless and cruel. *All* criminal behavior should be treated as mental illness. No more courts. No prisons. Just hospitals, clinics and benevolent doctors who treat sick people.

Dr. Menninger, however, failed to draw the nightmarish conclusion from his punishment-abolitionist argument.

> *Our world, the modern world will be*
> *an asylum – only doctors and patients*
> *inside.*

"Make me, make me your victim,

Resistance is only a symptom…

Of bigotry

You are so guilty, so

Make me your victim.

Make me, make me your victim,

My 'guilt' is just a crude fiction…

They treated me poor

I evened the score

Can't you see I'm a victim?"

—**Backseat Baby**, Parody of Barbara Lewis,
Make Me your Baby, 1965, as sung by
Eric Menendez

The hostility that blew back on me for publishing *Make Me Your Victim* convinced me that I should continue writing books that challenged the thinking that made the modern world the kind of place it had become. This was my calling. Prophet? Contrarian? Fool? Whichever it was, I developed puritanical rituals of self-reflection and the habit of prolonged solitude. My mantic calling was to extract realities from their manipulated distortions and reattach them to whatever solid fixtures I could find remaining in the world.

"And indeed there will be time

To wonder, 'Do I dare?'…

Disturb the universe?

In a minute there is time

For decisions and revisions which a minute will reverse."

—**T.S, Eliot**, The Love Song of J. Alfred
Prufrock"

Meanwhile, there was my mother, still toiling away in Babylon. She was about to take another step.

28 Oh Danny Boy, the Pipes, the Pipes are Calling

"For it is mutual trust, even more than mutual interest that holds human associations together. Our friends seldom profit us but they make us feel safe. Marriage is a scheme to accomplish exactly that same end."

—H. L. Mencken

After Roger died, Sally's third husband, I mistakenly believed that she had given up on marriage. For several years, immersed in my research and writing, I had only minimal contact. I was surprised then one evening when she called to tell me that she was going to get married, once again.

"Are you serious?" I murmured to myself. To Sally, after she told me about her new love, I said, "I assume the wedding is going to be a small, intimate occasion."

"No. What have I told you about 'jumping to conclusions', Joe? Actually, it is going to be a big wedding," Sally responded in her motherly manner.

She wanted me to be there – very much. For Sally's first wedding to Arnold, I lived too far away to attend. For the second, I pretended to be sick. I was mercifully spared. Sally's wedding number three to Roger was a small affair. I couldn't make it. In the middle of final exams in Austin, I was unwilling to make the trek to Alexandria for the nuptials for a guy embarking on marriage number four to a gal hoping that *numero tres* would go in a different, more fulfilling, direction. This was just going to be another episode in the TV reality show, "Serial Wives of Babylon." My thinking was: "Really? Was this going to be a serious occasion?" Well … in Babylon, there are no alternatives to "serious" – every occasion, gesture, conversation must be meaningful and significant. Power is enhanced when it is conspicuous and asserted, and when everyone pretends accordingly. The actors in Babylon are better than the ones in Hollywood.

Back to Sally's wedding number four. For that one, I was there. I had a sense that it would be the last. So, I resolved to be a dutiful son for a change, for once. Number four was not the quiet, low-key, understated, minimalist ceremony that you might expect from a bride whose batting average of matrimonial success in her previous trips to the plate was floundering at nil. A guest list beyond best man and bridesmaid you would think might be considered by most people as, well, inappropriate.

The big wedding *was* appropriate, and I wasn't displeased to be there. Sally's fourth husband-to-be was Danny O'Brian. Unlike his three predecessors, Sally did not find Danny in any of Babylon's trendy salons or in the back rooms where the power brokers wheel and deal. He wasn't a lawyer, politician, lobbyist or legislative aide. He didn't manage hedge funds, didn't run an NGO. He wasn't an "advocate" for a cause. He didn't make his living wrestling with abstractions. Concerns about the future of "the planet" did not interrupt his nocturnal slumber. His vocabulary was refreshingly concrete. Doing your job well, he believed, made your community a better place: "the world" he didn't worry about. His job? He was a plumber. Well, he started out as a plumber. He "made a difference." A toilet that flushes properly – that's a "difference" to be appreciated, one worth paying for. Think of how shitty your world would be without plumbers. Then think about how less crappy the world would be with a few less lawyers and a deficit of advertising executives. Think of how little would be lost with an epidemic that felled governors, political campaign advisors, cable TV talking heads, pollsters, fundraisers and most of the long-in-the-yellow-tooth congressmen who pretend to be statesmen. Would any of them be missed? Would a single soul be worse off?

By the time Danny met Sally he owned a large, successful plumbing-service business in Fairfax county, Virginia. He earned his wealth in a way to be proud of. Also, unlike his three predecessors, he was younger than Sally – by three or four years. Finally, unlike Arnold, Dave and Roger, Danny was never divorced.

Sally met Danny through a match-maker friend outside of her regular circle of worker colleagues. He was a widower. His wife of thirty-five years had died four years before he met Sally. They had dated for a year before they got married. Danny came from a big Irish family – three brothers, two sisters, three grown children from his marriage.

It was a happy wedding, one of the few I can remember. I drank. I danced with Danny's family's ladies. I danced with Sally – the first time ever.

Danny was good for Sally – mostly. He brought to her "the basics" that are a rarity in Babylon. He was faithful, kind and decent. He set himself to take care of her, to be someone she could put her arms around and feel like he understood her. His expectations of her were formed by an appreciation of her best qualities – her charm, her wit, her beauty. Oh, Danny was useful too. He could fix stuff, anything – cars, washing machines, lawn mowers, toasters – you name it. The only suit he owned was the one he got married in. He bought it off the rack at Men's Wearhouse – $300. They were happy together.

29 Eva, Beware of the City (Buenos Aires)

"The city can be paradise for those who
have the cash

The class and the connections, what you
need to make a splash

The likes of you get swept up in the morning with the trash

If you were rich or middle class ..."

—Madonna & Antonio Banderas, *Eva,*
Beware of the City

Shortly after Sally's marriage to Danny I completed my plans to live in Argentina for an indefinite period of time. The reason? It's complicated, but I think I can lay it out so it makes sense, given my struggles to understand the modern world and what was wrong with it.

How did Argentina fit into my efforts to achieve the insight and understanding I had been searching for? My starting point was the concept of entropy which is one of the consequences of the second law of thermodynamics. Entropy turns out to be a measure of disorder: the higher the disorder, the higher the entropy of the system. My suspicion was that modern societies are highly entropic – increasingly disordered and rapidly moving toward disintegration. Two examples of this on a micro-level are the cities of Detroit and Baltimore. They were once vital, thriving, culturally rich, relatively safe metropolises with productive, law-abiding citizens. Now, in spite of copious infusions of studious good will, expert guidance and government assistance, they are crime-ridden, murder-plagued, broken down slums that struggle to provide the minimal human services. Anyone who can, flees. Witness the flight:

> Population of Detroit, circa 1950 – 2,000,000
> Population of Detroit, circa 2018 – 670,000
>
> Population of Baltimore, circa 1950 – 950,000
> Population of Baltimore, circa 2018 – 600,000

For a firmer grasp on the vast disparity between the "ideals" of a modern system in high gear and the reality of disorder, scratch at the surface of Cabrini-Green and Pruett-Igoe (Chicago, St. Louis) public housing projects. The ideal – safe, low-cost housing for poor people: the reality – murderous, filthy, drug-infested jungles of complete social dysfunction. There up close for study is entropy in its final stages. Why are there so few takers? There are some reasons, if you catch my drift.

Argentina is a country-benchmark of decay, one I could use as a comparison with what I saw as the growing disorder, entropy, that was enveloping my homeland. At the beginning of the twentieth-century, both the U.S. and Argentina bore amazing similarities in their stages of modern development. Both were huge, proto-modern countries possessed of vast natural resources augmented by human resources in an immigration flow from Europe. Looking back over the twentieth century, one might rightly say that Argentina has been a *huge* disappointment.

What went wrong in the land of the Gauchos? It was a country with all of the raw energy and modern potential of the U.S. Now? We contemplate its ignominious slide into the third world.

Reading and thinking about it were not enough. I was a psychologist by training and inclination. I had to go there and observe life up close for myself, to meet and talk to the people and dig into the psyche of the nation. Which meant that I needed to be able to speak Spanish.

So, I enrolled myself in a three-month, total immersion, Spanish language program in San Miguel Allende, a beautiful colonial era city in Mexico's central highlands mountains. I lived with a non-English-speaking family with very talkative children who focused their attention on me. I spent nine hours every day at the school immersed in Spanish. On the evenings and weekends my Mexican family gave a delightful language immersion. To my relief, I discovered that my aptitude for languages was quite good. After those three months I could converse with reasonable fluency in Spanish and experience the melancholy of Spanish songs.

"No sé por qué te quiero

Será que tengo alma de bolero

Tú siempre buscas lo que no tengo

Te busco en todos y no te encuentro."

—**Ana Belen**, *No sé por qué te quiero*

I finished the program, prepared for a long residence in Buenos Aires, Argentina, then vacated my apartment in Burbank. Karen was most unhappy to learn about my plans.

> "What about your son? What kind of father can you be 5,000 miles away from him?"
>
> "Don't give me grief about this, Karen. It's temporary. I have to do it."
>
> "Ok, Harry. I mean, Joseph."
>
> "Touché."

In Buenos Aires I immersed myself in those mundane daily activities of life – shopping for essentials, doing laundry, working. In a small grocery store near my apartment I mopped floors and stocked shelves part-time. I pursued acquaintances and friendships. Argentines are warm, friendly people. They love to talk, to vent, to share their misanthropic opinions. They come out colorfully uncensored with passion. The frustration they experience with daily life made them enthusiastic to vent their spleen on an interested gringo. I listened, smiled and responded, showing a naïve wonder at what I was hearing. Within a short time, I had developed a social network. We went to the bars, restaurants and concerts. I got a crash course in the tango. From my daily experience I began to grasp the extent of the entropic forces at work. This country was a dark and fascinating place – for its tumultuous legacy of Juan and Eva Peron, the hospitality it extended to fleeing architects of the Third Reich, its love affair with the sadomasochistic tango. The food, the wine, the restaurants were fantastic.

Equally, if not more fascinating for me, however, was the frustration and vexation that arose from my daily efforts to make simple things work. It took me six months and three bribes to get a telephone in my apartment. Mail was iffy. The constantly fluctuating currency value made buying things more challenging than back home. Almost all transactions involving exchanges of services or goods of any kind were much more "complicated" in reaching a satisfactory conclusion – broken agreements, shoddy work, insolent service.

The conversations to make things happen were predictable. Thus, my phone conversation with a man who was supposed to fix my kitchen sink.

Ring, ring, ring, ring... another ten or fifteen times. Finally:

> "Hello. Just a minute." Some yelling and
> swearing in the background. Minutes
> later:

"Sorry, who is this?"

"This is Senor Martin. You were supposed to come last week to fix my sink."

"What?"

"My sink. It's plugged up. I called you two weeks ago, and you said you'd come last Friday to fix it. You didn't come. You didn't call."

"What's your name again?"

"Martin."

"Oh, yeah. Well my truck wouldn't start. I'll come tomorrow or Friday."

"Your truck is running now?"

"No, but I'm working on it."

"Will you come tomorrow or Friday?"

"Don't know right now."

"When will you know?"

"What?"

"Will you call if you can't come?"

"Sure." *"Como no,"* in Spanish.

Right, Como no.

In the background is the sound of a quarrel going on between a couple of women and a little kid.

"I gotta go." Click.

Who gets a working sink? Me, but only if, *"Si Dios quiere."* "If God wants it." *"Come no."*

These sorts of exchanges were standard fare.

The unions control many of the service industries in Argentina. After some experience with the union workers there, I can tell you that the hombres running them make American union bosses look like choir boys.

I quickly realized that I was experiencing a level of entropy, disorder, that did not (quite yet) exist back home. I was also disturbed to realize that the sewer that the American popular culture had become had no rival with Argentina. Back home was no longer "Take me out to the Ballgame" or "Paddlin' Madeline Home" – more like Snoop Dogg's "Fuck you" with its poetic lyrics: "I just wanna fuck bad bitches." Who would have guessed? Soon the dysfunction and disorder approximating that of Argentina would be so pervasive that no one would believe the "good old days" ever existed. Ahead? The disintegration of trust, the chaos of institutional corruption, and the triumph of a rotted-out culture where obscenity passes for art.

Why was that? I had now penetrated to the core of a quest for an answer to the question of Argentina's decay and what lessons it might hold for the future of my son thirty or so years later in his country. It was a question about the loss of confidence in those "systems" that are supposed to provide stability, predictability and fairness in their application of the rules. Here was the conundrum of "cause or effect?" Was the systems failure an effect of the growing cynicism and distrust? Or, were cynicism and distrust effects of the inefficiency and corruption of the systems? It was both. It was reciprocal causation. Which means that cause–effect relationships are bi-directional. A cause would later become an effect and vice versa.

Of course. Argentina was in an accelerated state of entropy (disintegration) brought about by the reciprocal causation of cynicism and system failure. Argentina's social institutions and systems were riddled with corruption, so much so that it was obvious to everyone. There was no confidence in them. No one believed that they worked the way they said they worked, i.e., fairly, impartially, efficiently. The government, elections, the legal system, unions, the church, business – no one saw them as anything other than systems rigged for the benefit of those with the most power and connections. Back to Blake: "What is it that distinguishes honesty from knavery, but the hard and wiry line of rectitude and certainty in the actions and intentions?" That hard and wiry line had long ago collapsed in Argentina, the only "certainty," the certainty of corruption. The collapse was well underway in the U.S. In Argentina, the knaves were running the show. Everyone knew it. No one pretended otherwise or hesitated to say so in private conversation. In the U.S. the knaves are running the show, but it is going to take more time for everyone to stop pretending that they are not. We are still in the pretending, denial stage. How much longer will it take? The Argentines were well past "denial." They are firmly in the "anger-cynicism" stage of dealing with the slow-moving train wreck that their country had turned into – anger-cynicism, that is, combined with fatalism.

This was the depressing conclusion I drew from the many conversations I had during my time in Argentina. The cynicism was a permanent, justified fixture of Argentinian public life. America at some point in the near future would be like Argentina and worse. The crooks would be open and blatant. No one would deny it. Everybody would know it.

> "Everybody knows that the boat is leak-
>   ing
>
> Everybody knows that the captain lied
>
> Everybody got this broken feeling
>
> Like their father or their dog just died."

—Leonard Cohen, *Everybody Knows*

Sitting in my apartment after spending an evening with friends at a restaurant, an anguished call came from Sally: "Danny's been murdered! Please come!"

30 Oh Danny Boy, the Summer's Gone, and All the Roses Falling

*"Evil people always support each
other; that is their chief strength."*

—Aleksandr Solzhenitsyn

Danny. I had said that Danny was good for Sally, "mostly." Here was the downside with Danny. Like Sally, he drank a lot. He had a good excuse. He was Irish. He and Sally drank together – too much. But they were happy drinkers. That made a difference. They could be happily tipsy together. And they were. That was until Danny, while waiting at the Anacostia Metro Station in DC, was stabbed to death by a knife-wielding druggie. The Anacostia Station is the most dangerous of the Metro stops. Danny was there by mistake. He had been drinking with some old friends from the District and, a wee bit muddled, got on the wrong train trying to get home.

The man who killed Danny was twenty-year-old, LaShawn Evans. Danny was the first person LaShawn had killed. Since the age of fourteen or so he had been working his way on up to reach the pinnacle of his career – homicide. Sooner or later he was going to kill someone who was simply going about his own business. It was just a matter of time. That person would be the man happily married to my mother, Danny.

As a juvenile, LaShawn had moved through "the system." Yes, another modern "system." At fourteen he was a burglar, sixteen, narcotics distribution, seventeen, armed-robbery, eighteen, aggravated assault. There is more, but you get the picture. He was on the move. LaShawn had been stepping into and out of the criminal justice system with predictable regularity. Abstract systems are constructed to serve the interests of the designers, not the interests of the folks they are supposed to serve. This particular one did nothing to make LaShawn less of a criminal. It did zilch to protect productive, law-abiding citizens like Danny from the predators that the system churns out by the boatload. No consideration is given to meeting concrete human needs, like protection from aggressors. No, the system is procedurally focused. Its ritualized, internal hoopla is designed to meet the useless standards of paper pushers and form-lovers. Protecting predators, like LaShawn and sustaining the illusion of their eventual reform are the goals that animate the designers.

The "modern" take on LaShawn was a variant of the Leslie Abramson presentation of Eric Menendez to the LA jury. Eric was a "victim" of uncaring, abusive parents. LaShawn was a "victim" of an abstraction, an uncaring, abusive society – poverty, poor education, single mom, racism – many abstract "causes" to account for the maladies and their victims. So many wars on abstractions to be launched, and on so many fronts – on poverty, on social injustice, on racism. Someday, we will overcome them all – all together or one at a time – but not soon. Not soon enough for the victims of the victims. Not for Danny. Not for Sally.

LaShawn's case history was routine, much like that of the thousands of young men that pass though the criminal justice system in Babylon. "Criminal justice" is a crowning achievement of systemic failure and, given how the system actually works, the term itself takes on the perverse, ironic formulation of "justice criminalized." The criminal justice system is a tribute to the men and women camped out in the chambers of power. They pretend to be about governing but devote themselves to managing a system designed to reward them, the designers, but does nothing for "the governed." These "guardians" of the public order are distinguishable from the dangerously disordered only by their superior command of grammar, accouterment in conventional business attire and gated-community home addresses.

Danny's murder was not a crime that was addressed by an institution that was supposed to uphold the law and administer justice; rather, it was a "feature not a bug" as a software developer would put it. It was a regular feature of a "system" designed to combat abstractions, a system whose premise is that crime is a symptom of societal illness, a medical problem with medical solutions, as envisioned by Karl Menninger.

Racked with the sorrow of Danny's senseless death, I thought about what G.K. Chesterton a century ago had said about this kind of system. "[T]his is the real objection to that torrent of modern talk about treating crime as disease, about making prison merely a hygienic environment like a hospital, of healing sin by slow scientific methods. The fallacy of the whole thing is that evil is a matter of active choice whereas disease is not."

"Evil" is a word now debased, used exclusively to express disapproval of someone you dislike – particularly someone with differing political or religious opinions. With crime and criminals, "evil" has no place in the modern lexicon of moral language.

I flew from Buenos Aires to Dulles Airport. Sally's devastation was complete. The funeral was the saddest moment of my life – a large gathering of Danny's family, friends and associates in mourning, contemplating the stupid, senseless circumstances of his death. Within, I was raging against the feckless elites who preside over the unnecessary destruction of decent people while pretending to care about them.

> "The apparition of these faces in the crowd;
>
> Petals on a wet, black bough."
>
> —**Ezra Pound**, *In a Station of the Metro*

31 Deviance or Disease?

"History has many cunning passages, con-
    trived corridors

And issues, deceives with whispering am-
    bitions,

Guides us by vanities. Think now

She gives when our attention is distracted."

— **T.S. Eliot**, *Gerontion*

It was the early spring of 2016. I flew from Los Angeles to Minneapolis, Minnesota. Upon arrival I rented a car and drove sixty miles south on State route 52 until I got to Rochester. There I made my way to the Mayo Clinic to see Sally where she had been a patient for two weeks. The Mayo Clinic was the best hospital in the country for the treatment of liver disease. My mother was in the advanced stages of alcohol-induced cirrhosis of the liver. Danny's murder a year before had pushed her into retirement and a deep depression which she treated with her life-long medication – this time in very heavy doses. I had stayed with her in DC after the funeral for a month, trying to comfort her. I couldn't.

I found Mom sitting up in her bed in her room looking like … well, like a person whose remaining days are in the double digits. Still, she was cheerful and joking with her brother Paul. He had flown in two days before from Dallas. The last time I had seen Paul was at Richard's funeral thirty years ago. He was now a retired minister and a widower. His wife, Mary, had recently died from a hemorrhagic stroke. Sally's older sister, Ruth Ann, remained in her home in Oklahoma City. She had been battling Alzheimer's and had already slipped too far into the darkness to make the journey.

Sally and Paul were, like their father and their uncle Daniel, estranged and had had little contact over the years. Paul looked like his father with many of his mannerisms, which drew me to him. We talked about Sally and her career. I was surprised how little he knew about her life. Paul was a life-long, tea-totaling Baptist. The consumption of alcohol he considered a vice. Imbibed in moderate amounts, easily to look away from and little to condemn. Tea-totaling merely cuts off the possibility of a slippery slide. Heavy drinking, he believed, is an affliction of a soul lost to God's calling. Paul knew that I was not a believer. But he wanted to know what I thought had happened to Sally, what had gone wrong in her life that so immersed her in alcohol and failed marriages. Paul was clearly looking to me for some insight into what kind of person his sister had been. He wanted to understand her. He was open to my thoughts.

Sally was on her deathbed. Responding to him in a helpful way was a tall order. I was too close to it.

Moreover, I was heavily implicated in whatever it was that made her do what she did from the moment I was conceived. But I knew that I'd never see Paul again. He was my uncle, a blood relative. That organic relationship meant something to me. I wanted him to understand his sister and what her life was about. What I came to offer him was paradoxical, contradictory choices, conflicting explanations. That was the best I could do.

Like his father, Paul was a deeply religious man, a conservatively religious man for whom sin explained so much of human failure. For him, Sally's struggles in life – her failed marriages and her heavy drinking were the result of sin, of moral failure. For the doctors at the Mayo Clinic, Sally had a disease, alcoholism. The disease of alcoholism has deleterious effects on your life's choices – the failed marriages and interpersonal conflict that afflicted her were, at least in part, due to the disease and its addictive power.

Sin implies agency: you look to the sinner, to the choices made to understand what went wrong. Disease has causes: you look away from the patient to understand what forces were in play to make her sick.

Two radically different explanations of human failing. Two theories about what went wrong in the life of Sally. Sally's life and Sally's death symbolized a cross-road of life-interpretation and belief: one, theological-religious; the other, scientific-medical. Which one do you follow? You can't travel down both of them. Those two paths are not clearly marked out. Sometimes they converge then diverge. Still, you must finally choose one over the other. Whichever one you do, something human is lost. Trying to sort this out puts you up against the most stubborn of antinomies. An antinomy is a contradiction between two beliefs that are in themselves reasonable. Thus: freedom and moral accountability or scientific causality; punishment or treatment; sin or sickness; evil or dysfunction. I was not enough of a philosopher, a psychologist or a mystic to know where to go for an answer. Paul listened respectfully and understood my limitations.

Sally died peacefully on a Wednesday afternoon in her hospital bed with Paul and me at her side. Shortly before her death, she asked me if I would forgive her. I told her that I already had. It was the truth.

A lament for her life from Baudelaire came to me as I sat alone that night she died;

> "And it is foolishness to trust in hearts,
>
> For hearts will break and beauty dies,
>
> Till Darkness with his hod picks up the parts
>
> To haul them to Eternal skies!"

—*Confession*

I arranged for the cremation of her body. I took her cremains to Bad Axe where they were interred next to the graves of her Mother and Father as she had requested.

32 The Best of Babylon

"For God, our God is a gallant foe

That playeth behind the veil….

To love your God as a gallant foe that
plays behind the veil;

To meet your God as the night winds
meet beyond Arcturus' pale."

— **Ezra Pound**, *Ballad for Gloom*

Sally's memorial service was the perfect, final touch for a woman who spent her life surrounded by the "hollow men." It was staged a month after her death in, where else? In the citadel of counterfeit respectability and entrenched self-veneration, Babylon. It gathered an impressive exhibition of Washington DC's most prestigious ruling class elites – a tidy, well-scrubbed rabble of mountebanks – Democrats and Republicans, "two arms on the same monster," as Jim Goad would say. They assembled at the Cathedral of St. Matthew the Apostle. You might be unaware that St. Matthew was the Patron Saint of Civil Servants. So, where else but in Babylon would you find a house of worship festooned with such a patron saint? Stop laughing, Reader. The irony, I am sure, escaped this illustrious congregation, wholly impercipient of the magnitude of their iniquities. No one there was a "servant" of anyone. Any respectable saint would have shunned this cluster of picturesque parasites with a disdainful whisper of "unclean." The only "worship" conducted in such a place was the ritual of self-adoration that an unfortunate, pressed-ganged observer would experience as a diarrheic effusion of mystery-laden vocables. From these practitioners of exaggerated politeness and audacious hypocrisy, on display was a "cringing affability," as Somerset Maugham described it, that the powerful put on to disguise the haughtily tinged airs of their self-regard and to pretend that they are just "regular folks."

The Cathedral was on Road Island Avenue NW, a short walk from Dupont Circle. Matthew the Apostle, among other things, was a tax collector, which completes the sainted, tainted irony. How fitting. A conclave of the sleek foxes, all of whom frolic in tall clover outside of the coup, courtesy of the taxes extracted from the chickens pecking and a-cluck-clucking inside. The Cathedral is the seat of the Archbishop of the Roman Catholic Archdiocese of Washington. The Dingells, in-name-only Catholics, pulled strings and secured the beautiful sanctuary for the service to stage the adios-ceremony for Baptist-born Sally. I'm sure she wouldn't have minded. Baptist, Catholic, Methodist – quaint anachronisms for any Babylonian who might pause to wonder why the differences could ever have been a "big deal." The service was presided over by the Pontifex Maximus of Babylon, Reverend,

Monsignor priest, Rex-Arthur C. Dix. A most impressive churchman he was to contemplate – tall, regal bearing, middle-aged handsome with a closely cropped salt-pepper beard – a fine ecclesiastical prop, polished and shiny, a perfect human veneer of religious ornamentation to attach to the gathering of a gussied-up, high-priesthood of pseudo leadership.

Finding myself in temporary association with this "high-priesthood," I was reminded of Wyndham Lewis's sardonic reflection on the subject of politicians and power. "[W]e to tend worship the politician – the wielder of power so dread and so inclusive – as once man worshipped the thunder and the lightning, earthquakes and volcanoes. And who can do otherwise than tremble, when he reflects on the power that some not very intelligent little man holds in his hand? It is his mental and moral limitations that are so terrifying." So many limitations were on display, and so much terror to be felt.

Sally's career with the Dingells spanned forty years. She was a grey eminence. Mom knew everyone in this troupe, players of *verlorene Tugend*, easy virtue, no *en honnête homme* to be found. More importantly, Sally knew everything *about* everyone who was pushing and pulling away at the levers of power. She had worked with many of the House Representatives, including the leadership, on both sides of the aisle over the years and their high-ranking staff members. Not a few of them she drank under the table on occasion.

The entire Michigan House delegation of Representatives in all their flabby sophistication was there.

It included the bulwarks of avarice and malice, John and Debbie Dingell, two maestros of a slippery, insidious insincerity that barely glossed over their smug sense of social superiority. The cadaverous, septuagenarian Steny Hoyer from the House leadership suddenly materialized, employing, as always, his rehearsed expressions of false warmth. Maxine Waters representing the Congressional Black Caucus arrived in a classic stretch limousine. Aloof and haughty, oozing with insolence, this seventy-eight-year-old harridan accoutered herself like a person who spurns every obstacle of cost for the wardrobe and jewelry. Her pricy adornment, sadly, could only be an imperfect disguise of a circus-tent trouper. In a sane universe she'd be the star attraction in the dementia unit at the Crazy Horse Retirement Village.

No one came on the Metro. A couple of Senators surfaced. First, Michigan's Debbie Stabenow with an anodyne face and a doughy physique most suitable for casting as an aging milkmaid in an Ingmar Bergman production of rural life in a Scandinavia of times past. Her orations on the Senate floor were as inspirational as soggy Cheerios languishing in a bowl of warm milk. Then there was the earnest Marco Rubio of Florida raised to an acceptable level of manly stature with his best pair of elevator shoes. Wearing a daffy smirk, this boy-man looked like a cross between Little Lord Fauntleroy and some two-bit, junior ward heeler. Mom detested the fake wunderkind from his first appearance in the Senate. A few other Republicans of "distinction" attended. Newt Gingrich who had acquired some additional plumage in the way of poundage since his days as House Speaker. His face was moving in a slow transformation from a chubby but menacing firmness to fleshy dilapidation – but oily and self-promoting as ever. Former Governor of Michigan, John Engel with his carefully-contained obesity appeared to be an ideal candidate for Weight Watchers. He trundled in with his wife, the trim Michelle. I chatted briefly with Mike Turner, a House of Representatives member from Dayton, Ohio. Mike bears a striking resemblance to Corneliu Codreanu, the Fascist founder of Romanian Iron Guard in the 1930s, murdered at the end of WWII. Turner, so far managing to avoid assassination, was accompanied by his third or fourth wife – or girlfriend, not sure. She was definitely in the "trophy" category – more interesting to look at and even to talk to than the ex-mayor of Dayton. He was better suited for employment, perhaps, as a Burger King restaurant regional manager.

At this event I recalled the perfect description for a gathering of motley dragons from Balzac: "Corruption thrives, talent is rare, so corruption is the weapon of [this] mediocre majority, and you will feel it pricking you wherever you go." You couldn't move anywhere with this bunch without feeling pricked and in need of a shower. Geryon, the monster of Fraud, who terrified Dante in his tour through the *Inferno*, must have been overseeing this gathering.

At last, giving off the final fumes of insincerity, this phony debauch of dear-departed respect sputtered to a conclusion. I rendered a fawning thank-you to the Dingells on my departed mother's behalf, extracted myself from this vortex of hypocritical slush, solicited a cab and made my way to my hotel.

Sally had left me a detailed diary of her working days covering four decades. I could have lived like a Pasha with the proceeds of blackmail. Several years before she died, she came to visit me in Burbank. We sat talking late into the evening. A bit "in her cups," she told me that when Al Gore was a Senator he had hit on her once when she was alone with him in his office.

"What did he do?"

"He tried to kiss me."

"What did *you* do," I asked her.

"I fought him off. I told him, 'Al, I'm sorry, I can't. I really like Tipper. I'd feel terrible. Please, no.'"

"What did he say?"

"Not much. He looked embarrassed. I made a fast exit."

"Did you 'really' like Tipper?"

"Oh, yes. I did. She was a very decent person. I don't know what was inside of him, but he was one of the few people who by comparison could make Hillary Clinton seem almost like a normal human being."

"You didn't like Hillary?"

"Don't get me started on that woman."

When I got to my room after the service, I removed all of my clothes and put them in the plastic laundry bag I found in the closet. I showered, dressed, went out and found an incinerator to put it in.

Sally's uncle Daniel, who had launched her career, had died several years before. During the service, I couldn't help but wonder what her father, Richard, would have thought about the memorial service and what it said about her life.

33 Assembling Harry

"He who is living is now dead
We who were living are now dying
With a little patience."

—**T.S. Eliot**, *What the Thunder Said*

I wasn't prepared for it. I just didn't see it coming. I was going to take Sally's death in stride. She was sixty-nine, a good run for someone with a life-long affair with demon rum. But … there were so many pieces that I had to pick up and fit together to form a coherent picture of her life: the renegade Baptist preacher's kid from a small town; the serial marriages to lousy men (one exception); success as a power broker in Babylon, power center of the world; the heavy drinking; and … the circumstances of her casual dalliance, the effects of which brought me into the world. Your mother and father are the people who made you. I could not put all these pieces of her life together in a way that made sense, any sense of the mother-half of who I was.

I know. It was obvious. I had to find the other half – Harry. Maybe the histories of Harry and Sally put together might form something resembling a Rorschach inkblot. It might help me understand my continuing insurrection against the modern world and whether it made any sense to continue with it.

Sally had never shared anything with me about Harry, other than what she told me about the drive-in-movie date and the circumstances that led to her pregnancy. My grandparents knew only what Sally had told them about him, which was almost nothing. They had always discouraged me from seeking any knowledge about him. Whatever, whoever he was, they despised him for what he had done to Sally – not for the pregnancy, but for abandoning her and his son.

It was a month after her death. I was going through some of her effects she had left in Bad Axe with her parents when she headed for DC shortly after I was born. In a folder I found a letter to her from Harry. The envelope had no return address, but its postmark was "Kansas City, MO," and the date was February 3, 1970. The handwritten letter read:

> Dear Sally,
> I got your letter. I'm so glad to hear that you got through the tough delivery and your baby boy is healthy and happy. I say "your" rather than "our" because having abandoned you I have no right to say it.
>
> You know almost nothing about me. Like you, I grew up in Michigan in a small town, an even smaller one than yours. I want to tell you some things about my

family. Someday Joe may want to know about his father's side of the family. If so, my mother and father, George and Kathleen Harrison live in Beal City which is not far from Mt Pleasant where my mother works at Central Michigan University as a secretary in the English department. I have three sisters. Two are married. Kay Kowalski is the oldest. She lives in Houston, Texas. Jeannette Davis lives in Three Rivers. Dorothy is still in high school.

My father, George, is a wonderful man. It's not his fault that I am the way I am. He was a minister for a time. Not like your Dad, he was a lay preacher and a social worker, a Methodist. He has worked at a lot of different jobs since then. Now he's a mail carrier and drives a rural route. My mom, too, is a fine person –very smart and perceptive. Dad was the dreamer-idealist: Mom was the practical-realist.

I guess I'm the black sheep of the family, neither practical nor an idealist. Not sure at this point. It's a long story. Maybe someday I'll figure it out.

But for now, enclosed is a check that I hope will cover most of the doctor and hospital costs of the delivery. I'll try to send more as time passes.

I hope you are doing ok. I'll try to stay in touch.

Harry

This was the only correspondence I could find from my father to my mother. If there was more, it had been lost or destroyed. With the family details he had included in the letter I was able to locate a current address for Jeannette. His oldest sister, Kay, it appeared, had died some years ago. Jeannette still lived in Three Rivers, population of about 7,000 in southwest Michigan, not far from the Indiana state line. I couldn't find Dorothy. She must have married, and I had no married name with which to search for her.

Determined now to meet Jeannette, I debated about calling her first. But I decided to appear in person and see if she would be able and willing to tell me about my father and his family. Was he even alive?

Jeannette lived in an old, but well-maintained two-story house, early 20th-century Neoclassical style, eight or ten blocks from downtown. I got there about two in the afternoon, mounted the steps to a large, covered front porch and rang the doorbell. A petite, attractive, nicely dressed woman in her early seventies opened the heavy wooden door and looked at me through the screen door. How, I had been wondering, would I approach her without immediately putting her off? I decided that I would be direct.

"Hello. I'm sorry to bother you. I'm not a salesman, a Jehovah's Witness or a

Mormon missionary." She started to interrupt me, but with my next sentence she looked startled and remained silent. That sentence: "My name is Joseph Martin, and I'm trying to find information about my father, Harry Harrison."

I continued. "He left my mother shortly before I was born. I've never met him. I have no idea where he is. My mother recently died. Going through her things I found a letter from him to her with information about his family, including where they lived – Beal City. Until I read that letter, I knew little about him and nothing about his family."

Jeannette was now staring intently at me with grave anticipation. I paused and looked back at her with what must have been a desperately imploring expression.

"In the letter my father mentioned three sisters and their names. One was your name, Jeannette Davis, his middle sister." Long pause. "I believe that…. That you are my aunt."

I'm not sure how long we both stood there in silence facing each other through that screen door. A long time it seemed, and I was beginning to think that I had made a mistake in coming here.

Slowly the screen door opened. I moved back, and Jeannette stepped cautiously out onto the porch. She paused and then seemed to recover her lost composure. Then she gestured at a couple of chairs off to the side and gently said: "Maybe we should sit down."

As I was descending into the chair, she remained standing while she looked intently at me. "You look like him," she said, as she finally settled into her seat across from me.

I could see that her hands, which she had clasped together, were shaking slightly from the effects of the news brought by this unexpected messenger.

> "I realize this must be a shock for you. I'm sorry. I couldn't think of another way to approach you. You didn't know your brother had a son?"

She nodded grimly in the affirmative.

> "I wasn't sure what, if anything, Harry had told his family about my mother. Nothing, I guess."

> "No. He never said anything to me or anyone else in the family. I am pretty certain of that. I was never around him much during his college days. I was already married then with children. After he graduated, he left Michigan in a hurry for a job in Kansas City. He

got married there soon after that – to a civil rights lawyer lady, I believe. That marriage didn't last long. I saw him at the wedding there, but after that, I didn't see him until many years later. By then he was in a heap of trouble and on the move. How and where did he meet your mother?"

"He and my mother met casually in their last semester of college – real casually." I paused and laughed. "I was, you might say, a blind date accident. That was the extent of their entire relationship. When I was young, I would ask my mom about my dad. She would always put me off. 'It's complicated. I'll tell you later when you're old enough to understand,' she would say. Eventually, I quit asking. I guess she figured I was never old enough. She did tell me, though, how they met and the crazy circumstances around it.

Please. I need to know. Is he still alive?"

With that question her face took on the features of great distress. She looked at me, then looked away.

"Yes, he is very much alive. Alive and in prison, a Federal prison." That news was startling to hear. Not what I had expected.

"For what?"

She laughed. "For a lot of things."

"How long has he been in prison?"

"Two or three years. I lose track of time. He was a fugitive for decades. Part of the time he lived outside of the country – Cuba and some other places, I think. He seemed to want to go wherever there was trouble and then add to the mix. Have you heard of the Weathermen from the 1970s?"

"Yes, of course. I've read about them – radical terrorists – they did lots of bombings, robberies and kidnappings. Much of it all was related to the Vietnam War and the civil rights movement. My God, he was involved with the Weathermen?"

"Oh yes. Harry was part of that crazy Bill Ayers bunch and quite the terrorist himself. He bombed a government building in San Francisco – didn't kill anyone, fortunately. After that is when he took off for Cuba because the Feds were hot on his trail. He was on the FBI's 'most wanted' list. I have a copy of that list with his photo if you want to see it. From there? Well, he went to South America, teamed up with some Central American communists. They killed Somoza who lived there after the communists ran him out of Nicaragua. He was a bad man, I guess. But he was minding his own business when they blew him to pieces. Not sure if I should go on."

"No, please, continue."

"Alright. Harry came back to the States. Eventually he settled down, if you can call it that. He went to Ohio where he ran some sort of religious scam on a TV cable channel. From there he moved to Chicago, then on to Alaska. In Juneau he operated a restaurant and, if you can believe this, got involved in politics – with Sarah Palin. Finally, he moved to Pennsylvania where he was apprehended. He was lucky to get away with all that stuff for so many years without getting himself killed or thrown in prison at a young age."

Jeannette then paused. I was sitting quietly trying to digest these details of what seemed to me a life story too incredible to believe.

"Did he ever remarry?" I asked.

She laughed. "Uh, yes, several times. Just a minute," she said: "I'll be back." She went into her house. After a couple of minutes, she walked back onto the porch with a thick binder and handed it to me.

"It's sort of his life's history. He finished writing it a short time ago in prison. His life was quite an adventure in crimes of various sorts. It reads like a novel. I've just mentioned some of the highlights – 'lowlights' is maybe better. The details are there, including the marriages and other women, if you want to get a more complete picture. He never mentions the affair with your mother. Maybe it's because he was ashamed. I don't know. It's quite something to think about. You'll be impressed. I was. It's an extra copy. You can keep it. It's your Dad's autobiography, I guess. Who from that conservative village we all grew up in would have guessed that my little brother would lead the wild and crazy life of an international desperado and would end up in a Federal prison?"

We continued our conversation for another hour or so. I told her about my mother and grandparents – the early years in Bad Axe and growing up in DC. She told me more about her brother and the rest of her family.

She then paused and asked me: "You don't know about my younger sister Dorothy?"

"No. She was a teenager when Harry wrote the letter, so she had no married name that I could use to find her."

"Well ... she's the 'political' star of the family. She got involved in state politics very young. She's always been ambitious. After a brief career as a social worker she got elected to the Michigan State House as a Republican. Then to the State Senate."

"Is that where she is now?"

"Oh, no. She's moved up. She was Michigan's Lieutenant Governor during the 1990s under John Engler. After that she was elected to the U.S. House of Representatives from Holland."

"Oh my God. She's in the U.S. Congress? My mother worked for years on John Dingell's congressional staff. As I mentioned, I grew up in DC. You know who Dingell is, right?"

"Oh yes, I've actually heard a lot about him from Dorothy. He's an institution in himself."

"Well?"

"No, I don't feel comfortable talking about him to you. Listen. You absolutely have to meet your other aunt, Dorothy. She's back home in Holland on Congressional break. She's only an hour or so from here. Let me see if I can get in touch with her. I want her to come over and meet you. I hope she can do it. Just give me a couple of minutes."

Jeannette went back into the house. Ten minutes later she stepped back onto the porch.

"She'll be here in an hour. Can you stay?"

"I can, but what did you tell her about me?"

"I told her that someone with extremely important family history information had unexpectedly shown up, and that she needed to get over here asap. She pressed me and was pretty annoyed that I wouldn't tell her more. But she finally agreed to come. She said: 'This better be good.' I said: 'Oh, believe me. It will be.'"

Jeannette and I were still sitting on the porch when Dorothy pulled up in front of the house in her silver BMW M340i Sedan. Out of it stepped a tall, slender, attractive, late-50ish blond casually dressed in tan slacks and a grey turtleneck sweater. She briskly made her way up the sidewalk. When she reached the top of the porch steps she stopped and bore down on me with a look that was a mix of curiosity and suspicion.

Looking at Dorothy I had this nagging feeling that I had seen her before.

> Jeannette: "Dorothy, meet your nephew, Joseph Martin."
>
> "What," she gasped and stepped back. "Is this some kind of practical joke, Jenny?"
>
> Jeannette: "No, it's no joke, Dorothy. Joseph, why don't you explain. Dorothy, you're going to need to sit down, though."

She did.

> "Dorothy, thank you for coming. Like I told your sister, my mother died three months ago. I was her only child. My father never married her and left when she was pregnant just after they both finished as students at Michigan State University. I never knew anything about him. My mother refused to talk about him. Going through her things, I found a letter he had written to her shortly after I was born with details about his family. That is how I found Jeannette. Over the last couple

of hours, she has been telling me more about my father and your family. My father is your brother."

Dorothy looked like she was struggling hard to come to grips with this. Finally: "I had no idea. This is a complete shock to me. I'm having a difficult time believing this. How old are you?"

"Forty-six. My mother and your brother met briefly at MSU."

"How did they meet?"

"A blind date. That was it. They got acquainted in a hurry. Too much booze; too much libido; none of her Baptist upbringing kicked in that evening. Unfortunately, well fortunately for me, she got pregnant. The timing wasn't so good for Sally. Harry wasn't interested in sticking around and being a Dad. My mom went back to her parents, had the baby, me, and went on her way."

"Yeah, that sounds like Harry. Did your mother ever marry?"

I laughed: "Ah, yes, many times."

Jeannette: "There's more, Dorothy. Brace yourself: Joseph's mother worked for Dingell."

"John Dingell?" Dorothy looked stunned. I nodded.

"In what capacity?"

"She was hired initially as an intern by Dingell's chief of staff, Daniel Martin. Daniel was her uncle, her father's younger brother. She grew up in Bad Axe. Daniel put her through law school. Then she signed on in the late '70s as a congressional aide, doing research, drafting legislation and negotiating with lobbyists. She rose high up on the staff and was with the Dingells until she retired."

"What was her name? No, wait a minute. I thought that I'd seen you before. You're Joseph Martin. So, your mother was Sally Martin?"

"Sally Martin, that's right."

"Oh my God. I knew her, of course. I was at her Memorial Service in DC. I knew I had seen you before. That's where it was."

"Yes, I remember you now too. The entire Michigan House delegation was there."

"What did she die of? There was really never any explanation other than a long illness."

"From liver disease. Sally was a life-long alcoholic, but a highly functioning one. Only a few people knew."

"I'm sorry. I work with the staff from the other side of the aisle. Did Jeannette tell you that I'm a Republican? Anyway, Sally was very good. I'll be honest with you, Joseph. I never had a high opinion of John Dingell. His wife, Debbie, stepped in when he retired and filled his seat like it was a family heirloom he was handing down to her. She's tetchy and rather mean. I like her even less than her husband."

That remark brought to mind a scathing quip I'd read about powerful people: "Usually a public detestable has some private offset. But of this nullity [Debbie Dingell] there is not even a record of private pleasantness." It was originally directed toward Emperor Franz Josef by Ezra Pound.

Dorothy went on: "That's all I want to say about the Dingells. But they had some good people on the staff. They were decent to work with. This blows my mind that this woman I knew for several years was, well, sort of, my sister-in-law.

Did you grow up in DC?"

"Yes, after my first five years with my grandparents in Bad Axe. How can I say this? Sally was not what you'd call a 'traditional mother.' She had bad taste in men with a few exceptions – went through four husbands. I had to endure the first two as surrogate Dads – anti-role models. The third one was a deadbeat and not much use, just a failed academic type. The last one was actually a great guy. A druggie murdered him at a metro stop in DC just a couple of years ago. Growing up, my direction was entirely self-direction. The family situation was what they call today, 'dysfunctional.'"

"Are you married?"

"No, I'm twice divorced."

"Do you have any children?"

"I have a son from my second marriage."

"What do you do?"

"For a living?"

"Yes, for a living."

"I used to be a clinical psychologist."

"Used to be?"

"Well, that's a long story. I made a career change years ago as the result of an experience that changed my perspective on the world in general and my profession specifically."

"What do you do now?"

"I write books."

"About what?"

"About what's wrong with everything."

Dorothy studied me for a few moments thinking most likely: "Something's not right with this man, but I can't put my finger on it."

She was right. There was something wrong with me.

34 My Prism Goes to Prison

"An honest man is the common enemy."

—Honoré de Balzac

*"[B]ut were I king, my acts would run
counter to my will."*

—Creon, *Oedipus Rex*

I spent the rest of the afternoon and the early evening at Jeannette's house talking to Harry's sisters, my newly discovered aunts. I learned about his arrest in State College, Pennsylvania, his arraignment in Philadelphia and the sentencing after he had pleaded guilty to a multitude of federal crimes. Harry on his sixty-fifth birthday was sentenced to thirty years in prison on terrorism acts and unlawful flight to avoid prosecution – his first eligible date for parole would be fifteen years later.

Jeannette and Dorothy had visited their brother, my father, in prison. His incarceration was in the high security block of the Terre Haute Federal Correctional Complex. From Jeannette's house in Three Rivers, it was a five-hour drive to visit her brother.

My newly discovered aunts encouraged me to visit my father. They didn't have to. I knew I had to meet him. I contacted the prison officials by mail and told them that I was the son of inmate Harry Harrison and would like to arrange for a visitation. They responded that their records showed that inmate Harrison had no son. I called and after making my way through a labyrinth of prison personnel, found a woman who was willing to listen to my explanation as to why the prison records were not accurate. Harry had left my mother during her pregnancy, I told her. His omission was simply part of his failure to take responsibility for the paternity of a child he had never seen.

> "Well, this is a problem," the prison lady said. "He states on his intake documents that he had no children," was her initial response.

> By this time, I was getting exasperated: "Of course he wouldn't lie, would he? Or maybe he forgot. It's not like he ever *acted* like a father. I've never even met him. Come on! He's a career criminal for Christ's sake," I said. "The guys you have locked up aren't in the cells because of their uncompromising honesty. He's my father. I want to see him and talk to him. If you ask him I'm confident that he will acknowledge paternity and will want me to visit him."

That seemed to clinch it. She said that she would be willing to accept a proof-of-paternity document in the form of a birth certificate and proceed with the request.

To be honest, I wasn't that confident. Why should I be? To be accepted at the prison as a visitor, the request would have to be approved by the inmate. That was part of the visitor protocol. Harry had to want to see me. Would he? I sent a copy of the birth certificate, waited and wondered which way Harry would go. Two weeks later a response came in the mail. My date for a visit to Terre Haute was set. In ten days, at age forty-six, I would meet my Father for the first time.

I flew from LA to Indianapolis and rented a car. From there, I drove seventy-seven miles to the prison complex outside of Terre Haute. The entrance to the section where Harry was housed was a totalitarian-modernist, two-story, concrete structure with the words "United States Penitentiary, Terre Haute" high above glass doors. The USPTH was a maximum-security unit that also housed the death row inmates convicted of federal crimes. Oklahoma bomber, Timothy McVeigh was executed there in 2001 as well as drug king pin and murderer, Juan Raul Garcia.

The USPTH is also loaded with history that speaks volumes to its dark legacy. Conducted there were medical experiments in 1943 and 1944. With approximately sixteen million American men mobilized during WWII, gonorrhea was rampant in the armed forces as well as in the civilian population. Dr. John F. Mahoney, the head of the Venereal Disease Research

Laboratory of the U.S. Public Health Service was searching for an effective treatment for sexually transmitted diseases. The Feds selected 241 USPTH prison inmates who "volunteered" to be exposed to gonorrhea. Researchers injected various strains and concentrations of gonorrhea into the inmates' penises. They were paid $100 to get the clap via a painful jab. What an opportunity for a comedy troupe like Monte Python to do a skit on the "Gonorrhea Gang" with some catchy tunes like:

"In the USP,

Model inmates are we;

Though our peckers hold puss

We don't make a fuss

We each got a C-note

Now we bellow "Hurray!"

Gonorrhea's the reason

We're hap-happy today."

This clap I got, I sure did mind

This clap I got, it might make me blind,

The bulls, you know, they're real unkind

But a cure they say, they're gonna find

Chorus:

In better days I'll be on the mend

Toward better days I'm so inclined

> So, you my friend I need not remind,
>
> Gonorrhea's on my mind
>
> Gonorrhea?
>
> Is 'Gentle on my Mind.'"

—**Backseat Baby**, *Gonorrhea's on My Mind*

The Terre Haute experiments set the foundation for the Guatemala syphilis experiment conducted from 1946 to 1948. Guatemala, a poor, nowhere country, crappy even by third world standards, was the perfect site to do Dr. Jekyll experiments on throw-away people. No need to bother with the ethical constraint of individual consent. No adverse legal consequences and bad publicity to contend with. Guatemalan soldiers, prostitutes, prisoners and mental patients were infected with syphilis and other sexually transmitted diseases without their informed consent. At least 83 of the Guatemalans died as a result.

The USPTH was full of bad vibes.

The visiting hours at the prison were from 8:00 to 3:00. I arrived in the early afternoon and went through the security checks. An attendant escorted me to the visitor's center where I stood next to a set of two chairs and waited. Accompanied by a guard, Harry suddenly debouched from a dimly lit corridor into the visiting room. He was wearing khaki colored pants and a matching buttoned shirt, short sleeves over a grey, heavy long-sleeved undershirt. Clean-shaven with thick, short greying hair, bright blue eyes, I was struck by how much younger he looked than his age. This inmate was not the broken old man I was expecting to see. Broad shouldered, thick chested and strikingly muscular, he must have stood about 5'8'' and weighed in at around 180 pounds. He looked like a man who in his younger days was nobody to fuck with.

Without saying a word, Harry sat down while I remained standing. Unsmiling, he leaned back in his chair, looked up at me and threw his arms out wide to his side, palms flat-up in a gesture that seemed to say … "well?" Then:

> "Ball's in your court … uh, son."

Coming in, I had no idea of what to expect from him, but this somewhat inhospitable how-do-you-do took me back. I took a deep breath and dropped into a chair.

> "Ok, I'll get to it … uh, Dad. I have always wondered what my father would be like. Sally, you remember Sally? She never talked about you. Over all these years, I had no idea of who you are, where you were, what you were doing. I had to construct you completely from my imagination. Which, at the risk of immodesty, is fairly powerful."

> "And how do I match up with your, uh, 'powerful' imagination?"

> "I'll let you know after we've had some time to … get acquainted. At this point, I'm not feeling 'the love.'"

There was a long pause. Harry was studying me. I could see him relax slightly. Finally:

"How is Sally?"

"Dead."

Harry flinched, bent slightly over and tapped his closed fist gently several times against his lightly closed lips.

"I'm sorry. I didn't know. When did she die?"

"Three months ago."

"What did she die of?"

"Too much booze."

Harry straightened, then leaned back against his chair and folded his arms tightly against his chest.

"So, she was a drinker?"

"Drinker? You might say that. Yeah, she put it away – early on she was into white wine; later she moved to vodka and gin. It never seemed to affect her career that much. She worked for a long time as a congressional aide to Michigan Congressman, John Dingle Jr. and did well – rubbed elbows with a lot of big shot politicians. But the booze didn't help much in her choice of men – she went through a bunch.

Finally, it did a number on her liver – cirrhosis."

"How about you? Are you a drinker?"

"I've no strong inclination toward alcohol and little interest. Good thing. Someone in the family needed to stay sober."

"Yeah well, sober is usually a good move in the long run. You're a handsome guy – take after your mother."

"I don't know about that, but she was a beauty. Maybe that was one of her problems."

"I suspect so. You married?"

"Twice divorced."

"Runs in the family, I guess. Any kids?"

"A son. Didn't know you had a grandson, did you?"

"No. What's his name?"

"Richard Thomas Martin. 'Richard' for Sally's father; 'Thomas' for Thomas Hobbes, the philosopher. He's eleven years old." He's smart too, like his mother, my second wife and a bit of a contrarian already."

"Hobbes, really? One of the few philosophers who makes sense."

That gave me a jolt.

Another long pause.

> Harry: "Do you know about the brief history of … us?"

> "Yeah, I know – very brief history, I would say. I know about how you two met – the blind date, the drive-in movie, the pregnancy and your escape to Kansas City. That's pretty much it. Sally told me about it around the time I went off to college – all the details. She didn't hold back. 'Avoid blind dates. Don't go and get any girls pregnant on the first date, like what happened to me,' she joked. I didn't. Not on the first date. Not on any.

> After she died, from a collection of her folders in storage I found that letter you wrote to her shortly after I was born. That was the first I learned about your side of the family. I used that letter to track down your sister, Jeannette in Three Rivers. I went to her house last month and shocked the hell out of her. Dorothy came over and got the shock treatment too. I guess you never bothered to tell anyone in your family about Sally or me."

> "No, I didn't, and I'll tell you why. You may have a hard time believing this,

but my father was a deeply religious man. He had very old-fashioned notions about what guys who get girls pregnant out-of-wedlock are supposed to do. 'Wedlock,' now there's a word you don't hear these days, do you? Anyway, he wasn't disposed toward shotguns, but he was firm on what ought to happen to boys who get girls into trouble. These notions were already out of favor back then and, of course, non-existent now. Nobody thinks, much less talks that way anymore. I knew if I told him, he'd push me very hard to marry Sally even though I barely knew her. My Mother? She too would have pushed me toward the altar. There was no way for me; it wouldn't happen. Plus, I can't believe your mother would have gone that route, even under extreme duress. What can I say? Booze, lust and youth – and opportunity. Everybody was … well… I also knew that even if I didn't marry her, my Mom and Dad would want to know their grandchild, maybe try to get custody. This would be a complication for Sally, her parents, my parents and me. I wasn't up for it. I didn't think she would want it."

"Well … that makes you a pretty rotten bastard in my view. I don't buy the 'complication' argument, Harry. Yeah, you weren't up for it, but that's it. The rest is bullshit. I dearly wish you had told them. Your parents? Really? They died never knowing that they had a grandson, your son. Goddamn you! That's beyond painful for me to hear. The grandparents I did know, Sally's Mom and Dad, were wonderful people. They were my parents for the first five years of my life. Having met Jeannette and Dorothy and hearing them talk about their family, I'm guessing your Mom and Dad were in that category. It grieves me that I never got a chance to know them."

Harry hunched his shoulders over and dropped his head down.

"Yeah. That's just one of the many things in my life I did that makes me a supremely rotten bastard. Being one was my MO I guess. Which is why I am here."

I was silent after that while I fought back the tears. Finally:

"I guess I can't blame you completely for me not knowing your Mom and Dad.

Sally had that letter you wrote her. She knew who your parents were and where they lived. She could have made contact. She should have. She didn't. You both fucked me over in hiding me from your Mom and Dad. It doesn't matter now. I don't know. Maybe it still does."

We both fell silent.

"Well," I said, finally, "Jeannette gave me a copy of your 'memoir.' I have to say: you've had quite a life of adventure. Amazing, really. I've read it multiple times and, yes, confirmation – you are a supremely rotten bastard. But…" I was looking distressed and hesitant.

"But… But what?" Harry's eyes were boring into me.

I started sighing and shaking my head. The agitation I had been feeling for weeks had finally broken out. Harry was now fixed on me with an intensity I hadn't seen before.

"But … I can't believe I'm saying this. As I finished reading what you wrote about your life, I couldn't help but be struck by this feeling that – your selfish and criminal ways aside – I saw the world much the way you do. How could this be? Hell, I never knew you, nothing about you. I lived a completely different life than you. I've been personally well ordered, disciplined, law-abiding, responsible, highly educated. I'm in a different universe. I'm struggling to understand this. That's the main reason I came to see you."

Harry continued his piercing stare. Then suddenly it broke. He laughed gently for a few seconds, then he said:

"That question I put on the last page. Got to you, didn't it?"

"Which question?"

"The one I said I hope haunts the reader in his quiet moments, 'Who will guard the guardians?' From the Roman poet, Juvenal."

It was my turn to laugh.

"Yes, it did, Harry. It hit hard, real hard. I grew up in Washington DC, Babylon, I call it. It's where our 'guardians' gather to conduct their business of 'guarding us.' Sally was close to some of the highest-ranking members of our guardian class. She worked for them, with them. She schemed with them and pushed their agendas. She drank with them. And with a few of them, fought off their passes at her. She married a couple of them. I got a close up look at this band of high-class pillagers – miserable excuses for human beings. Their guardianship was riddled with corruption, debauchery, lying and treachery – and no one guards *them*. I say this with all respect to your sister, Dorothy. She is no doubt an exception."

"Well, I hope so. But…"

"But what?"

"She's family. I'll forgive her if she slips. She's forgiven me."

"But, it's more than just the corruption of the guardian class that your memoir struck me with. It's the broader notion of corruption, how it pervades everything – our vocabularies, our thinking, our institutions, everything. I'm in a private, personal mutiny against the modern world. I have been for years."

"Well, it looks like the apple didn't fall that far from the tree. Welcome to my world, our world… Son."

35 Pardon Me?

*"As democracy is perfected, the office
of the president represents, more and
more closely, the inner soul of the people.
We move toward a lofty ideal. On some
great and glorious day, the plain folks
of the land will reach their heart's desire
at last, and the White House will be
adorned by a downright moron."*

—H. L. Mencken

We continued our conversation in that ominous direction. It was disturbing for me, but I knew I couldn't escape the conclusion. The father I'd never met until I was 46 was of the same mind as me. I would need time to digest all of this.

I had gotten up and was in the motions of leaving. Harry said "Wait a minute." He looked a bit hesitant and cast a cautious glance around us. I paused. Then he said: "Sit back down for a minute. I have something I need to tell you. Wasn't going to, but what the hell." I sat down and looked expectantly at Harry. He then leaned far over the table, his arms extended toward me. His right hand clasped down on my wrist – hard. The look on his face was unforgettable. His eyes were almost ablaze. He had the look of a man reborn. Then, very softly:

> "Until a month ago, I thought the only way
> I'd be leaving this place would be in a
> body bag. But, in thirty-six days and
> fourteen hours, I am going to be walk-
> ing out of this prison a free man."

That hit me like a jolt of electricity. Harry's sisters told me that he was riding out a thirty-year sentence; his earliest parole date would be at age 80. Terre Haute was probably his last stop. Was this a weird mind game he liked to play to pass the time in his dungeon?

> "What are you talking about, Harry? Jean-
> nette told me…"

Harry put his right hand up. I stopped in mid-sentence. What was the punchline?

> "I've been pardoned."

> "Pardoned? Bullshit! You're joking! How
> could you be…"

Harry's left hand went up. Stopped again in mid-sentence.

> "No. Dead serious, my son. Bad choice
> of words. My pardon is the real deal.
> President Obama is getting ready to

leave office. It's pardon-lottery time. He's been handing them out. I'm one of the lucky ones."

"I don't believe you."

"Believe me or not. Soon, I'll be hauling my outrageously pardoned-ass out of here. Ok, listen! Seriously, here's how it happened. You read my memoir?" I nodded yes. "So, you know. I was with the Weathermen in the early 1970s. We were blowing up government buildings all over the Goddamn country. Bill Ayers and Bernardine Dohrn wanted to make 'a statement' in California. They sent me to bomb the State Attorney General's office in San Francisco. Well, I did just that. That put me on the FBI's most wanted list. I fled the country. Went to Cuba. Hung out with Fidel and Raúl. I did some heavy lifting for those two guys – high-risk stuff. Really! Taking out Somoza right under Alfredo Stroessner's nose in Paraguay was one their highest priorities. I helped make that happen, not something I'm proud of now. I was out of the U.S. for a long time doing those things you read about, not things that would make you proud of your father. When I came back the heat was off. I behaved myself, more or less, and managed to avoid apprehension for decades. A DUI stop by the locals in State College, Pennsylvania triggered a computer search in the fugitive data bank. That's how I got here. Until a month ago, I'm thinking, 'Ok, I'm here to the end.'

But not so fast. 'It ain't over til it's over,' as old Yogi used to say. What happened was that Bill Ayers got wind that I was in prison for Weathermen shenanigans most of which were his ideas. AP picked up the news of my arrest. My sentencing made the back pages of the *Washington Post* – short column, which is where Ayers must have learned about it. He never cared for me all that much. I punched his lights out once. And, I wasn't too crazy about him or his nutzo hot pants wife Bernardine either. But I think it bothered him that I was rotting away in the slammer. He and the Mrs. are living the good life in the Windy City sucking up to the power structure – actually, they *are* themselves high up in it now. Maybe Ayers felt guilty. More than likely it was his ego and self-righteousness that pushed him benevolently in my direction. I don't know for sure. He still thinks that what he and his people did was brave, noble, truth-to-power stuff. So, he doesn't want any kind of stigma attached to anyone he was involved with back in the days of glory. He wrote a book about it, his memoir called, *Fugitive Days*. It's a work of true romance, a story about a man who has a life-long love affair with himself and his 'ideals.' Ayers continues to think he was a modern-day Robin Hood, and so do a lot of other folks. In any case, post-terrorist, he got to know Obama through the Annenberg Public Policy Center grant they worked together on when Obama was a state Senator. They were 'neighbors in Hyde Park.' That was the way Presidential-candidate Obama put it in 2008. The Republicans tried to make a big deal of him supposedly being bosom buddies with a former radical terrorist who bombed the Pentagon. The joke was that most of the voters didn't know who the hell Bill Ayers was. The rest who did didn't seem to give a flannel fart. As bad boys go, he was boring, ancient history, a has-been. He was no threat to anyone. No one was all that interested in what he and Obama had been up to, no one important enough to make a difference in the election. But, hey, now that I think about it, maybe blowing up the Pentagon wasn't such a bad idea after all. I don't know anymore. I could be convinced.

Anyway, Ayers morphed into a respectable commodity with the smart set. He is a retired education professor. His wife is a retired law professor. They have pensions to dream of. How's that for irony? They're 'radical chic' trim and in good shape for their age. The 'Amerika' they were so eager to destroy has been generous to them. They write books, draw royalties and get puff interviews by fawning 'journalists' to expound on their 'youthful idealism' – pure bullshit. But it sells like hot cakes to goodie-two-shoes lefty types. Sixties/seventies radical nostalgia – delusion-ridden schlock that would make a normal person puke. Bill, I think, really believes it. Why wouldn't he? He gets little pushback and lots of attaboys from the opinion makers.

Ayers, I am sure, had a back channel to the President and lobbied him for a pardon for me. Obama must have thought, 'why the hell not?' He was already drawing heat for kicking loose some young, hard-core drug dealers. An old radical has-been from the 1970s like me would barely make a stir, assuming anyone noticed. I'm no Marc Rich. Remember him? Clinton's pay-back-pardon for the half-mil he got for his Presidential library from Rich's ex-wife, Denise. Obama and Ayers were tighter than most people know. I think it was a favor. No. More like repaying a favor."

"How did you know Ayers lobbied for the pardon? No way you'd have gotten that information from the White House people. From Ayers, himself?"

"No. From Ayers, indirectly. It came through a channel to a reliable connection here on the inside. The networks coming in from outside sources are sophisticated. The message was coded, but Ayers had to have been the one who pushed on Obama. There's no other explanation that would make sense. Obama had no idea of who I was or what I had done. He couldn't have cared less if I rotted away in here for the rest of my life. The move could not have come from anyone other than Bill. Ayers knows that I know. I owe him. That's the way he would want it. Good for his ego. I can live with it."

"Do Jeannette and Dorothy know about the pardon?"

"No. It's hush-hush. The President's staff, I was told, wants to hold a lid on it and let it slip into a slow news cycle. It will go through without a lot of hoopla. Please don't tell them or anyone. I want to surprise them when I get out."

36 Whatever It Is, I'm Against It

"For months before my son was born

I used to yell from night till morn

'Whatever it is, I'm against it.'

And I've been yelling since I first com-
menced it

I'm against it."

—**Groucho Marx**, *I'm Against It*

Harry got his Obama pardon. He walked out of the Terre Haute Federal Correctional Complex a free man on December 18th, 2016, my forty-seventh birthday. He was 69 years old. The "correctional" efforts the Terre Haute Complex had spent on Harry? Wasted. I am confident that a "corrected Harry" would not be an improvement. Correction wasn't even a possibility. I can't imagine what it would look like.

I drove to the prison on that December day to gather my father and bring him to Jeannette's house in Three Rivers, Michigan. Dorothy was there. They knew I was coming that evening. They didn't know that I would be bringing their brother with me. The reaction? Astonishment followed by joy.

Harry was back. Let loose in the Land of the Free, the Home of the Brave. But how was this unreformed rascal supposed to spend his remaining days? He'd enroll in Medicare. Maybe he'd go on daily walks and monitor his cholesterol. For entertainment he'd select an NFL team to root for on Sunday afternoons while downing a few Bud Lites. Joining him, perhaps, friends his own age to reminisce with about the olden days. He'd hope they wouldn't die off too quickly.

With most people in similar circumstances the story would end here; nothing more of interest to report. As an ex-con with a few remaining years, Harry didn't have much to offer or to look forward to. He could rent a modest apartment. Maybe he'd put up a big Obama poster on his bedroom wall to acknowledge his eternal gratitude. Drinking coffee and listening to NPR would take up most of his mornings. He could get a part-time job in the afternoons to help maintain a modest existence – maybe a greeter at Wal Mart. To pass the evening, a Netflix movie, microwave popcorn and a Diet Coke. The largess of his sisters, perhaps, would make this possible. At least Jeannette and Dorothy still cared about him.

No. Harry had the fire left in him. Where did it come from? The guy was the hardest of hardcore in the club of contrarians. He had proudly taken up the attitude of Groucho Marx in "Duck Feathers" – "Whatever it is, I'm against it." He was against everything, including dying in place. No going "gentle into that good night" for this charming rascal.

"So what," you'll say, "that and 25 cents …" Well, "that" was the foundation of a new calling for Harry.

I'll get into it shortly, but some of his early history is in order.

In his youth and through his university days, Harry was what you might call a "fuck off." A traumatic experience in his teens poisoned his view of the world. The people who ran it he studied with contempt. By his 17th birthday he'd convinced himself that the best way to make his way through life was to enjoy himself at the expense of other people, and he became a conman. The world was going to be his mark. That night at the drive-in movie with Sally – case in point. His self-indulgent conniving took him down the road of life-long trouble-making. Early on though, Harry stopped making enjoyment his full-time hobby. He experienced a religious-like conversion to anti-establishmentarianism to which he applied his considerable conman skills. To the establishment's "overthrow" he devoted himself with the zeal of a true believer. In his prime, "the establishment" was what left-wing radicals like the Weathermen thought they were about to bring down. So … why not? He became a Weatherman.

> *"Our intention is to disrupt the empire... to incapacitate it, to put pressure on the cracks, to make it hard to carry out its bloody functioning against the people of the world, to join the world struggle to attack from the inside."*

> **—Weatherman book**, *Prairie Fire: The Politics of Revolutionary Anti-Imperialism (1974)*

> Borderline Personality Disorder (BPD) = a mental disorder characterized by unstable moods, behavior and relationships. Symptoms may include: grandiosity; distorted self-image; risky behavior.

BPD, I think it's safe to say, captures the personality profile of your typical Weatherman – "grandiosity" on the edge of insanity and "risky behavior" that scores eleven on a ten-point scale. Harry was BPD, at least for a time, but he was smarter – meaning wiser– than that crew of Johnny Come Lately Bolsheviks. He figured out that *every* "establishment" is a successful take-over by an anti-establishment movement. One way or another that anti-establishment becomes the next establishment with newish internal rot and hypocrisy. It takes on the same essential features: the corruption and collusion, the rationalizing of its grabbing the goodies for itself, self-serving propaganda to keep its grasp on power, the predictable, deluded self-worship. Same old shit, but with a stronger, nastier smell – more hypocrisy, more coercion. Every anti-establishment begins as a con-operation. "Support us, help us; we'll rid you of your oppressors. We are different from them." Wink-wink. Yes, they turn out to be different – worse.

The Russian Revolution is, perhaps, the most illustrious example of this. Once in power, the rule of the modernizing Bolsheviks was much more repressive, cruel and autocratic than the medieval Tsarist ruling class they had overthrown.

The Bolshevik-imitating, anti-establishment radicals of the 1960s were successful conmen; their game was to become the establishment, which they did. But they continued to imagine or maybe to pretend that they were pure, virtuous and selfless, unlike the oligarchs they replaced. While we "imagined" "living for today," they were busy putting the apparatus in place to make "tomorrow" an easy street for themselves and their comrades.

The new, "pure" establishment is like Leonard Cohen's girlfriend.

> "Everybody knows that you love me baby
>
> Everybody knows that you really do
>
> Everybody knows that you've been faith-
> ful
>
> Ah, give or take a night or two
>
> Everybody knows you've been discreet
>
> But there were so many people you just
> had to meet
>
> Without your clothes
>
> And everybody knows."

Everybody doesn't know. But that's another story.

During his years of adventure, when Harry wasn't blowing up buildings or plotting against right-wing dictators, he was reading voraciously – history, politics, economics. That reading taught him that the worthiness and good intentions of the ruling class we are taught to believe in are fictions. We embrace an elaborate web of fictions as historical truth. Which brought Harry to focus himself on the origin of popular beliefs. Belief, he came to understand, is the most important feature of how people organize their lives, specifically beliefs that relate to who should be trusted with power. "Who among us, do you *believe*, are trustworthy enough to be our guardians?" Answering that question is a study in the manipulation of belief. Successful manipulation of belief obviates the need for the more expensive and the less predictable resort to force. An internalized belief that leads to compliance works better than externalized threats. A life of examining popular, manufactured beliefs, as Harry came to see it, was a calling for contrarians courageous enough to expose the motivation of self-interest behind the facades and the belief structures built by the powerful that sustain the false trust. Harry was intent on exposing the self-interest behind these manufactured belief structures used to cover the depredations.

Every ruling class is composed of an elite that asserts its authority to rule on its claims of incorruptibility, while it exempts itself from the rules it imposes on those it rules over. Thus: "who will guard the guardians?" Try to answer that question in a way that gives you any comfort. It merely puts you into an infinite regress of disquiet. There is no happy answer. There are no guardians who don't need guardians who themselves are found to be unworthy of trust. That applies to "aspirant" guardians, like the Weathermen who imagine that they are more virtuous and hence more trustworthy. Harry embraced the unhappiness rooted in his question and applied his contrarian approach to showing how the "guardians" operate, how they lie and cover up their usurpations. He called it the "3-cs" approach – corruption, collusion, coercion." Harry's "antennae" for corruption had developed to a point where he noticed everything and was shocked by nothing. Twenty-first century America under Harry's scrutiny was an interlocking "system" that operated with the 3-cs. At age sixty-nine, Harry used the 3-cs to launch a new career.

37 Talk is Not Cheap

*"I would rather be an opportunist and
float than go to the bottom with my
principles around my neck."*

—Stanley Baldwin

Harry walked out of the Terre Haute Federal Correctional Complex that December at age sixty-nine. Even at this advanced age he had good things going for him. In the prime of health and physically fit, he looked at least 10 years younger than his age. In prison he did two things: read and work out. His mind was sharp. His body was hard. Pushups, sit-ups and chin-ups were a big part of his daily routine along with dead-lifts and bench presses in the weight room.

Harry emerged from incarceration as a life-long survivor who instinctively knew at any given moment where to position himself to take advantage of opportunities whenever and however they presented themselves. He was the consummate opportunist with a lifetime of practice. And, most important for his future, he had put together a profound indictment of the modern world. He just needed to find a way to deliver that message. He did. And, he would not be surprised at how favorably it would be received by so many.

Upon his release, Jeannette found Harry an apartment in Kalamazoo, Michigan not far from where she lived in Three Rivers. For anyone who might be curious, the comedic sounding "Kalamazoo," derives from a Potawatomi Indian word that means "place where the water boils in the pot." The city's name was popularized nationwide in 1942 when Glenn Miller recorded a number one selling single, "I Gotta Gal in Kalamazoo." The Modernaires did the vocals – with a hard accent on the "Kal".

> "A B C D E F G H, I got a gal in *Kal*ama-
>   zoo
>
> Don't want to boast but I know she's the
>   toast of *Kal*amazoo
>
> Zoo, zoo, zoo, zoo, zoo
>
> Years have gone by, my my how she grew
>
> I liked her looks when I carried her books
>   in *Kal*amazoo
>
> Zoo, zoo, zoo, zoo, zoo."

Catchy, no? Perhaps in a way that captures the wholesome, Blondie and Dagwood ethos of America in the 1940s.

After a couple of months of experiencing life in a place where water boils in a pot, Harry got a job at WKZO 590, the top radio station in the area. He was a "station office assistant," a gofer, on the third shift. His job was basic, office work. He sorted mail, answered the phones and made coffee for the staff. A foot in the door was all he needed.

WKZO's late-night talk show host was Denny Mc-Lain. No. He was not the Denny McLain who pitched for the Detroit Tigers in the 1968 World Series against the St. Louis Cardinals. And, by the way, lost the first game to the Cardinal's Bob Gibson who struck out 17 batters from the Tiger's murderer's row. WKZO's McLain was a portly, local radio personality, lively but limited. Like most AM radio talk shows, Denny's tended toward the conservative side. He encouraged listeners to call-in, and he chatted them up with his late-night "wisdom" about politics and the politicians who were making current headlines. It was standard fare for regional talk radio and one of WKZO's most listened-to programs. But, it needed a boost. Denny was status quo.

Harry, as always, grasped where he was – the limitations, the potential. He knew where he wanted to go. It wasn't the status quo. Denny was Harry's exit ticket out of the status quo, and he paid assiduous court to Mr. McLain. Denny didn't know it, but he was going to help the vigilant ex-con launch his new career. Harry carefully observed how Denny operated his studio equipment and how he managed the call-ins and the commercial breaks. He closely followed his monologues and became his most fervent studio admirer – and his friend. During his fugitive days Harry had served Fidel and Raul Castro. He knew how to suck up to heavy hitters a lot "heavier" than Denny. He and Denny became "close." After a couple of months, Denny's secret understudy had acquired a basic grasp of how McLain managed his program. In the meantime, Harry continued to think about ways he could be good at Denny's job, better if he got the chance. Longshot, but...

In his late fifties, Denny suffered from GERD, gastroesophageal reflux disease. One night on the air he had a ferocious attack of GERD. It was during a commercial break. Perhaps it was brought on by that hefty plate of spiced-up, take-out sausage lasagna Harry had special-ordered – just for him. Harry had devoted himself to absorbing Denny-details, and not just his lack of will-power to resist no-no cuisine as ordered by the doctor. He was observing Denny close up on the job. One time he jokingly told him: "if you ever need an emergency stand-in for a couple of minutes, I'm up for it." As a life-long conman, Harry projected confidence and was the king of savior faire. If anyone had the aplomb and the derring-do to pull off such an improbable stunt, it was Harry.

Well, while Mr. Radio talk show host, McLain was taking forty minutes to recover from his discomfort, he gave Harry the nod figuring he would be off only a few minutes. No one would notice the short gap with extended commercials. On the air Harry went. He had planned for such an opportunity and had prepared a short monologue consistent with the program's basic format and content. He did some fast talking, took several calls with his own version of "chat" that worked amazingly well for an upstart. He even managed the commercial breaks with no problems. During that 40 minutes, while the extra spicy lasagna of Harry's procurement was roiling Denny's digestive tract all the way down, so to speak, Harry had launched his new career – a talk-radio host.

"Who was that guy?" The next day WKZO's station manager, Karl LaFong, had his phone ringing with calls from regular listeners expressing enthusiasm for that "different" voice on the air the previous evening. They were wondering: who was the guy subbing for Denny – powerful voice, different style, high energy, fast on the uptake, great jokes. The execs ran the previous night's recording of the show; they could not help but be impressed. He was one, droll, funny guy. Harry's impromptu debut led to his newest duty as assigned. He would be a "relief pitcher" for Denny McLain if needed in a short pinch. Harry at his insinuating best had maneuvered his way into a position where his experience and skills might move him higher.

Then the senior slickster caught another break. One month after Harry's stand-in debut, Denny had to undergo an emergency gall-bladder surgery that put him out of commission for a week. With no regular sub available on short notice, Harry got a full week of air time as WKZO's late-night talk show host. That sealed the deal for him. His popularity had eclipsed Denny's. Denny went back to a position in morning-programming for local news stories. Harry went full time on WKZO's late-night, radio-talk show as Harry Hammer. He took his new name from the title of a book by Friedrich Nietzsche, *Twilight of the Idols, or, How to Philosophize with a Hammer*. The words in the title were powerful metaphors for how Harry conceived of his new calling in decadent, twenty-first century twilight-America – a man with a hammer in a china shop of idols.

Harry was a natural for talk radio. He had a low, powerful, raspy voice that was authoritative and at the same time edgy. The monologues were spontaneous, droll and witty. His instincts with the call-ins were perfect, using them as foils to boost the impact of his dark, corrosive humor. Harry brought to his program an incredible mass of knowledge from his years of world travel and dumpster diving into the smelliest bins of human "accomplishment." He'd seen it all – the corruption, up close and personal. He was involved in some of it. It gave him the confidence to push down into the perfumed sewage and examine those kinds of human failings that no one else wanted to touch. That, combined with his sardonic commentary and quick, smart repartee with his callers, made his ratings soar.

Harry's formation as a radio-talker was based on two models from radio history. The first was the controversial priest he had read about with great interest while in prison, Father Charles Coughlin. Harry's grandfather was an avid listener of Father Coughlin. From the National Shrine of the Little Flower Basilica church he had founded in Royal Oak, just north of Detroit, Father Coughlin broadcast his radio show to millions of Americans during the 1930s. National politics and economics were the focus of this muckraker priest. His popularity grew, and he became one of the most widely heard critics of FDR's social and economic policies – a truth-to-power guy with a Roman collar. His message was a mix of populism that called for the nationalization of major industries and the railroads and for greater protection of labor rights. The U.S. entry into WII brought wartime paranoia: FDR wanted it and exploited it. He shut down Coughlin's radio program and blocked the dissemination through the mail of his newspaper, *Social Justice*. Here, Harry noted to himself, was one of the 3-cs at work, authoritarian-style coercion by a sainted "savior of democracy." Conscripted American soldiers were dying for the cause of freedom across the ocean. Freedom of speech at home was expendable.

Then there was Joe Pyne. Pyne was an ex-marine who earned a purple heart in South Pacific combat in WWII. His nationally syndicated talk-radio show in the late 1960s was carried on 250 stations nation-wide. Teenaged Harry, enamored with the originality of Pyne's aggressive interview style, became an avid listener of his radio show. Pyne began his career as a radio talk personality in Pennsylvania. He moved to Los Angles where he was fired by KABC. LA's KLAC was dead last in the ratings. Its execs gambled and hired the acerbic, combative Pyne at $25,000 a year, a huge salary at that time. A smashing success, he lifted the station to the top with his confrontational, sarcastic approach to his listeners and guests. "Go gargle with razor blades," was Pyne's back-at-ya to callers who disagreed with him. His talk format eventually spread into radio programming across the country. Pyne rushed into controversy like a prize fighter jumping off his stool at sound of the bell. He would interview and go mano-a-mano with the most fringe elements in American politics from black militants to neo-Nazis to Klansmen.

That was the golden era of free speech in America. PC censorship, the primacy of feelings and the rule of comforting banalities had not yet arrived. No topics were off-limits. No personalities were banned from public forums. One of Harry's most memorable free-speech recollections was from his student days on the campus of Michigan State University in 1967. There he attended a talk given by George Lincoln Rockwell, head of the American Nazi Party. Rockwell had been *invited* by one of the student organizations. He was received and treated with the same consideration any guest of the university could expect. This would be unimaginable at any American university today where a former Secretary of State is regarded as too reactionary to be allowed to speak.

Harry modeled himself after Joe Pyne, but with his 3-cs probing that brought in and turned on huge listening audiences. His contrarian commentary on contemporary events and on the shortcomings of celebrity personalities and politicians was the driving force. His confidence soared with his airtime. He pushed the fruits from his search of the 3-cs into more of his monologues. They came with biting satire and withering sarcasm. His corrupt targets ended up with crude nicknames using Spoonerisms. There was Kalamazoo city councilman Matt Farrell who was taking kickbacks for city contracts. Harry would "slip" and call him Fat Merrell. Bart Figlio, a state house representative from Portage on the take, became Fart Biglio. Harry's mockery was infectious. The clever inversion of the names struck the listeners with mocking hilarity. Bart was no longer "Bart." He'd been christened with a potty moniker, a scatological twist that captured his status as a low life on the take. Bart should have been behaving himself, peradventure. There was something Dante-esque about Harry's approach: every program was a tour through the *Inferno* with a fresh look at the damned and a commentary on their vices. When Harry wasn't on-air he was scouring local and regional news sources that would provide grist for his skewering of the local and regional politicians. Every show had a different scandal to dissect or a new sleazy operator to pursue and put into his trophy case. Harry had unleashed a feeding frenzy for listeners hungry to know the truth that was regularly hidden from them.

The broadcasts also appealed to Harry's listeners with a back-and-forth shifting of focus from debauched individuals to the rot of institutions. Sometimes his broadcasts turned its fumigation engine on a particular individual – a city councilman, school board member or school superintendent, a utilities commission CEO. Then he would switch to the corruption of an organization. A prime target was the public-school teacher unions for their outrageous protection of incompetent teachers – teacher salaries, benefits and huge amounts of paid time off. He talked about the "Reassignment centers" in New York City maintained by the Department of Education, yet another corrupt "system." In the "Rubber Room," as it was so aptly called, were parked the behinds of hundreds of "teachers" accused of misconduct – drunkenness, lechery, gross incompetence and classroom unfitness – collecting a full-time salary to warm the seats. The Rubber Room housed the protected dregs of the system passing their days with video games or surfing the internet – doing nothing to earn their paychecks for months or years while awaiting the resolution of their cases, deliberately dragged out with the union fighting their termination.

The cowardice of university presidents and administrators for caving to the PC-ers shutting down speakers they didn't like was another subject Harry eagerly dove into. To add insult to injury, he made a special point of their astronomical, seven-figure salaries, benefits like paid country-club memberships, huge bonuses, free housing, cars, do-nothing jobs for their spouses. The incompetence and corruption of county governments and state bureaucracies he targeted for their pay-to-play contracting and fake jobs for family and friends. Sometimes he switched gears and went back with "refreshers" on forgotten scandals. Harry did a show on forced bussing in the 1970s. Black and white blue-collar kids spent hours on busses. The judges and politicians who waxed eloquent about the need for "diversity" sent their kids to expensive private schools far away from the poor black kids and blue-collar whites.

Harry had devoured Edward Gibbon's *Decline and Fall of the Roman Empire*. From it he took away the centerpiece of Gibbon's wisdom: "History is indeed little more than the register of the crimes, follies and misfortunes of mankind." "Crimes" and "follies." Harry just couldn't escape from them. Much of his life he had lived them. He could still feel them. He remembered what they smelled and tasted like.

38 Demolition Derby

"Oh, that deceit should steal such subtle
shapes
And with a virtuous vizard hide foul guile."

—William Shakespeare, *Richard III*

Nothing, however, topped the demolition job Harry did on Saint Arthur. "Un-sainting" the sainted Senator from Michigan, Arthur Vandenberg, looking down upon us now from his high perch in heaven, was a loving piece of scandal excavation work, long overdue. Sometimes you just have to turn back and dig up the old garbage and put it out for pick up. This particular smelly stuff was Vandenberg's seigniorial reign, thirty-three years from 1928 to 1951. Harry was a native of Michigan. He believed he owed his fellow Michiganders something besides the whitewashed, magisterial version of Michigan's greatest statesman.

"I'll strip the ragged follies of their time
Naked, as at their birth…"

—Ben Johnson

To be stripped naked was Mr. Vandenberg, a star performer of ragged follies." Harry would vindicate the couplet in Thomas Mann's *Bekenntnisse des Hochstaplers Felix Krull*," his confessional novel of a conman.

> "However fair and smooth the skin,
>
> Stench and corruption lie within."

Vandenberg was a native of Grand Rapids, a little north, up yonder from Kalamazoo. This was to be a piece of façade-wrecking close to home. On tap was un-manicured American history, the kind you'll never get in school – for a reason. Listeners were astonished to discover the decades-long cover-up on Vandenberg. Schools, civic centers, concert halls and university buildings all over Michigan bear his honorifically bestowed name. (A helpful rule of thumb for thinking about dead politicians: the more stuff a politician has named after him, the more corrupt and ruthless was his time in office.) Harry contemplating Vandenberg, perhaps, recalled Lord Byron's masterful, poetic takedown of Napoleon.

> "'Tis done---but yesterday a King!
>
> And armed with Kings to strive---
>
> And now thou art a nameless thing:
>
> So abject---yet alive!...
>
> Thanks for that lesson—it will teach
>
> To after-warriors more
>
> Than high Philosophy can preach,

And vainly preach'd before.

That spell upon the minds of men

Breaks never to unite again,

That led them to adore

Those Pagod things of sabre sway,

With fronts of brass, and feet of clay."

—**Lord Byron**, *Ode to Napoleon*

Ah yes. Thanks, Harry for "that lesson," an "Ode to Arthur." You stepped up to the plate when no one else would. Better late than never. Decades of false adoration laden with "high Philosophy" preaching and casting its spell over all the minds of those nice folks in Michigan. *This* idol Harry would shatter with this hammer. Vandenberg, falsely adored, a Midwest Pagod with feet of clay, "so abject," but he was "yet alive" in false memory. Harry was making history "come alive" delivered by radio.

The "isolationist" Republican senator was celebrated as a mid-20th-century giant in the Senate. That was the American *Pravda* version – a man of principled opposition during those years FDR was riding roughshod over the GOP. He had contended for the party's nomination to run against FDR in 1940. Then – surprise, surprise. Just prior to 1941, Senator Vandenberg experienced a sudden "conversion" from his "isolationist" resistance to American involvement in war-torn Europe to FDR's interventionism. Doing a political 180, he threw his support to Roosevelt's Lend

Lease program, a violation of FDR's promise of neutrality in the ongoing European war. Thirteen Democrat Senators had voted against the Lend Lease Act. It was the first slip in the slippery slide toward America's entry into the war. Vandenberg's admirers to this day portray his sudden switcheroo as "principled," a maturing of his perspective.

> "I saw the light, I saw the light
>
> No more darkness, no more night
>
> Now I'm so happy no sorrow in sight
>
> Praise the Lord I saw the light."

—Hank Williams, *I Saw the Light*

Praise, God. Arthur had seen "the light."

So much for loyal opposition. It wasn't the light Arthur saw: God wasn't paying much attention to Arthur. That man, he figured, most likely was beyond his reach.

Instead of seeing the light, the Senator was staring at the end of his tenure high up in the ruling class regions of Babylon. The end, that is, if he didn't join the crew that was beating the war drums. The majority of the American electorate in 1940 was "isolationist." FDR during that Fall election season promised to keep the U.S. out of the war in Europe. "I have said this before, but I shall say it again and again and again; your boys are not going to be sent into any foreign wars." Yes, just like Woodrow had (fingers crossed) promised back in 1916 with the first go-around. (Another helpful rule of thumb for judging politicians: give the promise of a politician the same level of credibility as the email from the Nigerian Prince wanting to send you ten million dollars.) The polls told Roosevelt that he would lose the election if he didn't make that promise – "again and again" – he knew he was going to break. Secretly, he was conniving with Winston Churchill to get us into it. Still, he wasn't yet one of those all-powerful dictators like the one from across the pond he was yearning to remove. He needed an assist from powerful, influential leaders in the opposition party to move things along. "Assist" as in betray their constituents who didn't want their sons, brothers and husbands getting killed to save Europeans from each other – again. They had seen Act One of Woodrow Wilson's "war to end all wars" tragedy thirty years ago. "Fool me once, shame on you." They had no interest in Act Two of making "the world safe for democracy" with Americans playing the lead role on the slaughter house stage. No matter. "Fool me twice" was furtively underway. Franklin got his "good war." In 1940 American unemployment topped out at 8.1 million. Near the end of 1942, it was at 1.5 million. President Roosevelt had *finally* put Americans back to work building a vast charnel house. FDR's toast to his military Joint Chiefs of Staff: "Make love *and* war."

Post war documentation assembled by contrarians like Justin Raimondo, Harry used to tell a different story than the sanitized one of America to the rescue. (Rule of thumb number three: always resist the siren call of the politicians to send the young men somewhere far away to fight the "evil ones." The courageous Eugene Debs did it with a speech in Canton, Ohio, and Woodrow Wilson threw him in prison for a long time.)

The Vandenberg conversion-myth of maturation was just that – a myth, an "invention" to cover the corruption and coercion that moved him to "maturity." Sex and blackmail, two of Santa's little helpers, make "naughty" (independent-thinking) politicians into good (obedient) ones. First, the sex part. Arthur, as Harry's listeners discovered, was quite the fancier of the fairer sex, and not from afar. His abundant indulgence in romancing ladies other than his Mrs. was not the best kept secret around the town – and beyond, as in around the circles of the British MI6, its Foreign Intelligence Service.

Now the blackmail. At the time of his road to Damascus conversion, Vandenberg was keeping himself "busy" with a hareem he'd assembled – three fetching ladies with strong ties to British intelligence. One was Betty Thorpe, a femme fatale wife of a dashing British diplomat. From Buenos Aires she was ordered to fly to Washington to arouse the Michigan Senator's interest. Arousing male "interest" was her assigned responsibility, one for which she was well endowed. Thorpe was a British Mata Hari, her *nom d'espionage*, "Cynthia." Mrs. Vandenberg's husband was *very* interested.

Providing Cynthia an assist with Vandenberg's "principled conversion" was another seduction specialist, Mitzi Sims with, shall we say, her own interests in the Senator other than the dimensions of his … well … Mitzi just happened to be the wife of Harold Sims, attaché at the British embassy. The aristocratic Mr. Sims also ran the code room at the embassy. Mitzi's special talents were in the field of espionage. And, she was employed by guess who? British Naval Intelligence. She was the bait that "honey-trapped" Vandenburg and set him up to be press-ganged into the retinue of Franklin's warmongering yes-men. The British Office of Naval Intelligence had amassed an impressive file on Vandenberg's bedroom dalliances with the professional ladies it had dispatched.

The story of Vandenberg's conversion – between the sheets, so to speak – is incomplete without mention of Brit spy-lady number three in the Senator's handsome hareem, Eveline Paterson. Ms. Paterson was quite the charmer and a statuesque blonde for good measure, who practiced her "arousal" ways with Arthur. She was also a professional publicist for the cause of Great Britain. J. Edgar Hoover and columnist Drew Pearson tagged her as a British intelligence operative. They would know. They were in on the set up.

"This could be our last goodnight together

We may never pass this way again

Just let me enjoy 'till it's over or forever

Please don't tell me how the story ends."

—Ronnie Millsap, *Please Don't Tell Me How the Story Ends*

The interminably "aroused" Senator was having himself more than a few "last goodnights together" with the Brit ladies. During which, no doubt, his enjoyment was never in question. His pillow-talking companions would continue to "pass this way" as bloody often as it took to make the Senator … see the light.

So, the powerful and highly esteemed Arthur Hendrick Vandenberg woke up one morning and found himself and his principles in a bind. He had to decide how well his principles were going to hold up against his competing interests. And now we know "how the story ends." What else could this randy Republican given to pillow-talk with sexy, lady spies do? Those straight-laced, starched-collar Dutch Calvinists from his home town of Grand Rapids would be awfully disappointed to learn about how far their fair-haired boy had wandered off the paths of righteousness. Insiders began to refer to him as the "Senator from Mitzi-gan." Vandenberg's vanity, arrogance – and overactive libido – made him an easy take down for the willy FDR and the conniving Brits who wanted American boys once again, "over there" to help them kill those recalcitrant Germans they'd picked a fight with. The Brits, it seems to be long forgotten by many, had declared war on Germany – not the other way around.

> "Over there, over there
>
> Send the word, send the word over there
>
> That the Yanks are coming
>
> The Yanks are coming

The drums rum-tumming

Everywhere…"

—George M. Cohen, *Over There*

A tantalizing, irresistible crew. Well chosen, and they executed their mission of seduction with perfection. The Three Musketeerettes, Mitzi, Cynthia and Eveline, were going to be sending "the word over there." Thanks Gals for your "rum-tumming" heavy lifting or, should we say, "heavy breathing." In any case: "The Yanks are coming."

Vandenberg's "conversion" remains an illustration of the maxim: power is found behind the scenes. It was best expressed by Wyndham Lewis in his novel *Self Condemned*: "You have to look for your criminal among the sinister background figures, and in the pressure-groups pushing the little front-line puppets hither and thither to left or right."

The Senator was reported to have said: "I had no youth. I went to work when I was nine, and I never got a chance to enjoy myself until I came to the Senate." Candid and so fittingly expressed. The man clearly understood why he was in Babylon and why Babylon was so accommodating to his recreational interests. He knew what his priorities should be. One question from Harry's takedown that still troubles me is this: how much of a conscience did Vandenberg ever have? Did what he had done ever trouble him? I'm inclined to think that the number of years spent in Babylon as a member of the ruling class is inversely proportional to the size of one's conscience; the more the years, the punier the conscience. At some point it vanishes.

Harry's radio show, and talk radio for the most part, succeeded with conservative-oriented audiences, less with liberal ones. The political spectrum of his reach was broader than the typical talk radio host. Harry's targets were not just on the liberal to left side of the political spectrum.

That said, talk radio was not a medium that seemed to work well for liberal performers. I pondered that for a time. I think now I know why. Radio, I believe, is the least modern of telecommunication media, the least mediated by technology. It moves the sound of the human voice directly to the human ear – not carried or animated by images or spectacle. No make-up needed. No beautified or gravitas-draped presenters like Walter Cronkite to influence the meaning or appeal of the message. "If Walter says it, it's gotta be true." Talk radio speaks directly to people who tend to make their way in a world less involved with or encumbered by abstractions. It appeals to mechanics, firemen, dentists, electricians, construction workers, hair stylists and barbers, people who work with *things*, with their hands. It has less appeal for the likes of English professors, tax lawyers, sociologists or actresses, people who work within systems. They manipulate abstractions and create, interpret or mediate an experience for the uninitiated. To properly "experience" suing your neighbor or divorcing your spouse, you must have a lawyer. To "experience" the televised news you must have Diane Sawyer or Anderson Cooper explain it to you. A mechanic's success is your car starting up when you need it. A sociologist's success is a theoretical interpretation of social interaction that gains approval from his colleagues. Think about which "success" is easier for most people to do without.

39 Meet Me in St. Louis, Louis

"Hell is empty and all the devils are here."

— William Shakespeare, *The Tempest*

Harry's success was WKZO's success. Advertising demand skyrocketed. The station management pulled out the stops on its rates. The increased revenue made the execs most tolerant with "the Hammer," as he called himself on air. In spite of the complaints they got, they were willing to embrace him and the mounting eccentricities of his on-air performances.

In Western Michigan Harry had become the most popular radio voice.

Then KMOX, 1120 AM, "the voice of St. Louis" came calling. WKZO was a minor leaguer in broadcast AM radio. KMOX was in the majors. With a 50,000-watt signal originating from a transmitter across the Mississippi River in Illinois, KMOX could be heard in as many as 44 states. It was the broadcasting home of St. Louis Cardinals' baseball. Best of all from Harry's perspective, it was in middle-America, where the most receptive constituency was waiting to hear him talk. "Eat your heart out, Bill Ayers," he must have been thinking to himself.

The KMOX executives made Harry an offer. He loaded up his 2010 Hummer and made the trek around northern Indiana, through Chicago on I-94, then down Interstate 55 across the Illinois cornfields and over the Mississippi river. With the St. Louis Gateway Arch in view from his studio windows, Harry took the mic. His *Blitzkrieg* talk show was about to hit radio listeners in fly-over country.

Harry's contract with KMOX gave him a wide span of control over his program content and his presentation formats. To the station he brought a unique combination of programming that hugely expanded KMOX's listening audience. There was the standard talk radio fare – exchanging comments with callers on current political-social topics. To that he added interviews and monologues that plunged into a range of forbidden topics.

Corrupt politicians in St. Louis were so abundant, it was hard to know where to start – from the precinct captains up to the mayor's office. The white ones in the suburbs were slightly less blatant than the black ones in the city. Then there was Kansas City and Jefferson City for geographical variety. He would invite the worst of them to come on his show and defend themselves. They never did. He made them suffer.

One of Harry's most ambitious inquisitions brought down the fury of the honchos from three of our modern industries – marketing/advertising, entertainment and the junk food corporations. The program's focus was the second of the 3-cs, "collusion." Harry began with the seemingly pedestrian observation that a large portion of every supermarket shelf-space is devoted to "snack food" – chips, candy, soda – processed, ready-to-eat food that is high in calories, low in nutritional value. "Snack food" is shorthand for food eaten to entertain or calm yourself. It is not produced to satisfy hunger. It's for people seeking escape from boredom, consumed as a supplement to passive entertainment, the kind spent sitting in front of electronic devices.

Junk food is expensive – chips versus vegetables. It also tends to be addictive, and it is high-octane fuel for stress eaters. "Betcha Can't Eat Just One." This was courtesy of the folks from Lay's Potato Chips who knew that they were making a sure bet and confident enough to brag about it as a memorable, commercial one-liner.

A suggested experiment: spend an hour in the junk food aisle of your favorite supermarket. Observe the shoppers passing through. (Be discreet.) Then estimate the average BMI. I did it on three different occasions in three different stores at three different times. For all three, I estimated the average BMI = 31. Approximately five percent of the shoppers I observed were in the morbidly obese range sitting on motorized carts. I attempted to be conservative in my estimates.

BMI Categories:

Underweight =   ≤ 18.5

Normal weight =   18.5–24.9

Overweight =	25–29.9
Obesity =	≥ 30
Morbidly obese =	≥ 40

That said, the normalizing of snack food consumption as a boost for passive entertainment is a relatively recent phenomenon. It wasn't a part of life before television. How did they pull it off? How did they convince people that what is not good for them is good for them, is wholesome and natural? How did eating – not at sit-down family meals, but while watching sports, movies, almost anything on a screen, become so, well … what everyone is supposed to do?

The driving force of this tripartite collusion is the advertising and professional marketing industry responsible for ensuring peak docility of the masses. The "father" of this industry is Edward Bernays, the nephew of Sigmund Freud. Bernays wrote *The Engineering of Consent*, which deserves a subtitle: "Confessions of an Expert Mass-Manipulator." Reflect for a moment on that title. Think about the sinister implications: *your* "consent," an expert's (an engineer's) *shaping* of what you come to believe is good and acceptable. As Bernays put it: "We [you and me] are dominated by the relatively small number of persons [Bernays and his fellow 'engineers'] who understand the mental processes and social patterns of the masses. It is they who pull the wires which control the public mind." This "small number of persons" appoints itself as our "guardians." And, back to the underlying question: who will guard the guardians? Harry was obsessed with the guardians – *their* best interests versus *ours*.

Bernays proudly announced that he understood how to use the power of mass media to shape tastes, change opinions and influence behavior. He considered "propaganda" to best describe the nature of his work, but given the bad associations with the term, opted for the anodyne "marketing." "If we understand the mechanism and motives of the group mind, it is now possible to control and regiment the masses according to our will without them knowing it."

In the late 1940s, Bernays signed on with the tobacco industry to apply his technical "understanding" to the challenge of expanding its customer base. He developed a successful advertising campaign that targeted American women with a glamorized, feminized messaging of cigarette smoking. "*Virginia Slims,* You've come a long way, baby," the first cigarette brand commercial from Phillip Morris advertised exclusively to women – celebrating the "liberation of women" with lung cancer.

In the 1950s, television became *the* delivery mechanism for "engineered" messaging for both commercial and political purposes. Television's dominance as *the* entertainment medium opened up a whole new world of sophisticated approaches for manipulating the tastes and preferences of the masses.

Televised – now digitized – entertainment dominates the regular leisure time of Americans. Its vehicle is advertising. Advertisers have captive audiences on which to practice their sophisticated, persuasive arts.

Sporting events – one major piece of the collusion – are venues for the marketers to promote snack food consumption as a natural, "necessary" accompaniment for digital entertainment. Harry told his audience: "turn on the NFL Sunday afternoon game. The commercial breaks are all enticements to buy beer, soda, junk food and fast food framed in the imagery of a frolicsome, middle class lifestyle. The Super Bowl is perhaps the single most dramatic – bread and circuses – spectacle that features this tripartite collusion – entertainment moguls, advertising executives, junk food producers – at the pinnacle of its success."

All three industries, as Harry demonstrated, are in cahoots. They collude to subvert the normal, healthy needs of nutritional food and temporary diversion from work. These they channel into enervating, compulsive distractions that chase themselves down a rabbit hole of self-indulgence. The destination? An inferno from which modern social pathologies swell. With these, Americans take on a physical and spiritual torpor, acedia – sloth and self-indulgence manifest in fat, apathetic minions of munchers indifferent to the world around them – and manipulatable by those "who pull the wires which control the public mind." Dante 600 years before said of his tour through hell with the poet Virgil: "I had not thought death had undone so many." Here is a massive "undoing" without death.

With the response Harry got in Kalamazoo – delight from his listeners and fury from the myth-keepers – with his demolition of Vandenberg, he decided to step up his game in St. Louis. This would be a close up look at two high-ranking "Pagod things of sabre sway," whose "fronts of brass, and feet of clay" had been scrupulously ignored by triumphalist historians. These would be the two Mr. Bigs of twentieth-century idolatry, FDR and Winston Churchill. Harry's corruption-focused antennae had picked up on a tawdry piece of WWII history that rarely makes it into American and British textbooks – the "feet of clay" chapters scrubbed away by the professional hagiographers. He turned his corruption spotlight on Winston Churchill and FDR – their forced repatriation of white Russians at the end of the war at the behest of Joseph Stalin.

What put Harry onto this colossal betrayal was *Victims of Yalta* published in 1976 by Nikolai Tolstoy, cousin of Leo Tolstoy and a Russo-British historian. Its appearance in the UK unleashed a firestorm of controversy and a libel law suit. Tolstoy accused members in the highest regions of the WWII British leadership of horrific war crimes, including the Stalin-loving, lickspittle, Anthony Eden who had been Prime Minister. Harry arranged for the author to be interviewed on his program. Tolstoy by then was an old man but still a brilliant speaker and an accomplished historian with his powerful and eloquent voice. He gave an electrifying interview.

First, the undisputed facts: over two million Russian POWs were handed over by the Western Allies to Joseph Stalin from 1944 to 1947. Their fate was forced exile to Stalin's Gulag where the majority perished from the hardships of slave labor in the harshest climate on the planet. Particularly egregious was the concealment from the public of what their governments, British and American, were doing. Worse, tens of thousands of the illegally repatriated Russians were Tsarist fugitives, Cossacks, who had never lived under Soviet rule, who had fled Russia in 1919 to escape communism. They considered themselves allies of the Americans and the British. Their betrayal and deliverance to the fate of slavery or death was engineered by Stalin, FDR and Churchill at Yalta. Stalin made his demands. The POWs at British and American gunpoint and bayonets were delivered to SMERSH, Stalin's counter-intelligence operation whose agents were savage in their treatment of their prisoners. When the British and the American troops were ordered to turn the Cossacks and their families over to the Soviets, widespread terror followed and mass suicides. George Orwell at the time was one of the few British intellectuals who protested the coverup by the press. He accused the left of being complicit in disseminating the "mythos" that Stalin's Soviet Union was a "peoples' democracy" and a "just" society.

This repatriation was a gross violation of the Geneva convention. Its dimensions must be judged as nothing less than a war crime of the same proportions that brought the Nazi leadership to the dock at Nuremberg and subjected the German people to years of Allied occupation and denazification. This betrayal was signed off by Churchill and FDR. Throughout WWII they were enthralled with Stalin, "Uncle Joe," as they called him. They turned themselves inside out to do what would please him including arming him (Lend lease) and pretending that he was something other than a mass-murdering tyrant. FDR and Churchill colluded in the cover up of the Soviet murder of 15,000 Polish officers at Katyn in 1940 – blamed by Stalin on the Germans until Mikhail Gorbachev confessed to the Soviet atrocity in 1990 – more truth tightly under wraps with the complicity of the guardians. Harry Truman completed the complicity at Potsdam and let Stalin put much of Eastern and Central Europe under his heel. Handing over two million Russians for him to enslave with the rest of his people was the culmination of the most cynical, papered-over collusion in history.

The Tolstoy interview brought down a storm of controversy on Harry and the station. But the audience for his program was exploding and advertising revenue was off the charts for the station.

40 When Harry Met Richard

"The surest way to corrupt a youth is to instruct him to hold in higher esteem those who think alike than those who think differently."

—Friedrich Nietzsche, *The Dawn*

Shortly after the Tolstoy program aired and the garboil ensued, I flew from Los Angeles to St. Louis with my son, Richard. Rick, as we called him, was fourteen. He was going to meet his grandfather, his only living grandparent. Karen's parents never came back for her. They just disappeared. We assumed, given their "lifestyle choice," that they were dead – OD'd or murdered. Karen and I would look at each other in sad amusement when we'd hear the hippie anthem drifting out of the oldies radio stations.

> "If you're going to San Francisco
>
> Be sure to wear some flowers in your hair...
>
> You're gonna meet some gentle people there."

—Scott McKenzie, *San Francisco*

That song came out in 1967. The "gentle people," such as they were, had gone somewhere else.

This trip was not my idea. I was opposed to it at the beginning. Harry was not a man I wanted to expose my son to. He'd abandoned a pregnant woman with his child. He'd led a life of crime, at times an agent of terror and murderous violence. Even so, I was drawn by the power of his personality and in admiration of his contrary mission taken up in his later years. His deep and corrosive cynicism was troubling, however. Was the talk-show Harry of KMOX different from the Weatherman Harry of the 1970s? I wasn't sure.

Rick was persistent. He was relentless. Harry was a famous, colorful, controversial talk-show personality with a national following. Rick was an avid listener of his radio program. He was fascinated with every aspect of Harry's performance. Knowing that Harry was his grandfather made him an irresistible attraction. He wanted to know more about him, what he was like, not just as a disembodied voice but as flesh and blood, as a living ancestor with secrets to divulge.

> "Dad. Why can't I meet him? Is it that he doesn't want to meet me?"

> "No, Son. I am confident that he'd want to meet you."

> "Then why can't I?"

> "I'm not sure. Let me think about it."

> I went to Karen. I wanted her advice.

> "What do you think I should do?"

She looked at me with an air of disagree-able tolerance that said: "I can't be-lieve I should have to tell you this."

"You've no right to keep him from his grandfather, Joe. He's old enough to decide. He'll hate you for it if he never gets a chance to meet him. Don't fight it. Take him, you dumb ass! What an opportunity for him – the good, the bad and the ugly – all three wrapped up in one big, colorful package of an old man at the top of his game. How can you argue against it? He's amaz-ing. You are, by the way, more like him than you imagine."

Well, I had argued against it, but maybe she was right. Except for the "dumb ass" part. And, in what ways did she think I was like Harry? I didn't ask. I was always a little afraid of Karen, of what she could see in me that I would rather avoid having to think about.

Rick and I arrived at St. Louis Lambert Interna-tional Airport. Harry sent a car and a driver to pick us up. The driver loaded our bags into a silver Mercedes SUV. Shaved head, dressed in a black tee-shirt, black jeans and crocodile-skin cowboy boots, he was about six feet tall and maybe 260 pounds. Those pounds were massively distributed around his neck, shoul-ders, chest and arms. They appeared to be packed with sheer, explosive muscle. He looked like he had been chiseled out of a block of granite and, if so in-clined, could go bear hunting with a golf club. His black sport jacket had the suspicious bulge of a semi-automatic pistol, a Glock, 9mm, I suspected. Polite and attentive, he had drinks and hors d'oeuvres to offer us. His accent was Russian. He drove us from the airport to Harry's apartment in downtown St. Louis. His rate of speed on the average exceeded the limit by 25 miles per hour. It appeared that he was immune from intervention by the traffic enforcement officials. Rick, as you can imagine, was highly impressed – blown away, actually. This was not the opening move I was hoping for.

Clearly, Harry was very concerned about security. His programming had made him highly unpopular with a certain listening segment. They were letting him know just how unhappy with him they were. Harry took a proud declaration from Mussolini as his own: "*Molti nemici, molto onore.*" "Many enemies, much honor."

All of this gave me great unease. I was thinking that I would blame Karen if things took a wrong turn.

Harry lived in a loft apartment on Locust Street a few blocks from the Mississippi river. The Gateway Arch was within walking distance. His apartment décor I would describe as "ultra-minimalist." Mono-chromatic – white walls, nothing hanging or attached to them except for a plaque that read:

> "Do not let me hear
>
> Of the wisdom of old men, but rather of
>   their folly…"

—T. S. Eliot

He had neither collectables nor knick-knacks. His furniture was simple and functional. No CDs, no music playing devices. Books and magazines were piled everywhere. His kitchen: a cheap table with two high-top chairs, a microwave oven and a small refrigerator that contained water bottles, cheese, a bag of walnuts and some apples. A box of Ritz crackers, bread and a jar of peanut butter were on a single shelf. Minimal décor; minimal interest in food. No romantic interests. Lots of women in his past; none in the present. For Harry, anything that didn't add power to his quest to smash the windows of the establishment, to expose corruption and hypocrisy, to rain down contempt on the powerful was a distraction from his mission.

His response to meeting his grandson, however, was most "un-minimalist." I had no idea of what to expect from him. Was our visit pro forma? Would Rick be an annoying distraction?

The opposite. I think he was overcome with the guilt of his abandonment of Sally and me. But there was more going on than just that. He was, how shall I say this? – ebullient to meet his grandson. Both Rick and Harry were astonishingly unimpeded by reticence or inhibition, as if they had known each other well from a different lifetime. There was something mystical about it, almost eerie. They bonded naturally, immediately. I receded into the background, fascinated to observe a blood connection that had skipped over a generation. How to explain it?

Before I met him, I had wondered if Harry was a psychopath. He'd been a conman for much of his life and a user of people, standard psychopathic markers. But, after I encountered him at Terre Haute I took away an impression that went in an opposite direction. He was too infused with raw, driving emotion and an arresting fearlessness. Typical psychopaths are marked by under-arousal. Harry was always angry. And he was still ... boiling, unappeasably angry.

This inexplicable connection between grandfather and grandson? It finally hit me. It was anger – an angry old man and an angry boy soon to be an angry young man. I had seen it in Rick at an early age. I thought it was normal child-development, oppositional behavior. It went much deeper than that, however. Later, I blamed it on the divorce, my long absence in Argentina, boyhood frustrations and insecurities. I was wrong again. Anger – *rabia, Verärgerung, colère, злость – was* the deep connection, whatever language you care to say it in. Rick was a born contrarian. It was in his blood. He was a young man whose future would be passionate, furious opposition to the lies of the status quo. His youthful calling was to swim upstream against the current. He was what they call in Oklahoma "an agginer," a popular Okie moniker because there are so many of them there.

Rick and I spent a week with Harry. Rick and Harry were inseparable. Harry took Rick to the KMOX station, and he sat beside him while he did his broadcast. Rick was enthralled. Through much of the week they sat up late into the night laughing and talking. I remained on the sidelines and wondered about it all.

On our flight back to LA I asked Rick about his encounter with his grandfather. What did he think of him? What impressions was he carrying back home of the time he'd spent with Harry? What would he tell his mother about him?

> "He was the most amazing person I've ever met, Dad. I want to be like him."

> "Why do you want to be like him?"

> "Because he cares more about the truth than anybody else."

> "How do you know that, Rick?"

> "It's obvious, Dad. Most people avoid the truth because it makes them uncomfortable. Harry lives for discomfort."

I couldn't argue against that.

Rick at fourteen had been reading Friedrich Nietzsche.

> "It's like Nietzsche said, Dad. 'There are two different types of people in the world, those who want to know, and those who want to believe.' Harry is in the first group. He wants to be a knower. I want to be one too. I have no use for believers. Harry," said Rick, "likes to quote Ezra Pound: 'the multitude of men thinks only thoughts already emitted, feels but feelings used up, and has but sensations faded as

old gloves.' I want to stand out from the 'multitude.'"

Well, "that was a successful visit," I thought to myself. "What the hell is Karen going to say? 'Nice going, dumb ass. You took Rick to St. Louis and brought back Friedrich Nietzsche Jr. quoting Ezra Pound. How soon before he grows the big mustache and goes insane? He'll be a hit in St. Elizabeth's in a few years.'"

Where do I go from here?

41 Left Field

"Let us die finely; our life is a long dying, amid which to be conscious is to capture melancholy satisfactions."

—Hugh Kenner, *The Pound Era*

"We die to each other daily. What we know of other people is only our memory of the moments during which we knew them."

—T. S. Eliot, *The Cocktail Party*

Where indeed?

Left field. How much of the big stuff in life that hits you and changes everything comes out of left field? You think you are going to lose your job. Perfectly healthy you see yourself. Boom! Stage four, pancreatic cancer. Your mother is in hospice. Your younger sister drops dead. Your kid on the way to West Point gets arrested for shoplifting. Poof! Off to the community college. You fall off the ladder putting up the Christmas lights. You never walk again without a cane.

Beware of left field. It's always out there.

"[T]he race is not to the swift, nor the
battle to the strong… But time and
chance happeneth to them all."

—Ecclesiastes 9:11

Left field came for Harry. Time and chance in St Louis. Harry's security broke down, so to speak. He and his muscled-up armed tutelary were gunned down by three Antifa shooters as they came out of the KMOX studio late one evening into the parking garage. Harry's driver killed one of them with return fire and wounded a second one, but he was outnumbered. Harry had been at the top of the St. Louis Antifa's list of "fascists." All three assassins had felony criminal histories, including assault. Rick had come out of that same studio with Harry a couple of months before the shootings. I still have nightmares from that memory.

The assassination sparked national news coverage. It was brief, however, much like when Bernie Sanders supporter, James Hodgkinson tried to murder a couple of dozen Republican congressmen in June, 2017. "Nothing to see here folks, move along," a weekend in the news cycle, and that was it. The usual, prolonged media hysteria that follows when the *wrong* sort of stooge acts up was mysteriously absent for that event.

How was the coverage of Harry's and his driver's murders mediated by the mainstream media? Those folks viewed Harry as a plague, and the coverage was, well, predictable.

I must take you once again to the hermeneutics of "flipping the victim." Recall Leslie Abramson and the Menendez brothers who "[were] not criminals, but sympathetic, decent people who [were] in *terrible trouble.*" José and Kitty were the "Hitlers." Eric and Lyle were the victims. They did what "decent people" under duress have to do.

The thrust of the CNN and MSNBC "flip the victim" coverage was that Harry's assassination was the result of his incendiary programming. It had created a "climate of hate." From an assortment of interviewed "experts," we learned that Harry was the source of that intolerable "duress." He had *provoked* an "unstable" element. Though troubled, they were like Kyle and Erick "decent" people who felt compelled to act – "activists," a word reserved to connote virtue and idealism of the approved kind. The criminal records of the assassins were downplayed. Harry's own criminal past, which came to the surface, made him an easy take down for this version of "flip the victim." Harry, like José and Kitty, was in the "you know what" class of people. And, those people as you know per Leslie Abramson, "deserve" what they get. Harry got "flipped." The story lasted two entire days. The news cycle then moved on to more important matters like the half-time show for the upcoming Super Bowl and how creative, clever and costly the special ads would be.

The final moments of Harry's life were permeated with a bitter irony. The "climate of hate" that summoned his assassins to the parking garage was grounded in "the truth" that he was determined to unveil for his listeners. Harry's death would thus become a profound vindication of his indictment of the modern world: *the modern world is organized to revile and betray truth tellers.* To paraphrase the Apostle John, so as to bring him into conformity with the ethos of the modern world: "Ye shall tell the truth, and the truth will bring about your destruction."

Harry had chosen his epitaph from Shakespeare's "Henry IV."

> Falstaff: "There live not three good men
> unhanged in England, and one of them
> is fat and grows old."

Harry was old. Good? A complicated question. He never intended to get fat.

> "I loved him and he loved me
>
> And lord, I cried the day he died,
>
> 'Cause I thought that he walked on wa-
> ter."

> **— Randy Travis**, *He Walked on Water*

For Rick, Harry "walked on water." He was devastated, inconsolable. I feared that the aftermath would permanently damage him – inconsolable grief would turn into unappeasable anger.

For me? It was desolation.

> "And without drums or music, long hearses
>
> Pass by slowly in my soul; Hope, van-
> quished,

Weeps, and atrocious, despotic Anguish

On my bowed skull plants her black flag."

—Charles Baudelaire, *Spleen* (IV)

For a time, we did nothing. After a month of staring angrily at the walls in sullen silence, we quietly gathered ourselves together and prepared to leave the country, a *pis aller*. America was becoming Argentina – worse. It was falling from a higher place. Its landing would be sheer ugliness and chaos. Thus, the words of Baudelaire: "Satan has blown the lights out at the inn."

"Get ready, little lady. Hell is coming to breakfast."

—Chief Dan George, *The Outlaw Josey Wales*

Uruguay was our destination – meeting my requirements of antediluvian – off the beaten track of hell where breakfast would not be a stopover in Dante's *Inferno*. It was the birthplace of the great nineteenth-century symbolist poet, Jules Laforgue who was also a model for Pierre-Auguste Renoir's 1881 painting Luncheon of the Boating Party.

We would be expats. But where? Uruguay, a place for renewal.

"And how knows if the flowers in my mind

In this poor sand, swept like a beach, will
   find

The food of soul to gain a healthy start."

—**Charles Baudelaire**, "The Enemy"

Yes, Uruguay and the hope to gain a healthy start. Uruguay was the proper place to make our retreat and begin the effacement of our psychic misery. It was a far-away country many Americans knew nothing about. The remote beaches, friendly locals, peace and quiet, extensive countryside and its traditional European culture helped to make our exodus bearable and eventually an act of prudence and wisdom. Montevideo was a step back in time, a classy city still operating as if in the olden days. Adults were in charge there. The city was a place where a "hard and wiry line of rectitude and certainty in the actions and intentions" still existed. There was less manufactured hostility between the sexes. The natural tension that existed was modulated by gentle sarcasm and good humor. Women there had not yet transformed themselves into pantsuit pugilists. Men there had not yet emolliated. They resembled stoic Gary Cooper or aristocratic John Kennedy instead of the femininely earnest Anderson Cooper or the blow-dried, elfish, lackey of the ruling class, George Stephanopolous. Absent were the ubiquitous antagonisms, the mounting tribal grievances and the visceral hatreds of back home. It was a good place to meditate on our fate and draw proper conclusions.

Shortly after we settled into an apartment in Montevideo, Karen made her exodus. She came to join us and embrace our rejection of the homeland. Weariness and disappointment had fallen upon her like a fine mist. It soaked her spirit and dissolved her faith in her mission of uncompromised self-denial. She had experienced enough moral decay and material decomposition. Her *orexia moralia* went into remission. It took the grim reality of life in San Francisco where she had been working as a public defender to put it out of commission. Daily she faced a title-wave of indigent criminality and was worn down and disgusted with the official endorsement – the "celebration" – of it.

The once beautiful City on the Bay? Think post-apocalypse – a place in the late stages of transmogrification. The downtown was an open-air, lunatic asylum. The inmates were the warders. The quaint city streets had been made into a toilet. When the sidewalks have become the acceptable locale for emptying your bowels, it's time for permanent relocation. "We are the world"? Yes, *we* are now the *third* world where distinguishing human from other animal semblances is more of a challenge. A disillusioned writer from *Taki Magazine* on a visit described the entropy that Karen experienced every day. "Those who defend the city where the streets are paved in dirty needles and bum-poo claim that their town is better than ever because of *freedom*, comrade. Every sidewalk is a bed for weary schizophrenics; every pot and planter a makeshift toilet where the homeless can expel the remnants of the stale pizza slices and dried box-cheese they picked from the trash earlier that day. After all, what's more charming than a city where dogs have to clean up after their owners?" Yes, the dogs in San Francisco offered more cultivation, class and consideration than the unkempt human occupiers of the streets – a world-class city, gone to the dogs, maintained by the dogs.

> "How much is that doggie in the window?
> The one with the waggly tail
> How much is that doggie in the window?
> I do hope that doggie's for sale.
>
> I read in the papers there are robbers
> With flashlights that shine in the dark
> My love needs a doggie to protect him
> And scare them away with one bark."

—*Doggie in the Window*

Patti Page released that hit song in 1953, the Pleistocene era in American history when men were men, and women did not seem to mind. Its lyrics, its tone, its style give you a depressing feeling of how much the roles for barking dogs and robbers have changed, and what a profoundly different place America now is.

The metropolis of San Francisco had become a fully modernist construct. The city "fathers" (using that word facetiously) had proudly demolished the boundaries to "freedom." The wisdom of Thomas Hobbes was long forgotten. The normalizing of "grief" was the order of the day – "no power able to overawe [anyone at] all;" "a great deal of grief in keeping company." And, more grief was on the way. As goes California, so goes the country – "gentle people" "keeping company" everywhere.

> "If everybody had an ocean
>
> Across the U. S. A
>
> Then everybody'd be surfin'
>
> Like Californi-a…"

> **— Beach Boys**, *Surfin' U.S.A*

Like Californi-a, Brian? No thanks, surfer Dude. Too late. Californi-a is just California now – too much "freedom." The line of rectitude and certainty, you might say, has been obliterated. Downtown smells of putrefaction. "Shit happened."

In Uruguay, Karen, Rick and I were finally at a safe, healthy distance from the "gentle people." We were "keeping company" with "a great deal [less] grief." Karen and I suddenly looked at each other through kinder, more understanding and appreciative eyes. Doubt and diffidence were pushed aside by caritas. We married again. This time in a small, colonial-era church. No fat judge in a polyester robe to officiously officiate. A wraithlike, white-haired priest with tender, pale blue eyes gave us the vows in soft, mellifluous Spanish. Karen wore a simple black lace mantilla. She was never more beautiful, and I was never less alone. Rick was my best man.

I thought of a marriage poem I'd read many years before.

> "At fourteen I married My Lord you.
>
> I never laughed, being bashful.
>
> Lowering my head, I looked at the wall.
>
> Called to, a thousand times, I never looked back.
>
> At fifteen I stopped scowling,
>
> I desired my dust to be mingled with yours
>
> Forever and forever, and forever.
>
> Why should I climb the look out?"
>
> —**Ezra Pound**, *The River-Merchant's Wife: A Letter*

42 Poetry Versus Facts

"The truth will set you free. But not until it is finished with you."

—David Foster Wallace, *Infinite Jes*

"Where all is rotten it is a man's work to cry stinking fish."

—F. H. Bradly, *Appearance and Reality*

Sally and Harry "connected" one night in a fleeting moment of lust in 1969. That connection stirred a wake. I was the flotsam that bobbed up from it, an unwelcome materialization, conceived beneath dark, cinematic shadows – retribution against immodesty. By 2020 the grim reaper had carried them both away. Their memories upon me weighed heavily as a stone.

Drinking coffee with my wife Karen and my son Rick beside me in a lovely outdoor cafe in Montevideo, I found myself staring into an abyss, a "dolorous abyss" of malignant perplexity. My mind was twisting into knots. In that singular moment I became Baudelaire:

"I am an artist that a mocking God

Condemns, alas! to paint the gloom itself."

Condemned to paint nothing but the gloom. How could I "reconnect" Sally and Harry in some way that would do justice to the tortured memories of them I had painted in my mind? I was speculating. Pouring over the impulses and ambitions that had animated them might tell me something – inauspicious clues that would help me better understand not just them, but the decadence of the society they lived and died in. I became the "Little Engine that Could" – "I think I can. I think I can. I think I can."

> "I suppose, when poetry comes down to
>   facts,
>
> When our souls are returned to the gods
>
> And the spheres they belong in,
>
> Here in the every-day where our acts
>
> Rise up and judge us…"

—**Ezra Pound**, *Au Salon*

Fleeting images grasped by the poets: the images are destined to tumble outward and downward. They fall heavily and make a bumpy hard-landing as facts – imposing, disquieting, often brutally felt with a devastating impact. Our lives are spent evading facts. Facts have fangs.

"Returned to the gods," what "spheres" did the souls of Harry and Sally belong in? What a disturbing question to confront, and what a stunning contrast to contemplate! Sally was a Babylonian: Harry, an anti-Babylonian to the core. My troubled soul was Babylon in turbulence – *impia civitas in bello*. I was an impious city at war. Here was the irony breathtaking in its implications. It plunged me into a state of turmoil, moral anguish and filial ambivalence.

Sally in and of *this* world was a highly talented, driven creature of conventional ambition. Her achievements were through an expertly choreographed form of pretending to operate by "the rules" while secretly subverting them – cynicism in service to power. The frosted, cynical surface of the *faux* cake was, to mix the metaphors, the self-righteous cloak in which the powerful wrap themselves. Pauline Kael described the disgust you feel when you come into close proximity of the poseurs: "But when they became political in that morally superior way of people who are doing something for themselves but pretending it's for others, their self-righteousness was insufferable." An outsider who finds himself in Babylon will quickly feel himself washed over by wave after punishing wave of cynicism and self-righteousness.

Harry entered center stage in ferocious opposition to the self-righteous ruling class – grubbing in the dirt for those fallen "facts," scraping them clean and holding them up to expose the corruption, the reeking hypocrisy, the cunning deceit of the guardians. This was cynicism in the destruction of the false legitimacy of power.

Sally and Harry were dueling cynics who came to "know" each other only for a passing moment – their precarious, *carnal knowledge* derived from a lascivious clutch that intersected the unfolding future of two young lives moving in opposite directions. That ludicrous backseat-coupling, I couldn't help but imagine, was ordained by some lewd, mischievous god as a metaphysical riddle. "What do you get when an irresistible modern-force meets an unmovable reactionary-object?" I'm still searching for the punchline. Plato believed that all knowledge comes from the excavation of memory. Someday, perhaps, I may be able to conduct a successful anamnesis and solve the riddle, and grasp that punchline.

How was I to judge Harry and Sally? What measures of culpability, of praise, of exoneration would I assert? How to judge if they failed or succeeded? By their own standards? They both succeeded. Mine? They both failed. Those of a modern system? Too treacherous a path to wander down. I held no map. I knew no guide I could trust. I was lost. I was:

> "A bewildered man, miserably
>
> Attempting a groping escape
>
> Out of a place full of snakes…"

—Charles Baudelaire, *The Irremediable*

Their messy personal lives and considerable shortcomings also had to be judged. This was turning out to be a massively complicated, painful mess to sort out. Who was I, so close up, to do it?

The pungent Uruguayan coffee had lifted me up; then it set me back down. My speculation quietly collapsed. It obediently rose again and reformed itself into a melancholy meditation. Harry and Sally came reluctantly together in my mind as moral antipodes, as archetypes of primal forces behind the entropy, the disorder into which modern society was descending. My memories of them came to form a hastily completed, black and white sketch of the modern world immersed in its pathologies of soul-killing distractions and constant manipulations.

Sally's life was about the seduction of power – its false promises, its allure, the dishonesty that makes it so irresistible, all-encompassing and enduring. "Who *are* you, Sally?" Gladys asked her twenty-two-year old pregnant daughter as she sat downcast in the kitchen at the end of her confessional. Sally was vulnerability and ambition; transparency and mystery; understandable, yet inscrutable. Albert Camus shocked the smart set when he said, "I believe in justice, but I will defend my mother before justice." Sally and the Babylonians she embraced were betrayers of justice. But she was my *mother*. I wouldn't hesitate to defend her. Inexorably, I am with *you* Albert: My mother. Yes, my mother comes before justice.

Harry's configuration was more difficult to trace. It was less of a recognizable pattern – wild and anarchical in his lifelong trafficking with other human beings. Of his later years, I would say of him what an admirer, George Saintsbury, said of the poet-critic, John Dryden: "He was not lightly moved by light things; and while his adversaries howled and gnashed and gesticulated, he swam steadily above on an easy wing pouring molten iron upon them." Harry's core-life conundrum: who will guard the guardians? The question is at one level merely rhetorical. We know the negative answer. But Harry moved it beyond grammar, beyond rhetoric. For him it was the articulation of a moral commission – to stalk the guardians who hide out in "death's other kingdom." And he did it with a mulish determination and concentrated contempt. He was reckless and defiant, possessed of a rare courage. But alas, all he could hope to do was to expose their untrustworthiness and unworthiness. We half-suspected the truth all along but were determined to resist the imposition with all of its meanness and ugliness. The carefully adorned, reassuring impostures that came under Harry's inspection he detonated and blew into pieces. The disintegration of the sculpted lies left the truth to be retrieved and reassembled out of the dust.

Yes, Plato and the promise of memory: I can only wonder.

I ask: what did Harry leave us? A big, fat *nothing* to believe in. *Nada*. Harry's late-life heavy-lifting in the service of unpalatable truth crashed down upon him – his commission an inevitable tragedy. His labors brought us to the barren shores of nihilism – truth collapsing under its own weight.

When poetry comes down to facts: what *is* the modern world that Sally served and Harry assaulted?

> *The modern world is a world of hostages*
> *to the complexity of abstract systems*
> *and their designers (hostage-takers).*

For the hostage-takers, people are entities that represent no more than the sum of their limited interests and impulses, not beings with needs, desires and aspirations that fall outside of the categories of the designers' invention and imposition. People are things shuffled into those categories. They are objects used to make them useful for the exclusive purposes of the designers: countable (to *tax*), manipulatable (to *buy* designer-made things), predictable (to *vote* for the designer-chosen guardians) and dispensable (to *die* in guardian-contrived wars). To be taxed, to buy, to vote then die is the sum, the *raison d'être*, the *Daseinsberechtigung* of life in the modern world. All resistance to the designer-categories, all manifestations of, and the reaching for, transcendence is subjected by the designers to *reductio ad minimum*, reduction to the lowest form, one fitted to make those imagining themselves made in the image of God into manageable higher primates.

> *Mystery* reduced to superstition,
>
> *Love* reduced to desire
>
> *Sex* reduced to technique
>
> *Beauty* reduced to pleasantness
>
> *Reverence* reduced to fear
>
> *Obligation* reduced to submission
>
> *Wisdom* reduced to ideology
>
> *Music* reduced to noise

Hostages and hostage-takers. Between the two, they sustain the illusions we embrace. They bespeak suspicion and surrender – suspicions of power, but the inevitable surrender to chimeras of legitimacy and virtue that cloak the naked venality, hypocrisy and corruption of the guardian class. "For what matters infamy if the cash be kept?"

Sally was a modern-world insider, a hostage-taker serving an abstract system. Harry was the outsider, its enemy, a hostage in opposition. Cynicism had enveloped them both, but it came from different directions and it played to opposite desires. How does one live with cynicism without it completely corroding the soul? Both were tortured human beings. Yet for a longtime they did. They lived as incompletely corroded souls that grappled in failure with the tragedies of the modern world.

Harry still meets Sally – the hostage and the hostage-taker – "the alpha and the omega," the beginning and the end of life in a modern world. You are either a hostage-taker – power as your narcotic – and the cynicism of Sally. Or, you remain a hostage – distracted by bread and circuses, content with the shadows on the wall of the cave. Bow to the nihilism of Harry.

Take your choice, gentle Reader. I don't envy you. Sally –

> "A woman drew her long black hair out tight
>
> And fiddled whisper music on those strings
>
> And bats with baby faces in the violet light

Whistled and beat their wings."

—**T. S. Eliot**, *What the Thunder Said*

Harry—

"I should have been a pair of ragged claws
Scuttling across the floors of silent seas."

—**T. S. Eliot**, *The Love Song of J. Alfred Prufrock*

About the Author

Stephen Paul Foster is a philosopher (Ph.D. St. Louis University) and world traveler who writes about politics, religion and contemporary culture. His *Toward the Bad I Kept on Turning* (2020) is an historical novel that takes the reader on a wild tour through baby-boomer America. After Harry met Sally is the sequel novel. Stephen is a native Midwesterner who grew up in Michigan, married and became a father in Missouri, and currently resides in Ohio.

Made in the USA
Middletown, DE
01 March 2024

50588899R00221